D1094635

Dear Reader,

You might have heard of Nessie or Champ, the legendary lake monsters of Loch Ness and Lake Champlain, respectively. But what happens when rumors circulate about a monster in picturesque Chickadee Lake? I hope you'll join in the fun as Jan and Elaine try to find out who is behind the tales while hosting Jan's twin grandsons for a week. In their search, they discover that similar rumors surfaced in town back in the 1940s. Are the two spates of stories related?

The cousins also want to help the local fire department raise money for new equipment, so they take part in a field day, selling cookies, lemonade, and iced tea on the school grounds. The small volunteer fire department runs on a shoestring, so local businesses and organizations come together to support their fund-raiser, and Jan uses a classic sugar cookie recipe to bake treats for the event. Her "Chick of Chickadee Lake" cookies are a big hit during the firemen's muster, and you can find her recipe in the back of this book.

Growing up in a small town in central Maine, I always enjoyed town events—parades, community yard sales, boat races, and firefighters' field days among them. Join us in the fictional town of Lancaster for some very real fun.

Sincerely,
Susan Page Davis

Tearoom Mysteries

TEAROOM *mysteries*

Beneath the Surface

SUSAN PAGE DAVIS

Guideposts

New York

Tearoom Mysteries is a trademark of Guideposts

Published by Guideposts Books & Inspirational Media
110 William Street
New York, New York 10038
Guideposts.org

Copyright © 2017 by Guideposts. All rights reserved.

This book, or parts thereof, may not be reproduced, stored in a retrieval
system, or transmitted in any form or by any means, electronic, mechanical,
photocopying, recording or otherwise, without the written permission of the
publisher.

The characters and events in this book are fictional, and any resemblance to
actual persons or events is coincidental.

Acknowledgments

Every attempt has been made to credit the sources of copyrighted material used
in this book. If any such acknowledgment has been inadvertently omitted or
miscredited, receipt of such information would be appreciated.

Scripture references are from the following sources: *The Holy Bible*, King James
Version (KJV). *The Holy Bible, New International Version*. Copyright ©1973, 1978,
1984, 2011 by Biblica, Inc. Used by permission of Zondervan. All rights reserved
worldwide. www.zondervan.com

Cover and interior design by Müllerhaus
Cover illustration by Ross Jones, represented by Deborah Wolfe, Ltd.
Typeset by Aptara, Inc.

Printed and bound in the United States of America
10 9 8 7 6 5 4 3 2 1

CHAPTER ONE

Customers filled the parlors at Tea for Two on a sunny July morning, spilling over to the tables on the shady side porch. The lake that drew tourists to the Central Maine community provided a picturesque setting for the tearoom in the old Queen Anne house. Tourists and regulars alike loved the tastefully decorated home and the cousins who owned it.

Elaine Cook helped their two servers, Rose Young and Archie Bentham, that morning by handling the customers sitting outside and helping prepare trays for the others. She and Rose met in the kitchen, where Elaine's cousin Jan Blake kept busy with the baking end of the business.

"Did you hear about the guy filming at the Pine Tree Grill last night?" Rose asked, flipping her long, wheat-colored braid over her shoulder.

Elaine poured hot water carefully into a porcelain teapot painted with dandelions on the sides. "No. Was it for a newscast?"

"From what I heard, it was just for his own curiosity. He's here for a wedding or something and thought it would be fun to get some footage of the small-town natives in their habitat." Rose consulted her order pad and opened a container of fresh blueberry scones. "Maureen was talking about it. Apparently she and Alan were over there for supper last night."

Elaine and Jan knew the retired couple well. They attended the same church the cousins did, and Alan Oakley served on the board of selectmen for the town.

Jan took a baking sheet of cookies from the oven. "Hot ginger chews, if anyone's in the mood."

"I'll pass the word," Rose said.

"Whose wedding is he here for? Is it Sadie Taylor's?" Elaine set the cover on the teapot and reached for a clean plate.

"You'll have to ask Maureen," Rose said.

Elaine went out the back door and around to the side porch to reach her waiting customers. The walk to the tables on the back end of the porch was shorter that way. Three women smiled at her approach.

"Here we go." Elaine set each one's order before her and filled their mismatched teacups. "Can I get you anything else?"

"No, this is wonderful," said one of the women.

Elaine checked on the other three parties on the porch. One group included Macy Atherton, a frequent customer, with two couples. "May I bring you anything else?" Elaine asked.

"No, thanks. We're about done," one of the men said.

"Thank you so much," the woman sitting next to him added. "Your menu is wonderful."

"How nice of you to say so." Elaine smiled at them. Macy had introduced them earlier as vacationing at her rustic cottages on the lake. She often steered visitors toward Tea for

Two, and Elaine and Jan were grateful, though Macy nearly always complained about some aspect of her visit.

"The tea was a little strong today," Macy said, and Elaine almost laughed. Macy just couldn't leave without registering a complaint.

"I'm so sorry. Are you ready for your bill?"

"In a couple of minutes," said one of the men. "Give it to me. I'm treating."

"I'll be right back with it."

Elaine went in the front door and detoured into Rose's station in the west parlor. Since the customer had said he'd be ready in a couple of minutes, she decided she had time to speak to Maureen Oakley. Maureen was seated at one of the tables with another woman, and Elaine walked over.

"Hi, Elaine," Maureen said with a smile. "This is my friend Dee. She's visiting from Anson."

"Glad to meet you. That's quite a drive," Elaine said.

"Yes, but I had to go to Augusta anyway, and Lancaster is on my way," Dee said. "Any excuse to stop in and see Maureen."

"Well, thanks for coming in."

"I'm glad we did," Dee replied. "This place is charming."

"It's one of my favorite spots," Maureen said. "How are you doing? You seem to be quite busy."

"We are," Elaine said. "Jan's two little grandsons are coming later today to spend some time with us. Their mom and dad are going away for a week, and the kids are going to attend the Vacation Bible School at Lancaster Community Church."

"How fun," Maureen said. "Now, are those Amy's boys?"

"Yes. They're twins, seven years old. It should be an active week for us." Elaine took a breath and plunged in. "Did I hear there was some excitement at the Grill last night?"

"You very well might have," Maureen said. "There's a young man here for his cousin's wedding, and he's doing some filming."

"Who's his cousin?" Elaine asked. "Anyone I know?"

"Sadie Taylor."

"Thought so," Elaine said. "Her mom was in school with Jan and me, and we got an invitation a few days ago."

"Well, apparently this young man used to live in Lancaster, but his family moved away quite some time ago. Long before you bought this place." Maureen sipped her tea.

"He'd be too young for me to have known him in school," Elaine said.

"Oh my, yes. He's thirty or so. And he was sticking that camera in everyone's face last night, asking what we liked about life in a small town. I got the impression he thought we were out of the loop way up here. He's been living in New York City, and now he thinks Lancaster is very quaint." She frowned for a moment. "Now, what was his name? Anyway, I told him there's no better place than here to raise children."

"Good for you," Elaine said.

Maureen laughed. "Alan told him he liked living in a small town because he didn't have strangers poking around asking him silly questions all the time. I hope it doesn't turn out to be an embarrassment for the town that he said it."

"That sounds like Alan," Dee said, picking up her teacup. "Personally, I love the small-town life, although Anson does have its feuds and dustups. But Lancaster is so slow-moving and congenial."

"Oh, right." Maureen winked at Elaine. "Nothing bad ever happens on the shores of Chickadee Lake."

Elaine chuckled. She could think of a few events that might not be considered either congenial or slow-moving, but she wouldn't mention them to a customer she didn't know. Lancaster did have a unique charm, and she wouldn't want to tarnish its reputation.

"Enjoy your tea." She went to the kitchen to figure up the bills for her outdoor customers.

"Are the parlors still full?" Jan asked when Elaine came in.

"Pretty much. When is Amy bringing Max and Riley?"

"Not until after lunch," Jan said. "It should be slower by then."

Elaine went out the front this time so she would come to Macy's table first. She rounded the corner onto the side porch that faced Sylvia's Closet across a strip of grass and shrubs.

To her surprise, all of her customers were bunched up at the opposite end of the porch, nearest the lake.

"What's going on?" Elaine asked as she approached them.

Macy turned toward her. "Clifton just came up from your dock and said he saw something odd on the lake."

"Oh?" Elaine realized Clifton Young, Rose's father and a town selectman, had joined the group.

"Hello, Elaine," he said. "I brought the boat over, and I was just telling these folks that I saw something large floating in the water off Turner's Point."

"What was it?" Elaine asked.

"I don't know for sure. If I was boating on the Amazon, I'd have said a crocodile."

Elaine laughed. "No, really."

"I need to get over to the town office—I'm late for a meeting—so I didn't go closer for a better look. Now I wish I had." Clifton shrugged. "Probably just a floating log, though it looked greenish. Trick of the light on the water, most likely. Have a nice day, folks." He strode the length of the porch, toward the street. It was only a short walk to the town office.

Elaine glanced down toward the dock. Clifton's boat was moored alongside it. Rose often brought the boat to work, but that morning she had ridden in with her neighbor, Jordy Quinn, on the back of his motorcycle. The customers were still staring out at the water, which licked the shore with gentle waves.

"Well," she said, "I expect Clifton's eyes played a trick on him. I have your sales slips here."

She handed out the slips. Two of her parties headed inside to pay, laughing about the "crocodile" and speculating as to what Clifton had actually seen. She heard Macy tell her cottage guests as they walked toward the front porch, "That reminds me of something the man who sold me Green Glade told me about."

The others settled back at their tables.

"Can I refresh your tea?" Elaine asked them.

After she had done that, she went in the front door. The two parties that had left the side porch had paid and gone, but apparently they had spread the word inside about

Clifton's reported sighting. Maureen and her friend were at the checkout.

Rose rang up their bill while Maureen said, "Didn't I hear Macy say something like that happened when she was a child?"

"She was talking about what other people told her," Rose replied. "She said the man who used to own Green Glade saw something in the lake years ago. But it wasn't like a crocodile. She said he described it more like a sea serpent."

"A sea serpent in Chickadee Lake." Maureen shook her head.

Dee chuckled. "Maybe it's a Maine version of the Loch Ness Monster. I must say this visit to Lancaster was an eventful one."

When the two women had gone out, Elaine stepped over to the counter.

"Rose, did Macy tell everyone what your dad said?"

"Loud and clear." Rose rolled her eyes toward the ceiling. "I'll be surprised if they didn't hear her clear over at Murphy's General Store."

"Rumors," Elaine said with a sigh.

"Well, maybe it will bring in more business," Rose said. "Not that we need any more. I'd better go check on my customers."

Archie came out of the east parlor. "What was that I heard? Some sort of large animal in the lake?"

Elaine threw her hands up. "You didn't hear it from me."

Suddenly Archie cocked his head to one side. "What's that?"

Elaine listened. "Sounds like a siren."

Archie went to the front door and threw it open. The sound immediately became louder, and they stepped out onto the porch. From the fire station up the street came the town's tanker, followed by the ladder truck, both with sirens screaming.

Elaine covered her ears as Rose and several customers crowded out the door to join them.

"I wonder what's burning," said Pearl Trexler, who had been having a leisurely tea with her friend Martha Nelson.

"I hope it's not Green Glade," Archie said, "after that fire a couple of years ago."

"I don't think they're turning that way." Elaine followed the path of the fire trucks. "No, they're going out Sugar Maple Road."

Several other vehicles zoomed past and turned onto Sugar Maple Road. Elaine recognized those of some of the volunteer firefighters.

"Look!" Archie pointed, and far over the trees and the buildings on the other side of Main Street, a gray column of smoke appeared.

CHAPTER TWO

I wonder what it is," Martha said. "I hope it's not the school burning."

"I think it's farther away than the school," Rose said.

Elaine sent up a silent prayer for the firefighters and whoever owned the property where the blaze burned.

More guests crowded out the door to see what was happening.

"Guess we'd better go inside," Rose said. She made her way through the customers to the checkout. Several people stepped up to pay and remarked on the fire trucks.

"Hope it's nobody's house," one woman said as she gave Rose her credit card.

Elaine hoped not as well. She went back to the kitchen, where Jan was placidly loading the dishwasher. She looked up when Elaine came in.

"I heard sirens. What's going on?"

"Both fire trucks and a pack of volunteers went tearing out Sugar Maple Road," Elaine said.

"I hope it's nothing serious."

"Well, we could see smoke from the porch."

"Must be something fairly big, then." Jan closed the dishwasher and pushed the start button. "Tag King was saying how they need some new equipment for the fire department. I hope they have what they need today."

"Yeah, that's why they're holding the barbecue and firemen's muster in a couple of weeks," Elaine said. "To raise money for new hoses. Tag said if they earn enough from the field day, they want a thermal imaging camera too."

Jan nodded. "Something like that could save lives."

"Yes. But I think the ladder truck needs some maintenance too. That will come first."

The cousins gazed soberly at each other. Tag King had recently been elected fire chief by the other volunteers. At thirty, Tag was a respected part of Lancaster's business community. He owned his own motorcycle- and snowmobile-repair shop on Pine Ridge Road, across from his parents' Hearthside Restaurant.

Noon was approaching, and many of the customers checked out after the excitement of the fire engines. While the tearoom was quieter, Elaine and Jan ate their lunch and went upstairs to their living quarters to make sure the guest room was ready for Max and Riley. Only recently, Elaine's daughter Sasha had stayed in that room after she'd made the official move to Lancaster to be nearer to her boyfriend, Brody. Now, she'd moved into her own apartment and was steadily building her personal training business. She'd already gained several new clients and Elaine had no doubt she would be a huge success.

Elaine took in the room. The boys would probably want to sleep in the tower room at least once, but Jan wanted them close by for the first night. The boys didn't usually stay over unless their parents or older cousins were there as well. At seven, they were growing right up, but she wanted to know they were adjusting to the old house before letting them sleep out of earshot.

When she and Jan were sure the room was as ready as they could make it, with a few boy-friendly toys and storybooks handy, they went downstairs. Archie stood on the porch, talking to Kit Edmonds and her eight-year-old daughter, Marcella. Kit taught school at the local elementary school, but she and Marcella were off for the summer and frequently visited the tearoom. Kit's husband, Russell, delivered the mail by boat to lakeside cottages and businesses, but he was also a volunteer firefighter.

"Hi, Jan. Hi, Elaine," Kit said as they reached the bottom of the stairs.

"Hello," Marcella said with a smile.

"Well, hi, Marcella and Mom," Elaine said.

Archie turned to her and Jan. "Kit was just saying Russell's gone on that fire call."

"Do you know where it is?" Jan asked.

Kit nodded. "Apparently it's a small barn at the Reynolds place."

"Oh, I'm glad it's not a house," Elaine said.

"Yes. Russell had just finished his mail route and had tied up at the marina, so when they paged him, he ran over to the firehouse, and Tag took him in the ladder truck with him. Russell called me when they reached the scene so Marcella and I wouldn't worry."

"That was nice of him," Archie said.

"Yes. I was just glad they didn't have a breakdown on the way to the fire. Russell says those old trucks really need some serious maintenance."

"Maybe the tearoom could send something over to the firehouse for the firefighters when they get back," Jan said.

Elaine smiled at her. "That's a great idea. Most of them probably haven't had lunch yet."

"I'll make up a couple of boxes of cookies." Jan looked at Kit. "Would you like to drop them off?"

"Oh yes, we would *love* it," Marcella said, bouncing on her toes.

Kit laughed. "We'd be glad to."

"I'll go get them right now." Jan hurried toward the kitchen.

"Maybe you'd like to sit down and have a cup of tea on the house," Elaine said with a smile. "I'm sure the firefighters will be out at the Reynolds farm for a while."

Marcella's eyes lit and she grabbed her mother's arm, grinning up at her.

"All right," said Kit, "but we haven't had lunch either. No cookies yet."

"I'll wrap a couple of them for you to take home," Elaine said.

An hour later, everyone seemed to have forgotten about the fire—everyone in the tearoom, anyway. Rose and Archie took their lunch breaks, and more customers began filtering in. About three o'clock, Beatrice Orwell came in. The elderly woman was one of Elaine's favorite customers, and she stopped by her table.

"Quite the excitement in town," Beatrice said, patting her wavy brown hair.

"Yes, that fire set everyone's heart racing," Elaine replied. She'd had several reports from customers over the past couple of hours.

"Fire?"

"Isn't that what you meant?" Elaine asked. "The Reynoldses' small barn burned earlier today. No one was hurt. They're saying it was probably caused by spontaneous combustion in the hayloft."

"That's too bad. No, I meant the thing in the lake."

"Oh," Elaine said. "I'd nearly forgotten that."

"Clifton Young saw something," Beatrice said firmly. She picked up her teacup and took a sip.

"Surely just a floating log," Elaine said.

"Maybe not," Beatrice said. "It makes me think of when I was a girl. There was a creature in the lake then, you know."

Elaine studied her face, but Beatrice didn't seem to be teasing.

"Tell me about it." She sat down opposite Beatrice.

"Well, this...thing appeared one summer. Right after World War II, it was. My sister Agnes and I were girls."

Elaine nodded. "What sort of thing was it?"

"An animal of some sort. A giant eel, maybe, or a water serpent. Big. People would see it in the twilight, near the outlet of the bog."

"Really?" Clifton Young would have motored past that place on his way to their dock.

"People called it Chick."

Elaine frowned. "But it wasn't a bird."

"No, no." Beatrice leaned toward her and said in a conspiratorial whisper, "You know—for Chickadee Lake."

"Oh, I see." Elaine smiled. "So it wasn't real."

"Some said it was."

"Did you ever see it?"

"Me? No. We didn't live on the water, but the stories made me too scared to go in swimming that year."

"What happened to it?"

"No one knows. People saw it now and again for a few years, and then it sort of faded away. Maybe it died, I don't know."

"Huh. That's very interesting." Elaine stood. "Thanks for telling me about it. I should get back to work now."

"Nice talking to you," Beatrice said.

Elaine took a few steps toward the dining room door and looked back at her. No, she was sure Mrs. Orwell was serious. She walked out to the kitchen. Jan sat on a stool at her work island, leafing through a cookbook.

"Jan, maybe Macy is telling the truth about there being a creature in the lake fifty or sixty years ago. Beatrice Orwell says she remembers it, back when she was a child, and it had a name."

"Oh? What was it?"

"Chick, for Chickadee Lake."

"That sounds very…lighthearted."

"Doesn't it?"

Jan's brow furrowed. "Wasn't there a lake monster in Lake Champlain back along? I seem to remember something…"

"You may be right," Elaine said. She and her late husband Ben had followed his military career around the world, and she had gaps in her US cultural knowledge.

Jan got up and closed the cookbook. "The twins will be here soon, but it might be worth looking that up sometime."

"Yes," Elaine said. "Especially if Chick makes another appearance." She looked out the window toward the side porch. "Oh, someone's sitting out on the porch. I'd better go wait on them."

She went out via the back door. A young woman with short-cropped strawberry-blonde hair sat at one of the round wrought iron tables with two men who looked to be in their thirties. Elaine walked over with a smile.

"Sadie, hello."

"Hi, Elaine," Sadie Taylor said.

"We got your wedding invitation. You must be so excited!"

"I sure am. Our house is in a frenzy, and we decided to sneak out for a little break." Sadie gestured to one of her companions. "This is my cousin Garrett Wolfe and his friend Adrian Holt. They came early for the wedding, and they're staying at the B&B."

"Nice to meet you," Elaine said. "Wolfe. That's an interesting name."

Garrett grinned. "It's my professional name."

"He was a Taylor," Sadie said, "until the show-biz bug bit him."

"Oh, are you an actor?" Elaine asked.

"No, I'm more of a director," Garrett said. "I like to get behind the camera too."

Sadie waved one hand through the air. "He's going to videotape the wedding."

"How nice," Elaine said. "I guess you wanted to spend some time getting reacquainted with Lancaster?"

"Yes," Garrett said. "I lived here until I was nineteen, and I have fond memories of the small-town life. I brought Adrian along thinking we might do a little filming for another project."

"That's intriguing."

Garrett shot a glance at Adrian, and his friend smiled.

"Well, what would you folks like this afternoon?" Elaine took out her pen and order pad.

Adrian's phone rang in his shirt pocket. He took it out and glanced at the screen.

"It's Danielle. Just get me a cup of tea and something to go with it." He got up and walked farther down the porch, where he could have some privacy.

Garrett winked at Elaine. "His girlfriend. He's crazy about her." He looked over at Sadie. "What do you say, cuz? Share a pot of chai tea?"

"That sounds good to me," Sadie said. "Why don't you bring us the cookie assortment plate, Elaine? Unless you'd like something else, Garrett?"

"Nope, cookies sound great." Garrett leaned back in his chair. "I'll want to get some footage of the lake, of course. You have a beautiful spot here."

"Thank you," Elaine said. "Where did you live when you were young?"

"Over on Oxcart Road. My folks sold it ten years or so ago, and someone else lives there now."

"The Farrises," Sadie supplied.

That name jogged Elaine's memory. "I know the place. Nice and quiet over there."

"Too quiet to suit Garrett." Sadie smiled at her cousin. "He had to move to the big city for some excitement. New York. He lives in Manhattan now."

"That's quite a change. Well, I'll go get your tea started."

Elaine walked past Adrian, close enough to hear him say, "I miss you too," and went across the screened-in back porch to the kitchen.

"Sadie Taylor's out there with her cousin and his friend," she reported to Jan. "Her cousin Garrett is a film director— the one causing the stir at the Pine Tree Grill last night, I take it."

"It's a small town," Jan said. "I suppose it was bound to happen. If you don't spill anything on him, maybe he'll put you in his next big movie."

"Ha. I don't think he's famous yet, but I may be wrong."

She fixed the tray for the guests and took it to them. Adrian had rejoined Garrett and Sadie at the table. Elaine arranged their cups, teapot, and cookie plate and left them. Almost as soon as she got back into the kitchen, Rose hurried in the door from the hallway.

"Jan, I think Amy's here. I saw a van pull in that looks like hers."

"Fantastic." Jan untied her apron.

"Are you ready for this?" Elaine asked.

"I am *so* ready." Jan smiled at her. "The question is, are *you* ready, Elaine?" She followed Elaine out to the front porch.

Amy was out of the van, and the rear door was up. One of the twins rocketed out of the side passenger door and sped toward them, followed by his identical brother. The first boy plummeted into Jan's arms. Elaine had frequently complained that she had trouble telling which twin was which, but Jan always knew.

"Well, Riley! Welcome!" She hugged him back.

Max was right behind him. Both boys wore shorts and T-shirts, but their shirts were different, so that would help Elaine—at least for a few hours. Riley's was solid blue, like a sports jersey, with a number eight on the front, while Max's shirt had green, blue, black, and white stripes.

After they hugged their grandmother, they both said, almost in unison, "Hi, Elaine."

She laughed and held out her arms. "We're thrilled to have you here."

After delivering hearty hugs, the boys retrieved their backpacks from the van, and Jan took them inside and straight upstairs, while Elaine went to help Amy with a few more items.

"I brought their lifejackets and a couple of swim tubes," Amy said apologetically. "I didn't know if they'd get to swim, but they'd sure love to."

"Oh, I think that can be arranged," Elaine said.

"Great. Their water shoes are in here, along with face masks and snorkels." She passed a bright-red carryall to Elaine.

"I guess they're eager," Elaine said.

"You bet. Riley said they saw a turtle last time they were here, and he's determined to catch one."

"Maybe we'll have a terrarium by the time you get back."

A couple of customers came out of the tearoom, and Elaine waved. "It's almost closing time," she said. "Things will quiet down then."

"Do you need to go help?" Amy asked.

"No, Rose and Archie will handle it. Let's get this stuff inside."

Since Amy was expecting another baby, Elaine grabbed the two bags that looked heaviest and let Amy carry the light, though more awkward, swim tubes.

"Maybe we should put those on the back porch."

"Sounds like a plan," Amy said. "They've got their suits in the backpacks, but this stuff doesn't need to be in your way."

They took all the swim gear around by way of the side porch. Sadie and the two men were drinking their tea and bantering. Elaine noted that more than half the cookies had disappeared from their assortment.

"Can I get you anything else?" she asked on the way by.

"No, this is great," Garrett said.

"Well, enjoy. I'll send someone out to check on you in a few minutes."

She and Amy arranged the boys' gear on the back porch, away from Earl Grey's cat shelter and feeding station. When they went into the kitchen, Archie was unloading a tray of dirty dishes. Elaine pulled her order pad from her pocket.

"Hey, Archie, my last party is still on the porch, but I think they'll be done soon. Would you handle this, please?" She tore off the slip with Sadie's party's order on it.

"Sure. Welcome, Amy."

"Nice to see you again, Archie." She looked at Elaine. "Guess I'll go tell the boys goodbye and hit the road."

"Are you sure you want to climb those stairs?" Elaine asked. "I can bring them down."

"No, the exercise is good for me. I just hope they don't wear you and Mom out." Amy went with her up to the guest room.

CHAPTER THREE

J an showed the boys where to store their clothing in the guest
room, where they could each have an entire dresser. This
was their first extended visit to Jan's house without their parents.
Amy and Van had decided to take a week off together before
the new baby came, and Jan was delighted for the chance to get
to know her grandsons better at this stage in their lives. They
were growing up so fast, and she didn't want to miss a thing.

Riley put his space action figures on top of his dresser and
stuffed his empty backpack in the bottom drawer.

"Can't we sleep in the tower room?" he asked.

"Maybe," Jan said. "But not tonight. You've got to show me
what good boys you are first. But we'll see if you can't have at
least one night up there later on."

"Well, guys, this is it," Amy said from the doorway. "You'll
be here seven whole nights."

"Yippee!" Riley cried.

Max ran to her and threw his arms around her waist. "Have
fun, Mom."

"You too."

Riley moved in for his hug, and Amy seemed reluctant to leave them.

"Help with the dishes."

"We will," Riley said.

"Your swimming stuff is on the back porch, but don't you go near the water without Grandma or Elaine, you hear?"

"That is absolutely correct," Jan said. "That's one rule that will get you banned from the tower room if you break it."

"We won't," Max said.

"Bye, Mom." Riley smiled angelically up at Amy.

"Oh, you two," she laughed. "Goodbye."

Jan went down the stairs with her daughter.

Elaine said, "Come on, boys, let's go check out the leftover cookies."

"Oh boy!" Max led the way to the kitchen.

Archie was coming in from the porch with the Open banner. Only a few customers lingered over their tea.

"Four o'clock already," Jan noted.

"Yes, and I'd better make tracks. Thanks again, Mom." Amy kissed Jan's cheek and went out.

In the kitchen, Rose was loading dirty dishes from a tray into the dishwasher.

"Well, hello, Kincaid duo," she said.

"Hi, Rose," the twins said in unison.

Rose laughed. "Let me guess—milk and cookies?"

"Yes, but we'll get it," Jan said.

"Can we eat outside?" Max asked.

Jan nodded. "I don't see why not. If fact, we can eat down on the deck if you want." Stairs marched from their back porch down to a platform well above the water, complete with a round white wrought iron table and chairs, where Jan and Elaine often enjoyed their breakfast or a cup of tea in warm weather. More steps led from the deck area down to their boat dock.

Elaine poured milk for the boys and tea for herself and Jan, while Jan selected paper plates, napkins, and two cookie boxes.

"All right, Riley, you take the plates. Max, you carry the napkins. Let's go." Jan opened the back door and held it while Elaine went past her with the tray of drinks. Jan closed the door firmly behind her and followed with the all-important cookies.

The twins' energy surged when they saw the sparkling water below. They flung their burdens on the table and raced down the lower steps to the dock.

"Hey! A fish jumped!" Riley yelled.

Max turned and looked up at the women. "Whose boat is that?"

"That's Mr. Young's." Jan grabbed for the paper napkins before the breeze could send them into the lake. "Rose's father. You boys be careful down there."

"I'll set things up," Elaine said. "You go and enjoy the moment."

"Thanks." Jan held the railing and went down the steps to the dock. Both boys were kneeling on its edge, peering over the side into the clear water below.

"See anything?" she asked.

"Minnows," Max said.

"I bet we could catch some if we had a bucket," Riley added.

Max looked up at her. "Grandma, can we go swimming?"

Jan considered that for only a moment. "Not tonight. Maybe tomorrow afternoon. Now, let's go eat our snack, or it will be too close to suppertime."

The boys raced up the stairs, and Jan followed at a more leisurely pace. The four of them settled down to eat on the deck.

"How many cookies can we have?" Riley asked, looking to Jan.

"I think two is plenty for this time of day."

The boys considered the choices in the plastic containers and each put two cookies on his plate.

"Want one?" Elaine asked.

"No, thanks." Jan sipped the vanilla chai tea Elaine had poured for her. "Maybe after supper."

Elaine covered the containers. The back door opened above them, and Rose and her father came out of the house and down the steps.

"Hey, Clifton," Elaine said. "Your adventure caused quite a commotion today."

"Rose was telling me," he said as he reached their level on the deck. "Sorry about that. I didn't mean to stir things up."

Jan laughed. "I think the fire got more attention."

"Yes," Elaine said, "but some of the older people were saying they remember tales of a lake creature when they were young."

"Speaking of that fire," Rose put in, "Dad says the Reynolds family had insurance on the barn."

"They did," Clifton affirmed. "But it's still a blow. And the fire department! The tanker went to refill, and they had a flat tire. Tag said they couldn't have saved the barn anyway, but we need to take better care of the town's equipment. It's there to keep us all safe."

"Can't buy many tires if the people vote down the budget," Jan noted.

"True." Clifton shook his head. "I still don't understand that one. It was really close at the town meeting. I think that item went down by two votes. Then someone moved to cap the department's spending at what they had last year. They need an increase instead!"

"Maybe the muster they're planning will raise money to make up what they're lacking," Elaine said.

Rose nodded. "Let's hope so. If we have a fire at our house, I want the fire trucks to make it out there."

"Maybe we could do something the day of the muster too," Jan said. "We could donate money to the fire department from it."

"Like sell cookies shaped like fire engines?" Rose asked.

"Yum, yum," Riley said.

"Hey, buster, you've got a milk mustache," Jan said. "Use your napkin."

Elaine said, "Let's give it some thought. We should be able to come up with something that would complement what the fire department is doing."

"They're letting merchants set up vendor booths that day," Clifton said. "Well, we'd better get going. Thanks for letting me dock here."

"Anytime!" Jan called after him.

Clifton and Rose went down to the dock and climbed into the small motorboat. Rose cast off, and Clifton started the outboard motor. They puttered away across the lake.

"Bye!" Riley jumped up and waved frantically.

Max pushed his chair back and joined him. "Bye, Rose! Bye, Rose's dad!"

Rose looked back and moved her arm in a sweeping wave above her head.

"Boys," Elaine said quietly, "can you settle down for a second, and I'll tell you something neat?"

They both turned toward her, big-eyed and nodding.

"The kitty is watching us," Elaine said.

Riley sucked in a deep breath.

"Where?" Max asked.

"Now, don't you go chasing him," Jan said. "Earl Grey doesn't like to be chased."

"But if you stay still, he might go onto the back porch for some supper," Elaine said. "And sometimes he lets quiet, polite people pat him."

"I can be polite," Max said soberly.

Riley didn't look so certain.

They watched the cat for several minutes, but Earl Grey didn't go up to the porch. When he had slunk away in the tall grass, Jan said, "Show's over for now. Let's take this stuff up to the house."

She gave each of the boys something to carry. When they reached the kitchen, Archie was just coming in from the hall.

"There you are," he said. "I put the receipts in the safe. I think we're all set for the night."

"Thanks, Archie," Elaine said. "We'll see you Monday."

"Righto."

"Say hi to Gloria," Jan said, knowing Archie's wife would appreciate the greeting.

She took the twins for a walk before supper. After they'd eaten, she had them help clean up the kitchen, and then she got out a board game the boys liked. They coaxed Elaine to play with them, though she didn't need much convincing.

They had a rousing game, but soon the boys were beginning to look a little droopy.

Max yawned. "Grandma, is Rose's house going to have a fire?"

"What do you mean?" Jan was distracted, putting the game pieces into the box.

"She said if it did, she didn't want any flat tires on the fire truck," Max replied.

Riley frowned at her. "Yeah. Is *your* house going to have a fire?"

Elaine met Jan's gaze, her face filled with concern.

"Oh, no, honey," Jan said. "They were just saying how we have those fire trucks to protect our town, and people are trying to raise money to keep them in good shape."

The boys were quiet, seeming to think about that.

"Do you have a smoke detector?" Max asked.

"Yes, we do," Elaine said quickly. "In fact, we have several. There's one in the hallway upstairs, right outside the room where you'll be sleeping."

"That's right." Jan put the lid on the game box. "And we have one in the kitchen, and one in each parlor, and a couple more of them upstairs."

"Is there one in the tower room?" Riley asked.

"Well, no," Jan admitted, "but there's one by the stairs that go up there."

Elaine stood. "Maybe you guys would like to see how the moon looks when it shines on the lake at night."

"Good idea," Jan said. "Let's go down to the deck. We might even hear some loons."

Later, when the boys were tucked into bed, Jan and Elaine sat down in their upstairs living room.

"Whew," Jan said. "I'm beat."

"Think we've got the pep to keep up with them all week?" Elaine asked.

"I hope so! And they'll start Vacation Bible School on Monday."

"That's true. They'll be over at the church during the busiest time of the day."

"From 9 a.m. to noon." Jan yawned. "I know it's early, but I think I'll hit the hay."

"Something tells me that when those boys get up in the morning, they won't be less energetic than they were tonight."

"Yes, and they're going to want to swim tomorrow afternoon and go turtle hunting."

Elaine smiled. "I can hardly wait."

Jan rose and picked up the sweater she'd dropped on the couch. "Just pray that this good weather stays with us. I can't imagine those two cooped up inside for long."

MAX AND RILEY didn't seem nervous about going into a strange Sunday school class the next morning. They ate a huge breakfast and pumped Jan with questions about the children their age.

"Hey, guys," Elaine said at a lull in their conversation, "I think I hear Earl Grey on the back porch. Do you want to feed him?"

"Yes!" both boys cried, jumping up with excitement.

"*Shh,*" Jan said. "You have to be very quiet, remember? Move slowly." She walked noiselessly to the back door, which Elaine had left open a crack.

Max and Riley followed, exaggerating their tiptoe walk.

"Aw," Riley said softly, peering under Jan's arm onto the porch.

"I see him!"

Max's announcement was a little too loud. Earl Grey leaped out the hinged cat door and jumped off the steps, then slipped underneath them.

Jan shook her head. "Well, I guess you have to wait to see him another time."

Riley said sternly to his brother, "Next time, be quiet!"

Max's head drooped.

Jan let them put cat food and water in Earl Grey's dishes. "Time to get dressed for church," she said. "Put on the best clothes your mom sent with you, and then come to me for inspection."

"Go ahead up with them if you want to," Elaine said. "I'll take care of the dishes."

She hummed as she went about cleaning up the kitchen. When she went upstairs to change her clothes a few minutes later, Jan had both twins in the living room. They looked extra cute in clean khakis and button-up shirts, and she could see wet comb tracks through their hair.

"Let me see your fingernails, Riley," Jan said.

Elaine smiled and went to her bedroom.

At the church, she volunteered to take the boys to the class for their age, but Jan turned her down.

"I want to make sure they know Grandma's expecting the best from them."

Elaine went into the auditorium, where the adult class would meet. Will and Pearl Trexler, Kit Edmonds's elderly grandparents, were already seated in their usual pew, and she stopped in the aisle to greet them.

"Well, hello, young lady," Will said.

Elaine let him get away with calling her that because he was eighty-two years old. She grinned at him and his wife.

"Hi, Will. Good morning, Pearl."

"Say, did you hear something about the Chick monster making an appearance?" Will asked. "I heard it was near your waterfront."

Elaine shook her head in exasperation. "I think it was just a log. Clifton Young said he thought he saw something from his boat as he was passing the outlet of the bog, but he didn't have time to investigate."

"Oh, down there," Pearl said.

Will's brow furrowed. "That's prime hunting grounds for Chick."

Elaine chuckled. "Beatrice Orwell told me people used to say there was a Loch Ness-type serpent in our lake. What do you know about it?"

"It's true," Pearl said.

Elaine was skeptical. She scrunched up her face. "According to whom?"

"I was just a girl, but my father saw it," Pearl insisted.

"Really?" Elaine had never heard that Pearl's father was unreliable. "For sure?"

"He always claimed that," Will said. "My friends and I went out looking for it, but I was never fortunate—or unfortunate— enough to spot it myself."

"What year are we talking about?" Elaine asked.

"Must have been '47 or '48. I was around twelve. My brother and I and a couple of other boys used to take my folks' rowboat out. We'd row over to the outlet and fish for hours, hoping Chick would surface."

"But he never did?" Elaine asked.

Will shrugged. "Not while we were looking."

"Somebody took a picture of it though," Pearl said. "Who was that? Do you remember?"

Will shook his head. "No, but I seem to remember something about it."

"Very interesting." The Sunday school teacher stood up behind the lectern, and Jan was returning from delivering the boys to their class. "We'll have to discuss that another time," Elaine said. She patted Will's shoulder and hurried to join Jan.

Between the services, she went with Jan to get the boys. Max and Riley bounced from the classroom, holding up their lesson papers.

"Look, Grandma! See what we made?" Max stuck his paper into Jan's hand.

"Nice." Jan gazed down at the drawing of David watching his flock.

Elaine stooped to look at Riley's work. "Oh, I like the way you made the sheep all different colors."

Riley grinned up at her. "We start VBS tomorrow. Do you know what that stands for, Elaine?"

"I sure do. Vacation Bible School."

"It's about Noah's ark," Max said.

A colorful poster on the wall of the hallway shouted the message as well. Elaine pointed to it.

"Look, this shows the animals going into the ark. What's your favorite?"

"The elephants," Max said, rocking up and down on his toes.

"Dogs are my favorite, but they don't show any dogs," Riley said.

"I'm sure there were dogs there too," Elaine told him.

"Yes," Jan said. "They just didn't have room on the poster for all the different animals."

"Maybe the dogs are already inside the ark," Riley said wistfully.

Elaine smiled at Jan over his head. "I'll bet you're right. They were probably the first ones inside, to pick a good spot."

The boys were fairly quiet during the worship service. Afterward, Will Trexler caught up with Elaine in the aisle.

"You ought to talk to someone at the town office about the lake monster," he said. "In the old days, the chamber of commerce made a big to-do over it."

"Really? I'm amazed."

"Sure, it was good for the town. Brought a lot of tourists. Half the cottage businesses were built then."

Elaine chuckled. "I meant I was amazed that Lancaster had a chamber of commerce seventy years ago."

"Oh sure. We had quite a boom after the war. And Chick was a big help."

"Thanks. We might look into that," Elaine said.

Riley had stopped walking and tugged at her hand. Elaine turned to face him.

"What is it, Riley?"

"Did the town blow up?"

"What? No."

"He said there was a big boom and a war."

Elaine couldn't hold back her smile. "A boom in this case means they did a lot of business, and more people came to live here and to visit Chickadee Lake."

"Oh. What was the war about?"

"That was something called World War II. Did you ever hear about that?"

"I think so. Maybe."

"It was a long, long time ago," Elaine assured him, "and it didn't come near here. It was mostly in other parts of the world."

"Okay."

She wondered if he had G.I. Joe toys, but maybe not. Everything seemed to be superheroes and space aliens these days.

Jan and Max had moved on ahead of them, and Jan looked back.

"Come on," Elaine said to Riley. "We can talk about it more later if you want to. But we have to get home now and eat lunch so you and Max can go swimming and look for turtles."

"Yeah!" He tried to run up the aisle, pulling her hand, but she held him back.

"Let's walk, but we can walk fast."

CHAPTER FOUR

Jan loved Sunday afternoons. They were so peaceful and quiet, a restful break from the business. She and Elaine sat on the dock in deck chairs, watching Max and Riley wade in the shallows on their turtle-hunting expedition. The boys wore their swimsuits, T-shirts, and rubber-soled water shoes, and Jan had slathered them with sunscreen and given them each a plastic pail.

"Lookee, Grandma!" Riley turned toward them from his place along the rocky shore just beyond their tiny beach and held up a three-inch turtle.

"Yay! Put him in your bucket," Jan called.

"I suppose we'll have to find something for the boys to keep them in all week," Elaine said. She took a sip of her mint iced tea and waved to Riley, who plopped the little turtle in his pail and turned back to the search.

"They're having so much fun," Jan said. "I suppose we can get some turtle food at the pet store."

"Probably. Is that old dishpan big enough?"

"How about that old galvanized washtub in the garage?" Jan suggested.

"Yeah. We can put rocks and a little lake weed in it."

Jan smiled as Max shrieked and turned, holding up his new find.

"Great!" she yelled. She glanced at Elaine. "I think we can keep the poor things happy all week, but I'll make the boys let them go before they leave."

"They might want to take a couple of them home for pets."

"Oh, wouldn't Amy love that," Jan said. "She's got enough to think about with the new baby on the way. No, I think these reptiles will remain mostly wild. That way the boys can catch them every time they come to visit."

"Unless the turtles wise up and hide when they see them coming," Elaine said with a laugh. "That's probably best all around though."

A motorboat approached across the placid lake, and Jan studied it. "Is that Jack?"

"Looks like his boat." Elaine stood and waved. Jack eased the cabin cruiser in toward them and brought it around a few yards out and killed the motor.

"Hi!" Elaine called to the young game warden.

Jan looked toward the twins. Excited, they were splashing toward the dock in the shallows.

"Hey!" Jack called. "Just thought I'd tell you I've been patrolling down near the outlet."

"Find anything?" Elaine asked.

Jack shook his head. "No floating logs, no snags, if that's what you mean."

"Too bad," Jan said.

"We hoped you could put the rumors to rest," Elaine told him.

"Well, if Clifton did see something, it's not there now."

Jan didn't like the implications—whatever had been there yesterday had moved. So maybe it was a live creature after all.

The twins scrambled up onto the dock at the shore end and ran out to where Jan and Elaine had placed their chairs.

"Is that Jack?" Max shielded his eyes and peered at the boat.

"Yeah, Jack!" Riley said. The twins had met Jack Weston at family gatherings, when their aunt Tara had brought him as a guest.

"Well, hello there, young Kincaids," Jack said with a grin. "What are you up to?"

"We caught three turtles!" Max shouted.

"Wow, three turtles. Are you going to have turtle soup?"

Max scowled at him. "No!"

Jan laughed. "It's not illegal for them to keep a few as pets for the week, is it, Jack?"

He shook his head. "No, those little painted turtles and box turtles are all right. Let me know if they start messing with snappers though."

"Oh, I haven't seen any snapping turtles," Jan said. "No big ones, anyway."

Jack nodded. "Well, I just wanted to tell you I didn't find anything, in case your customers are worked up about it. I heard there was a lot of speculation about what Clifton saw."

Elaine asked, "Did you ever hear of anything like that in this lake?"

Jack lifted his hat and ran a hand across his brow. "Just what the old-timers tell me, and I think they're pulling my leg."

"Well, thanks for stopping by," Jan said.

"Okay. Figured you'd help douse the rumors. I'm going to tell Clifton now, and then I'm going home to have a late lunch."

They waved to him as the boat pulled away and gathered speed.

"Grandma, what was he talking about, in the lake?" Max asked.

Jan couldn't think of a good way to word her reply without the boys getting more curious. "Nothing. Just that the lake is a good place to be. He said there's nothing bad in it. Now, do you want to swim, or do you want cookies?"

"Swim," said Riley, peeling off his damp T-shirt.

"Cookies," said Max.

Elaine laughed. "Have your swim, and I'll go fix a snack. Are you going in the water, Jan?"

"Sure, why not?" Jan didn't swim often, but it was a beautiful, warm day, and she'd feel better about the boys being in the lake if she was within reach. She unzipped her cover-up and dropped it on her deck chair. "You boys know how to swim now, don't you?"

"We had lessons at the Boys and Girls Club," Riley said.

"I thought so. So, show me your stuff."

She walked to the shallow end of the dock and followed the boys as they scrambled down into the water.

Elaine Skyped with her son, Jared, later in the afternoon and talked to her daughter-in-law, Corrie, and both of their children.

The family had vacationed in Maine with Elaine recently, and the kids missed the lakeshore and the tower room, not to mention their grandma, now that they were back home in Ohio. They'd asked about how Sasha was settling in, and the kids made jokes about Sasha and Brody "sitting in a tree, k-i-s-s-i-n-g."

"We've got Van and Amy's boys here this week," Elaine told Corrie after Lucy and Micah had grown distracted and moved on to another room to play.

"Oh, Micah will be so jealous." Micah was a couple of years older than the twins, and he enjoyed playing with his cousins when the entire family descended on Elaine and Jan's house. "If he had his way, he'd have stayed with you all summer. So, what are you up to with Max and Riley?"

"We're having lots of fun. They just got out of the water with Jan, and I think they're getting changed now. And they're starting VBS in the morning."

"Good. That will keep them busy and give you some breathing space."

"Yes, I think it's going to be a great week," Elaine said. "I just wish you could all be here too, even though it hasn't been that long."

"So do I," Corrie said.

They talked a while longer, and then signed off with a promise from Elaine to send a photo of the twins with their turtles. Jan walked into the living room as she closed the program.

"Amy just called from Nantucket."

"Oh?" Elaine asked. "Everything okay?"

Jan smiled. "Yes, but she couldn't not check on the boys. She said the ferry ride was a little choppy, but she's okay, and she and Van are going to walk around town this evening and soak up the atmosphere."

"Good. I hope they have a marvelous week. Lucy and Micah want a picture of the twins with their turtles. I told Micah we'd post one for them."

"Great idea. I'll get one as soon as they're out of the bathroom."

"Are they all set for tomorrow morning?" Elaine asked. "Do we need to do anything about their clothes?"

"No, they're ready." Jan sat down on the couch. "Did you notice how Max picked up on what Jack said this afternoon? I don't want these boys having nightmares because someone saw a log in the lake and people start crying 'monster.'"

"It was nothing," Elaine said. "We just have to tell them that. I was a little concerned this morning though. Riley heard me talking to Will at church, and Will said the town had a big boom after the war because of the lake monster thing. Well, Riley thought he meant there had been a war here, and the big boom was some kind of explosion."

Jan chuckled. "I'm sorry. I can't help laughing. We just need to make sure the boys understand what we say."

"Maybe we can make it fun," Elaine said. "I don't want it to be traumatic for them."

Jan looked over her shoulder toward the doorway. "Should we dig into it a little, so we can tell them exactly what happened back then?"

"That might be a good idea. So far, I don't think they've made the connection between 'Chick' and the lake they swam in today, but if they do, it could be scary." Elaine frowned. "Maybe we shouldn't mention Chick around them."

"Well, why not? I think it can be fun. Of course, we shouldn't use words like 'monster' and 'sea serpent.' But if they catch on to it from what people say, we'll need to be able to show them that it was just a fun tourist promotion or something."

"Yeah," Elaine said, "that might be a better approach than trying to hide it from them."

"Maybe we can go over to the town office in the morning, after we drop them at the church for VBS, and find out more about what really did happen back in the old days," Jan said.

"Sounds like a plan."

Noise from the hallway alerted them that the boys were approaching.

Jan stood. "I'm going to take them downstairs. They can help me start supper."

"Okay. And I think I'll do a little searching on that Lake Champlain thing you mentioned." Elaine reached for her laptop.

An hour later, when Jan called her to supper, Elaine was amazed to find that she had become a lake monster believer, at least so far as Lake Champlain and Loch Ness were concerned. She wasn't so sure about Chickadee Lake.

She went down to the kitchen and greeted Jan and the boys.

"Hey," Jan said. "The guys want to eat in the east parlor, in front of the fireplace. Feel like lighting a fire in there?"

"What fun," Elaine said. Even though the temperatures were pleasantly warm, it wasn't too hot to have an evening fire. "Would you guys like to help me lay the kindling?"

"Yeah!" the boys cried.

Jan smiled. "You can have them pull a table where you want it too, and I'll start bringing in the food. Here, Riley, you can carry the bag of chips."

Elaine said, "Oh, and I found quite a bit on that research project we were talking about. I sent you some links. We can talk about it later."

"Gotcha," Jan said.

By the time the boys were in bed, Jan was showing her fatigue, but she brought her laptop to the living room and read through the articles Elaine had linked to. When she had finished, she looked up at Elaine, who had done more browsing while she waited.

"Well, you made a believer of me on the Champ monster," Jan said.

"Yes, I was impressed," Elaine admitted. "The New York and Vermont legislatures have both passed resolutions to protect Champ."

Jan set her laptop beside her on the couch. "But Chickadee Lake isn't nearly as deep as Lake Champlain. Even if their creature is a huge water snake or a garfish like some people think, our lake just doesn't have the space for something like that. Not without everyone knowing about it."

"I think you're right," Elaine said. "If there really was something here in the 1940s, what happened to it? No one ever caught it, or it would have been in the papers."

"Maybe we should go through old newspaper files and see what we find," Jan said.

"That's not a bad idea. But let's go to the town office first. Mark Payson might be able to tell us something about it. Will Trexler said the chamber of commerce was active back then, and they were involved somehow."

"*Hmm.*" Jan leaned her head back against the couch. "We need to get the boys over to the church by nine for Bible school. We could hit the town office after that."

"Will you be done with your baking?" Elaine asked.

"I can be. But I'd better go to bed now if I'm going to get up early to do it."

Jan always rose early, but when they planned an outing she got to the kitchen even earlier. She always made sure the tearoom had plenty of baked goods for the day before leaving the house.

Elaine stood up. "You're right. I'll try to drag myself out early to help you. Our best time to look into this is while the twins are occupied elsewhere. We don't want them to be upset by rumors."

Her cell phone rang, and she took it from her pocket. "Hello?"

"Hi, it's Rose. Sorry to call so late, but I thought you'd want to know."

"Know what?" Elaine asked.

"Chad Prentice called my dad a little while ago. He'd been fishing near the bog tonight. Didn't quit until sunset."

"And?" The skin on the back of Elaine's neck prickled.

"Just as he was about to fire up the motor, he saw something in the water."

"I'm listening."

"He's not sure what it was, but it was big," Rose said. "Big enough to scare him. He said it looked like a huge black thing, just beneath the surface. He was afraid it might go under his boat and capsize him."

"That's pretty big." Elaine met Jan's curious gaze. "Did he think it was a fish?"

"The way he described it, it was more like a really big snake, or an eel."

"Yeah, eels can get big," Elaine said.

Jan nodded her agreement.

"Well, he'd heard about what Dad saw, and so he called to tell him."

"Has he told Jack Weston?"

"I don't know," Rose said. "Probably."

"Okay, thanks. Maybe you should drive to work in the morning, and not bring the boat."

"That's what I thought too," Rose said.

Elaine ended the call and looked at Jan. "There's been another sighting. Maybe we're wrong about how deep the lake would need to be."

CHAPTER FIVE

Jan had preregistered her grandsons for VBS, so on Monday morning it was just a matter of escorting them into the church, introducing them to their teacher, who was Kit Edmonds, and seeing them seated in the row with a dozen other lively children in their age group.

"Looks like Kit will have her hands full," Jan observed as they went down to the church's kitchen to deliver a quadruple batch of cookies they had promised the refreshment committee.

"She's got a helper to sit in with her," Elaine said. "I think they'll be fine. Although between the twins and Jayden Philips, things could get a little wild."

Jayden's mom had three boys and a new baby girl. Although the boys were adorable, they were also extremely active. Elaine figured their mother was happy to send her two older sons to VBS this week.

Annie Richardson and Maureen Oakley held sway in the kitchen that morning.

"Oh, Jan, fantastic," Maureen said when she saw them. She reached for the plastic containers. "What do we have here?"

"Eight dozen animal-shaped sugar cookies with a light icing," Jan said.

"Perfect."

"Jan had a lot of fun making them," Elaine said. "I did wonder about children who can't have sugar or gluten though."

"We've got something for them," Annie said. "I talked to all the moms of the three kids who are restricted, and I think we've covered it. Thank you so much for doing this."

"No problem," Jan said. "I plan to do this again Thursday, so let me know if you want something different."

"I think the animal cookies will be a big hit," Maureen said.

Annie nodded. "Especially with the ark theme. It's wonderful. But we do have some other cookies too, and fruit."

After they left the church, Elaine and Jan drove to the town office. Several cars were in the parking lot already.

"Looks busy," Jan said.

"Well, it's Monday morning. Everyone wants to take care of things they thought of over the weekend," Elaine replied.

"Should we come back another time?"

Elaine shook her head. "Let's at least see if Mark's busy. We won't have many opportunities when the boys aren't with us this week."

They got out of the car and went inside. Mark Payson, the town clerk, was a friend of theirs. His wife, Bristol, owned the Bookworm, the bookstore next door to the tearoom, and the couple attended Lancaster Community Church.

Three people stood at the counter where a clerk was helping them with routine business, and Mark was talking to a man near his desk. Jan and Elaine decided to wait until Mark was free.

About five minutes later, his customer left and he approached them, smiling.

"Hello. How can I help you today?"

Jan said, "We're hoping you can steer us in the right direction on some town history. Did you ever hear about there being a monster in Chickadee Lake back in the 1940s?"

Mark frowned. "I don't think I did, but it sounds intriguing. Tell me more."

"Saturday Clifton Young thought he saw something in the water," Jan said. "He wasn't sure it was alive, but older people started bringing up these stories about a creature in the lake."

"And then someone else saw something last night," Elaine added. "Chad Prentice was fishing around dusk, and he thought he saw a large snake or eel in the water."

"Where was this?" Mark asked.

"Near the outlet from the bog," Jan said. "It was in the same general area where Clifton saw a log or something else."

"*Hmm.* I haven't heard anything like that, but let me take a look in the computer files."

Jan and Elaine followed him to his desk, and he sat down. Mark clicked away at his keyboard for a couple of minutes, then shook his head.

"I'm not finding anything like that. The last invasive species scare was for a lakeweed that boaters were accidentally transplanting from one lake to another. That was about ten years ago."

Jan sighed. "We hoped there would be something. Apparently the chamber of commerce weighed in on it way back then."

"Postwar, you said?"

Elaine said, "Yes, just after World War II."

"A lot of our records from that time have never been computerized." Mark stood. "Let me check with Madeline. She's been here a lot longer than I have." He leaned toward them and whispered, "In fact, I think she might have been born in the '40s."

"Now, Mark, that's not so long ago," Elaine said.

Jan grinned at her. "Yeah. None of us are getting any younger."

Mark chuckled. "You're absolutely right. I was only thinking I'd be remiss if I didn't ask the older and wiser people here."

"That's what I did yesterday," Elaine said. "Will Trexler remembered it."

"Really?" That seemed to carry some weight with Mark. "Let's see what Madeline can tell us."

He led them to where an older woman was working at her desk. She didn't look nearly as old as Will, but Jan thought she was probably near retirement age.

She greeted them, her eyes twinkling behind her glasses, and Mark explained what they were looking for.

"*Hmm,* yes, there was something. I don't remember much about it personally, but I think there was an impact on business. Mark, you might check for an establishment called Chick's Ice Cream Stand. I believe it was where I Scream Ice Cream is now."

"Chick?" Elaine said. "That's what Beatrice Orwell called it."

Madeline nodded. "It was quite a phenomenon, if I'm not mistaken, and Bea Orwell is old enough to remember."

"All right, thanks," Mark said. "I'll see what I can pull up."

"Not in the computer files," Madeline said. "Try the older files out back."

"Okay, we will." Mark smiled at Jan and Elaine. "Would you like to venture into the storage room with me?"

"Are we allowed?" Jan asked.

"Why not? Everything in this building belongs to the townspeople."

Mark led them to a back room almost entirely filled by industrial shelving, cartons, and old metal file cabinets. A single window let in a little sunlight at the back of the building, and Mark turned on overhead fluorescent lighting.

"This is where all the old stuff is," he said with a smile. "The clerks peck away at it whenever they have a slow time, but I'm afraid it will take us years at the rate we're going to get all the old records into the computer."

"What's the system?" Jan asked. "Are documents filed by year?"

"In these cabinets, they are." Mark walked along the row, squinting at the labels on the file drawers. He stopped before a tall gray cabinet with four drawers and touched the next-to-bottom one. "Here you go, 1946. I'll check another place where we have business permits filed."

Jan let Elaine riffle through the folders and envelopes in the drawer.

"Chick, Chick," Elaine said. "I'm not finding anything." She sneezed.

"Want me to take a look?" Jan asked.

Elaine stepped back and let her continue the search.

"Hey, I might have something!" Mark called from deeper in the room.

"Good," Elaine said, "because we're not finding anything."

"It was in those old permits." He walked around the end of a row of metal shelving and brought over a yellowed sheet of paper. "June 1947. The Anderson Ice Cream Stand changed its name to Chick's Ice Cream Stand."

"Interesting." Elaine took the paper from him.

"I can make you a copy."

Jan straightened. "If that was in 1947, maybe I'm looking in the wrong year."

"Yes, it may have been sighted in '46," Elaine said, "but there might not be any official records until the following year."

Jan turned to Mark. "What sort of records would there be? The fact that Madeline remembered the ice cream stand's old name is terrific, but beyond that, how do we know what to look for?"

"I have no idea," Mark said.

"I guess we'll know it if and when we see it," Elaine told her.

The cousins took turns flipping through the dusty documents in the next drawer while Mark went to copy the page he'd found for them.

"Wait a sec," Elaine said, just as he returned. "Here's something about the Fourth of July parade in '47. The town budgeted fifty dollars for a float representing Chick the Lake Monster."

Jan stared at her. "So it was real?"

"At least the town acknowledged it," Elaine said.

"Wow."

"Where would the chamber of commerce keep its old files?" Elaine asked Mark.

"I think some of them are archived at the library. But we've got lists of the members from each year. Let me get you that."

Mark put the photocopy of the ice cream stand document in Jan's hand and disappeared again. Twenty minutes later, the cousins left the town office with that as well as a copy of the selectmen's approval of the parade float funding and a list of Lancaster businesses that participated in the chamber of commerce in the years 1946 to 1948.

"This should give us a place to start," Jan said as they went out to her car.

"Yeah," Elaine replied. "A lot of places to start. I just hope it all leads somewhere."

WHEN THE COUSINS got back to their house, Jan headed straight for the kitchen. Elaine left the papers they'd gotten from Mark in her office and looked out into the entrance hall. Archie was ringing up a customer's bill, and Diane Blanchett, the owner of Computer Gal, walked in through the front door. She looked around uncertainly.

Elaine hurried out to greet her. "Hi, Diane. May I help you?"

Diane gave her a grateful smile. "Thanks. I didn't get breakfast this morning, and I thought I'd grab a muffin and a cup of tea to take over to the shop with me."

"Sure. What would you like? We have blueberry muffins, bran, or zucchini-pineapple this morning."

"Ooh, sounds good. Green tea and a zucchini muffin—to go."

"You got it. Would you like to sit down while I fix your tea?" Elaine asked.

"No, I'll just wait here, if that's okay."

Elaine hurried out to the kitchen. "Diane wants a zucchini muffin to go," she said to Jan.

"I'll get it." Jan stooped to pull one of their small takeout bags from beneath the island counter while Elaine fixed green tea in a large disposable cup.

A minute later, Elaine placed the items in Diane's hands and went behind the checkout counter. "I used a tea bag, since you were in a hurry, and left it in the cup to steep while you go over to your store," she told Diane.

"Perfect." Diane swiped her debit card. "Did you hear about the lake monster?"

"Uh..." Elaine eyed her cautiously. "I heard that Clifton Young saw something—maybe a log."

Diane grinned. "Yeah. You never really know, do you? It gave me an idea."

"What kind of idea?"

"You know the field day that's coming up to raise money for the fire department?"

"Yes."

"I was thinking." Diane leaned toward her and lowered her voice. "What if we had some kind of show at the Grange Hall that afternoon, or even in the evening? We could do a readers' theater, or even a short play, about the Creature of Chickadee Lake."

Elaine gazed at her for a moment. "Well, I don't know. I suppose it might help raise more money…"

"Sure. And it would be great fun." Diane put away her debit card as she talked.

Elaine handed her the receipt. "I was thinking more along the lines of selling cookies shaped like fire trucks and dalmatians that day."

Diane laughed. "Those are good ideas too. If I have time, I'm going to work on a skit. There's not much time, but I think I can come up with something."

She left, and Elaine stood there for a minute, thinking about it. Everyone seemed to love the idea that the lake might hold some mysterious animal. Whether it was true or not didn't seem to matter. Unless she was mistaken, Chick of Chickadee Lake was unstoppable now.

She went to the kitchen. Jan had her loose-leaf binder of favorite recipes open on the counter.

"Jan, I think this thing about Chick is taking on a life of its own."

Jan looked up. "Oh?"

"Diane Blanchett is going to write a play about it for the day of the firemen's muster."

"That should be interesting," Jan said. "You don't think she helped start the rumors, do you?"

"How? You mean, putting something out there that people see and don't know what it is?"

"I'm not sure, exactly. How do these things get started? I know people do publicity stunts sometimes for their television shows and things like that."

"Yeah, to attract attention and make people want to see the show." Elaine frowned. "I don't think so. It seemed like Diane thought of doing a play after she heard about the sightings. And how could she make people see something in the water, anyway?"

"Beats me." Jan looked at the clock. "Guess I'd better start thinking about what we're going to feed the twins for lunch."

CHAPTER SIX

After the boys had spent an hour in the lake that after-noon, Elaine offered to take them over to the Bookworm so Jan could have a break and plan her baking for the next day.

"What about the turtles?" Riley asked. "Can we take them?"

They had four now, in a galvanized washtub well stocked with water and rocks for them to climb on.

"No, I'm afraid they wouldn't like it," Elaine said. "Leave them in the tub in the shade."

It took the twins only a few minutes to shed their swimsuits and pull on shorts and T-shirts.

"You need shoes," Elaine said when they came down-stairs barefoot.

"Why?" Max asked. "It's hot."

"Because store owners don't let customers come in with-out shoes."

They ran back upstairs and found their sneakers, and soon Elaine was on the way out with them. They walked down the sidewalk to the bookstore next door. Bristol greeted them as they entered.

"Hello, Max. Hello, Riley. I'm so glad you came to visit." Bristol smiled at Elaine. "Katelyn is in the children's section right now. I'm sure she'd love to help the boys find a new book."

"Thanks." Elaine took the twins to the area set up to be child friendly.

Bristol's helper, Katelyn Grande Conrad, grinned when she saw them. "Well, hi, guys. Did you come to pick out a new book?"

"Our grandma says we can each get one special book," Riley said. "She'll read it to us for a bedtime story."

"That sounds like so much fun." Katelyn looked at Elaine. "I'd be happy to help them, if you want to browse."

"Thanks."

"So, what do you guys like most?" Katelyn asked the twins. "Trucks? Animals?"

Elaine smiled as Max and Riley peppered Katelyn with suggestions. She went back to the front of the store. Bristol was taking books out of a carton and setting them on the counter.

"How's it going with the boys?"

"Great," Elaine said. "They're having a ball catching turtles. Chickadee Lake may be turtle-less by the time they leave."

Bristol chuckled. "They haven't seen Chick, have they? Mark told me you and Jan came to the office asking about it."

"We did," Elaine said. "Your husband was very helpful. Had you heard about this before?"

"Not a word." Bristol paused to count her pile of books and consult the packing slip.

"It's so bizarre," Elaine said. "Apparently it was quite a phenomenon in the mid-1940s. The people who owned the ice cream stand at the time changed its name."

"Yeah, Mark said he thinks the town ran with it to promote tourism."

Elaine shook her head. "I don't know what to think, with these new rumors. First Clifton Young, and then Chad Prentice."

"What about Chad?" Bristol asked.

"He says he saw something big in the water last night when he was fishing."

"*Hmm*. Hadn't heard that one. But then, I wouldn't call Chad the most reliable person in town." Bristol picked up a stack of books. "Walk with me?"

"Sure. Can I carry anything for you?"

"Nope."

Elaine followed her to a display of books by Maine authors, where Bristol began shelving the new arrivals.

"Imagine if people did that now, changing the names of their businesses. The Lakeworm, instead of the Bookworm," Elaine mused.

Bristol laughed. "Chick's Closet, and A Little Lake Monster. I don't think that's going to happen."

"I hope not. I'm not ready to jump on the sea monster bandwagon."

"Now that's a funny picture."

Elaine smiled. "Okay, I'm getting carried away. It's fun to think about, but it wouldn't be so fun if there actually turned out to be something in the lake."

"I don't know." Bristol set the last book in place. "Maybe. A little extra business never hurts, and it could be fun."

"Well, the kids are a little confused by all the talk." Elaine smiled. "Riley heard that we had a boom after World War II, and he thought it meant an explosion."

Bristol chuckled. "That's kids for you. I don't want them to be scared, but kids do love to talk about monsters and the superheroes who go after them."

"True. The boys enjoy swimming in the lake so much, but I don't think they would if they thought there was a big snake in there. I hope Jack Weston can figure out what's going on and put an end to it."

Riley and Max came running from the back of the store.

"Walk, guys," Elaine said.

"We got our books," Max said eagerly, holding up a bright picture book with an airplane on the front.

"I want this one." Riley held out a classic Dr. Seuss book.

Elaine took both and checked the prices. "Great. These look like a lot of fun." She smiled at Bristol. "I'll pay for them and settle with Jan later."

"Oh, I can put it on account for Jan." Bristol took the books to the cash register. As she rang up the purchase, several people entered the store.

"Thanks." Elaine took the Bookworm bag from Bristol. "I hope you have a *booming* day of business."

JAN WENT TO the cash register in the tearoom's entry, happy to help Rose and Archie out for a few minutes. She'd rung up the bill and had a nice chat with two guests who were staying at the

Northwoods B and B when Elaine came in the front door with the twins. The boys always made her smile, even if they were tired and cranky. Right now they looked happy.

"What did you get?" she asked.

Elaine gave her the bookstore bag, and she pulled out the boys' choices.

"Oh boy. We'll read these tonight, when you're in your pj's."

"Can we sleep in the tower room tonight, Grandma?" Riley asked.

Jan looked at Elaine. "Um, maybe. I hadn't thought about it."

"It's pretty far from the bathroom," Elaine said.

"Yes, let's think about it. You want to swim again this afternoon?"

"Yeah!" they both cried.

"Okay, go get changed." Jan set the books under the counter as three customers came out of the east parlor, ready to check out.

"Busy?" Elaine asked.

"Yes. Rose has a full parlor and people on the porch. Macy brought more guests."

"That's great. I can take over here," Elaine said.

"Would you? I've got one more batch of cookies to put in the oven."

Elaine slipped behind the counter and greeted the customers while Jan hurried to the kitchen. She would have to watch the boys while they swam soon. How was she going to get everything done? She slid a cookie sheet into the oven and opened a cupboard. She had a freestanding timer somewhere. Maybe she could set that and take it to the dock with her.

All too soon, her adorable little grandsons were back, wearing their Jamaica-short swim trunks and face masks, dragging their beach towels behind.

"Hey there," she said, unable to hold back a smile. "This batch of cookies has seven minutes left. Can you wait that long?"

"Can we wade until you come down?" Max asked.

"*Hmm,* I think you should stay on the dock and wait for me."

Max's mouth drooped. "Okay, but don't dawdle, Grandma."

She laughed. He'd probably heard her tell him that one time too many.

"Hey, aren't you going to swim?" Riley asked her.

"Oh, I think I'll pass today, but I'll be down soon. Don't you get wet until I'm there."

"Okay." Riley opened the back door and shrieked.

"What's the matter?" Jan strode to the door.

"The kitty was in there. Sorry, Grandma."

"I guess you scared him away again," Jan said.

"He scared me first."

"Well, don't worry about it. Just try to remember he might be out there the next time you open the door to the porch."

The boys scurried out and down the steps toward the deck and their wharf below. Jan shut the door and checked the timer. Five more minutes.

Rose bustled in with a tray of dirty cups. "Do we have any more cranberry scones?"

Jan checked the container. "Two."

"Perfect. I need those and a cookie of the day."

Jan fixed the pastry orders while Rose got the beverages.

"Are you waiting on Macy?" she asked.

"Yes. This isn't for her, but she is in my station. She wanted to sit out on the side porch with her guests so they could see the lake. I think she's hoping someone will come in off the water and report another monster sighting. That's what they were talking about when I took their tea out."

Jan shook her head. "It's so silly."

"I know, but people will sometimes believe anything."

"I think it's more a case of Macy wanting to get some free advertising. If these folks tell their friends about it, maybe their friends will be curious and come stay at Green Glade Cottages."

"Could be." Rose set the final cup on her tray and picked it up just as the timer rang. "Thanks, Jan."

"You're welcome. I'll be down on the dock with the boys for a while if you need me."

When Jan got to the dock, the boys were huddled on shore a few yards away, working at something they were building from stones, sticks, leaves, and strips of birch bark.

"What are you making?" Jan asked.

Riley looked up. "An ark."

Jan smiled. Apparently they were taking their Bible school lesson to heart.

"We want to put the turtles in it," Max said.

"No, only two of them," Riley corrected him.

"Right. But some animals had seven in the ark. Did you know that, Grandma?"

"I did," Jan said. "I think Noah and his family took seven sheep and maybe some of the other animals they might sacrifice to the Lord, so they'd have extra."

"They might need extra turtles," Riley said.

Jan held back a laugh. "Could be. I don't think it would hurt to put a couple of extra turtles in there."

"We want to put two ants and two ladybugs too," Riley said. "But not spiders."

"We don't like spiders," Max said gravely.

"I'm with you on that." Jan stepped off the dock and walked over to where they were constructing their ark. "*Hmm,* I'm not sure how many critters you'll be able to fit in there."

"Do you think we can put mice in?" Max asked.

"How would you catch them?"

"Maybe Earl Grey will catch some for us if we're nice to him," Max replied.

"We-e-ell, I wouldn't count on it," Jan said.

"How are we going to put the fish in?" Riley asked.

"I don't think they put fish in the ark," Jan told him. "I think they just swam around in the water near the ark."

"What about octopuses?" Max asked.

"Them too."

An hour later, Elaine joined Jan in the deck chairs on the dock. The twins were splashing about in waist-deep water below her. "How's it going?" she asked as she dropped into the empty chair.

"Not bad," Jan said. "Did you see the ark over there?" She pointed to the little structure near the shore.

"Oh, is that what that is?"

Jan laughed. "It's supposed to carry the turtles through the next great flood, along with a few bugs and whatever other animals the boys can manage to coax in there."

"They might catch a few frogs or a garter snake," Elaine said.

Jan held up two fingers. "Two of each."

"I walked over to Murphy's for a roll of tape, and I saw Diane again."

Jan arched her eyebrows, knowing more was to come or Elaine wouldn't have mentioned it.

"She's started writing her play," Elaine said. "She asked me if you and I wanted to be in it."

"What did you tell her?"

"I said maybe we could help out offstage, if it's going to benefit the fire department."

Jan shrugged. "I suppose we could do something. Help with the costumes or props, maybe."

"The fire department really does need new equipment, but I don't want to be up on stage." Elaine smiled at the boys as they dog-paddle raced from the edge of the dock to a large rock sticking out of the water thirty feet away. "I think the field day is a good idea."

"I just hope it doesn't turn into a circus," Jan said. "This whole lake monster thing has me wondering if someone might have cooked it up to get attention."

"If it draws attention to the fire department, that's okay, isn't it?"

"I suppose." Jan lifted her sunglasses and frowned at Elaine. "You don't think Diane started it, do you?"

"I thought Clifton did."

"Well, he was the first one to say publicly that he'd seen something." Jan pursed her lips. "And he's on the board of selectmen."

"Yes. What about it?"

"Remember how Will suggested the chamber of commerce had a lot to do with it in the '40s?"

"Yeah, and Mark gave us a list of all the old members." Elaine studied Jan's face. "Are you thinking the town leaders are trying to revive an old publicity stunt?"

"I don't know what to think," Jan said. "I just wonder."

Elaine nodded. "When I first heard about it, I was under the impression that Clifton didn't know about the old story when he saw whatever it was in the water. But I suppose he might have heard about it somewhere and elaborated. Maybe tomorrow while the boys are at VBS, we should try to dig up some old clippings and chamber of commerce records."

"Let's. I'll try to get tomorrow's baking done tonight." Jan put her sunglasses back in place. "Oh, and remember, we're going to try not to mention it around the boys."

"If you think that's best. Are you letting them sleep in the tower room tonight?"

"I guess so. They'd never forgive me if I didn't."

Elaine nodded, smiling. "We can leave the stairway door open, so we can hear them if they don't settle down."

"Yeah, and I'll make sure they've both got flashlights, in case they want to come down during the night."

"Remember the night we slept in the haymow in Grandpa Willard's barn?"

"The word 'sleep' is a misnomer for that one. I don't think I slept a wink," Jan said.

Elaine nodded. "It was the owl. It wouldn't shut up, and it sounded so weird."

"But we told Grandpa and Grandma that we slept just fine."

"We were stubborn, even then," Elaine said with a laugh.

"And we never asked to sleep in the barn again," Jan noted.

"Nope. Too spooky, and the hay was too itchy." Elaine looked over at Jan. "Do you think there are mice up there in the tower room?"

"I hope not. But if there are, maybe the boys will catch some for their ark."

CHAPTER SEVEN

Rose opened the back door and called, "Can one of you lend a hand for a few minutes?"

"I'll go," Elaine told Jan. She rose from her deck chair and hurried up the steps. "Sure, Rose, what do you need?"

"Sorry to bother you," Rose said. "We were already busy, and the volunteer firefighters decided to meet on our side porch and hash over their plans for the muster."

"Great," Elaine said. "Did you take orders?"

"Four coffees, two teas—a green and a chai—and a cookie assortment."

"Coming right up," Elaine assured her. The firefighters occasionally met at Kate's Diner. She wondered why they'd chosen the tearoom this time. Maybe the diner was full. She quickly set the teas to steep in small pots and prepared the cookie plate. Then she counted out six cups and small plates and took the coffee carafe off the base. She started a new pot and was out the door with the heavy tray.

Macy and her guests were still seated at the porch table nearest the water, and Elaine smiled as she passed them. She knew everyone in the group at the front table but one. Des Murphy, Tag King, Rachel Leon, Alicia Brooks, and Caden Gower greeted her with cheers as she approached.

"Hey, Elaine," Des said. "That looks great." When she lowered the tray, he helped take the items off and distribute the cups. Elaine went around and filled the coffee mugs for those who wanted it.

"The green tea is mine," Rachel said.

Caden claimed the chai tea. "Elaine, I don't think you've met my brother," he said, indicating the man next to him. "This is Jason."

"Hi," Elaine said. "Are you a firefighter too, Jason?"

"Me? No, I'm just horning in on the fun. I'm visiting Caden, and he let me tag along to his meeting."

"Well, it's nice to meet you." Elaine smiled and went back to the kitchen, where Jan was tying on her apron.

"I sent the boys to get changed, and I told them they can play in the tower room," she said. "I hope that's okay with you. I didn't want them down near the water without one of us down there, and I need to get on with my baking."

"That's fine," Elaine said. "I'll pop up and check on them when I get a minute."

She totaled up the bills for the firefighters and checked in with Rose and Archie, asking if they needed any help.

"I wouldn't take it amiss if you cleared a couple of tables for me," Archie said with a smile.

Elaine set to work and soon had two of his tables in the east parlor ready for new customers. She went back to the kitchen, picked up the fresh pot of coffee, and went out to the porch.

"Anyone here having coffee?" she asked at Macy's table.

"No, but we could use more black tea," said one of the guests.

"We're sharing it," Macy said, nodding toward their flowered china teapot.

"Sure." Elaine glanced at their plates. "Should I bring more cookies too?"

"I'd love to get one of those blueberry muffins to take back to my husband," said one of the women.

"I'll bring it out with the tea," Elaine said.

She moved on to the firefighters' table.

"I think we should invite the Oakland FD too," Tag was saying to the others. "It would mean more competition if we had four departments taking part."

"I like it," Alicia said. "Some of their fans might come watch and spend a little money."

"We'd have to borrow more equipment," Rachel told him.

Caden asked, "Why couldn't we ask them to bring whatever is needed with them? They'll be bringing their own turnout gear and ladder truck, anyway."

"That could work." Tag looked up at Elaine and grinned. "Oh good, more coffee." He held up his cup, and she topped it off.

"The cookies are great, as usual, Elaine," Rachel said.

"Thank you." She made the rounds of the table, filling the cups. "Anything else for you guys?"

Tag looked around at all of them, and they shook their heads. "I guess not."

"I'll bring out your slips in a minute," Elaine said. "You can sit and talk as long as you like."

"Thanks," said Tag.

Alicia smiled up at her. "This is a really nice spot, Elaine."

"Thank you." When she turned around, Elaine found Macy at her elbow.

"Oh, pardon me," Macy said. "I just wanted to ask Tag who's buying the chicken for the barbecue the day of the muster." She looked at the fire chief. "One of the auxiliary members can pick up the chicken if you want. We'll be right there with you that day, Tag."

"I know you will," Tag said with a big smile. "Your group always does a terrific job when we have to raise funds. We're counting on you to help set up and organize the barbecue. I'll call you tonight with particulars, okay?"

"Sounds good. I was thinking maybe you'd want to put Chick, the lake monster, in your ad."

Tag frowned at her. "Lake monster? Is that what Chad Prentice was talking about last night?"

"He's the second person to report a sighting," Macy said, "although I wouldn't say you can always rely on what Chad tells you. But there was something in the lake back in the 1940s, and it's starting to look like it's still there—or there again."

The firefighters all chuckled and glanced at each other uneasily.

"You don't really believe that, do you, Macy?" Des asked.

"Dana Austin believed in it. He told me all about it when I bought Green Glade from him, and I wouldn't call him a liar, God rest his soul."

"There could be *something* in the lake," Alicia said, "but I wouldn't be too quick to call it a monster."

"But it *would* be good advertising," Macy said. "It would draw in a lot of people to your event. You could gear one of the muster contests to fighting the monster."

Tag looked at Des. He shrugged.

"Thanks for the idea, Macy," Tag said. "We'll consider it. I'll call you later."

"Great. If the auxiliary can do anything, just holler. We're always happy to help you guys." Macy went back to her table.

Elaine had just been standing there holding the nearly empty coffeepot, fascinated to see Macy in action.

"What's the matter, Elaine?" Des asked.

"Nothing. I just…I can hardly believe people are taking this thing seriously."

Tag winked at her. "Well, you never know, do you?"

"And she could be right," Rachel said. "Maybe we should think about using these sightings—or claims of sightings—to help us raise more money. Make it a theme for the muster."

Mindful that she had promised Macy's group more tea, Elaine reluctantly headed for the kitchen. She would have loved to sit in on the firefighters' discussion.

While she switched out the coffeepot for fresh tea, she told Jan about the firefighters' confab. "Rachel seems to think the lake monster is a good thing and can pull people in for the muster."

"She may be right," Jan said. "Instead of fire trucks, maybe we should make cookies shaped like sea serpents."

Elaine laughed and bagged a blueberry muffin for Macy's guest. "That may be a good idea."

She took her tray out. Macy was seated again with her guests at the back table.

"I'd love to see that monster," said the woman who had ordered the muffin. "Wouldn't it be a blast to get a picture of it?"

"The papers would pay you big money for it," said another.

Rose came onto the porch from the front of the house. She paused and greeted the firefighters and then brought Macy's group their slips.

"Is Elaine taking care of you?"

"She sure is," Macy said. "Though my tea was lukewarm."

"Add a muffin to my bill," said the guest, ignoring Macy's complaint and holding up her takeaway bag.

Elaine excused herself and went back to the kitchen.

"I don't know, Jan. This lake monster thing is gathering momentum. People are going nuts over it."

Jan sighed and waved a rubber spatula at her. "I just hope it doesn't wind the boys up too much."

"So far, so good." Elaine glanced at the clock. "And speaking of the twins, I'd better run and see what they're up to."

"I'd appreciate it," Jan said.

Elaine went up the stairs. Chatter reached her from both parlors, and more people came through the door. She'd better hurry so she could get back down and help Rose and Archie.

On the upstairs landing, she paused and listened, but all was quiet. She peeked into the guest room, where the boys had slept the last two nights, but they weren't there. Elaine caught a murmur of voices from the tower room. What on earth was keeping them so quiet? She went on up the stairs.

They had their sleeping bags unrolled on the floor and their pillows in place. Both twins sat cross-legged on their sleeping bags, with clipboards on their laps. Jan had given them a supply of blank paper to draw on, along with new boxes of crayons and colored pencils. Max and Riley were hard at work.

"Hey, guys," Elaine said. "What are you doing?"

The boys looked up.

"Hi," Max said. "We're drawing."

Riley got up and pushed his clipboard into her hands. "I'm making a turtle."

Elaine looked at his picture and smiled. "That's pretty good, Riley."

"I'm drawing the ark," Max said. "I put two zebras going in the door." Elaine took his clipboard and studied the drawing. Two black-and-white-striped blobs with appendages that could be legs were indeed headed for a boat-like structure.

"I see them," she said.

Riley picked up another piece of paper off the floor. "And this is the monster."

"Monster?" Elaine looked down at the black, snakelike squiggle that reared up out of blue peaks that could only be waves. Her heart sank. They had tried to be careful about discussing Chick when the twins were around. "Tell me about the monster," she said, sitting down next to Max on his sleeping bag.

"It's in the lake." Riley looked at her with wide, innocent eyes.

"Oh honey, there's no monster in the lake."

"That's what Mrs. Edmonds said. That it's not real."

Max piped up, "But all the kids in our class at VBS say there is one."

"Yeah." Riley was very solemn. "They said it's bigger than a boat."

Elaine beckoned Riley to sit beside her and drew Max toward her. "Boys, those kids don't know what they're talking about. You know Jack Weston, Aunt Tara's boyfriend?"

Both boys nodded.

"Well, he knows about all the fish and turtles in the lake, and any other animals that might get in there, and he went out to check, and he didn't see anything big like that."

"Maybe it hid," Max said.

"Or it's just not real," Elaine said. "Sometimes animals do get in the lake and go for a swim. Last month, a moose was out there swimming around. And sometimes people see beavers, and loons, and all sort of things in the lake. But they're real animals, not monsters."

The boys eyed her uncertainly.

"Come on," Elaine said. "Let's go down and have a cookie. Your grandma is baking macaroons for the tearoom. You like those, don't you?"

"Yeah." Max jumped up. "Can we have chocolate milk too?"

"*Hmm,* I don't think we have any right now," Elaine said, getting to her feet, "but you can absolutely have regular milk."

They went down to the kitchen, and Elaine fixed the boys' snack.

"They've got their beds all made for tonight in the tower room," she told Jan. "And they drew some really interesting pictures with the art supplies you left up there."

"Great," Jan said. "How does it look out front now?"

"I think Rose and Archie have things under control," Elaine said. "I can go check."

"Yes," Jan said. "I think I'll sit down with the guys for a minute and take a little break myself."

Elaine nodded. She would wait until the boys were otherwise occupied to relate their conversation about the monster.

As Elaine walked out into the hall, Rose was seating two women in the west parlor. Elaine peeked into the east parlor, where she found Archie collecting used dishes from an empty table. She walked over to him, glancing around at the four tables in use.

"How's it going?"

"Just great." Archie looked up, catching movement outside the window. "Oh, there's another party on the porch."

"Would you like me to go?" Elaine asked. She thought she recognized Sadie Taylor's strawberry-blonde hair.

"Sure, if you don't mind," Archie said.

Elaine went out and greeted Sadie and her cousin with a smile. "Good to see you again."

"Thanks," Sadie said. "We decided this was one of the most peaceful places we knew."

"Not to mention the place with the best cookies," Garrett added.

Elaine laughed. "Both good reasons to come here. What can I bring you? The cookie of the day is macaroons."

"Oh, that sounds good." Sadie arched her eyebrows at Garrett. "Chai tea again?"

Garrett was scanning the menu card Elaine had given him. "I might try the orange spice and one of those scones."

"Well, I want the macaroons and chai," Sadie said with a stubborn jut to her chin.

Garrett laughed. "Get whatever you want, kiddo. You have only a few more days to enjoy your freedom."

Elaine wrote it down with a chuckle. "When is your fiancé arriving, Sadie?"

"Not until next Thursday. He's flying into Portland that afternoon, so we have to cram the fittings and rehearsal and everything in before Sunday."

"You can do it," Garrett assured her.

"I'm sure everything will be beautiful for the wedding," Elaine said. "Say, Garrett, where's your friend?"

"Adrian? He went to Waterville to pick up some supplies. He's around."

"Maybe we should take him some cookies," Sadie said. "He's still talking about the ginger ones he had here the other day. Do you have any of those, Elaine?"

"I'm sure we do. I'll bag up half a dozen. Or do you want a box?"

"No, six is enough. I'll save it for when Adrian's prowling the kitchen looking for a snack and toss it at him."

Elaine went inside to fill their order, still smiling.

THAT EVENING, AFTER a trip to the ice cream stand with the twins, they all settled down in the living room upstairs. Jan had borrowed a video from the Ryders for the boys, and they were eager to see it. She started it playing, and then she joined Elaine at the far end of the room.

In hushed tones, Elaine told Jan what the twins had said about the lake monster, and that they seemed to believe what the other children told them.

"I'm not sure what we can do, except keep telling them it's not real," Jan said.

"I know." Elaine shook her head. "We were being so careful. It was naïve of me to think wouldn't hear about it at VBS."

The doorbell for the front door rang, and they looked at each other.

"I'll get it." Jan stood and hurried out into the hall and down the stairs. To her surprise, her boyfriend, Bob Claybrook, stood on the porch.

"Well, hi," she said.

"Hi." Bob stepped forward and kissed her cheek.

"I didn't expect to see you tonight, but I'm glad for the surprise," Jan said. "Come on in."

"Thanks. I had dinner with a client, and it ended earlier than I expected, so I thought I'd drop by."

"I'm glad you did. Come on upstairs. Elaine and the twins are up there."

They went up to the sitting room, and Elaine stood with a big smile. "Hello, Bob. Good to see you."

"You too," Bob said.

Jan paused the boys' video long enough for them to greet Bob. The twins had met him several times before and weren't shy around him. They seemed to think he was a frequent part of the tearoom's furnishings.

When she had let them go back to their show, Jan led Bob to the other end of the room, where they sat down with Elaine.

"So, Bob, have you heard about the"—Elaine glanced toward the boys to make sure they were engrossed in the video—"lake monster?"

Bob laughed. "I heard something about it. Did Clifton Young start that craziness?"

"Maybe this round of craziness," Elaine said, "but it seems there was another bout of it back in the 1940s."

"Really? I didn't know that."

In whispers, Jan caught him up on what they knew, and what they had learned at the town office. Elaine brought out the papers Mark had copied for them.

"We thought we'd check with the chamber of commerce tomorrow while the boys are at VBS, and maybe the *Penzance Courier,* to see if we can find out more about the old-time sightings," Elaine said.

Jan nodded. "The twins have heard the rumors, and we don't want them to be scared. The other children were talking about it at VBS."

"Riley even drew a picture of the monster this afternoon," Elaine said.

Bob frowned. "So, what's your point in digging up information about the old rumors?"

Jan looked at Elaine. "I guess we hope it will help us show them it's not real."

"Yes," Elaine said. "If we could show them that the old one was proven to be a hoax..."

"Was it?" Bob asked.

"We don't know. The excitement about it seemed to die out after a few years." Jan looked helplessly at Elaine.

Elaine's brow furrowed. "So far as we know, nothing was ever proven."

"Well," Bob said, "it's pretty hard to prove a negative."

"I suppose so, unless we could cover every inch of the lake," Elaine said.

"All at once," Jan added. "So what can we do?"

"Let me think about it," Bob said.

"Would a cup of tea help you think?" Jan asked.

"That depends. Does it come with a cream puff?"

"Sorry, no cream puffs today," Jan laughed, "but we have scones, muffins, and cookies."

"Why don't you two go on down to the kitchen?" Elaine asked. "I'll stay here with the boys."

"If you're sure," Jan said.

"Oh, go on." Elaine waved them toward the door. "Great to see you, Bob."

While they drank their tea and Bob ate a raspberry scone, they talked about other things, but after about fifteen minutes, he leaned back in his chair and squinted, looking across the room at nothing in particular.

"What?" Jan asked.

"I was just wondering..."

"Yes?"

Bob shrugged. "What would happen if someone tried to prove the monster is real?"

Jan eyed him skeptically. "You're the one who said it's hard to prove a negative. It's even harder to prove something that's not true."

"Maybe not." Bob winked at her. "Why don't I give Nathan a call? If the four of us get together for lunch tomorrow, maybe we can come up with a plan."

Jan still didn't see how the three of them, plus Elaine's boyfriend, Nathan Culver, could put the rumors to rest, but Bob's cheerfulness gave her hope. "All right. Where do you want to meet? Elaine and I will be there."

CHAPTER EIGHT

E laine rose early on Tuesday to help Jan with her morning baking and get the boys off to Bible school.

"I wonder how the dinosaurs fit on the ark," Max said solemnly in the car. "Is that why we don't have dinosaurs now? They wouldn't fit?"

"I don't think so," Elaine said. "They could take little ones, or even eggs."

Max and Riley seemed to accept that. She led them up to the church door, hoping talk of dinosaurs wouldn't start them thinking about the lake monster again.

When she got back to the tearoom, Jan was ready to leave on their sleuthing expedition, but as they went into the hallway headed for the garage, Archie intercepted them.

"That film fellow wants to talk to you," he said.

"You mean Garrett Wolfe?" Elaine asked.

"That's the one."

"Is it about the menu, or what?"

Archie frowned. "No, I think he wants to do a little filming here. Or videographing—whatever it is he does."

Elaine looked at Jan.

"Could be good publicity," Jan said.

"Okay. Can you bring him to the office, Archie?"

"Righto."

Archie left them, and they went into Elaine's office next to the kitchen and placed an extra chair for the visitor.

"Hello," Garrett said cheerfully from the doorway.

"Good morning," Elaine said, extending her hand. "Garrett, I don't think you've met my cousin, Jan Blake."

"Are you the one who makes the delicious cookies?" Garrett asked, shaking Jan's hand.

"She sure is," Elaine said.

"Pleased to meet you," Jan told him with a smile.

"Sit down, won't you?" Elaine took her chair behind the desk, and Jan and Garrett sat down. "Now, what is it exactly that you'd like from us?"

Garrett's smile was charming, no doubt about that. His direct brown eyes and regular features put him in the handsome category, and Elaine had a feeling not many people said no to his requests.

"I've found Tea for Two so delightful, I wondered if Adrian and I could do a little filming here. Nothing serious, just a few interior shots, and we'd pan your view of the lake, and maybe interview a few patrons. With your permission, of course."

The cousins looked at each other.

"What do you think?" Elaine asked.

"I don't know..." Jan looked at Garrett. "You wouldn't say anything negative about our business, would you?"

"Absolutely not. I *love* your business. In fact, if you're agreeable, I'd even like to talk to you a little about how this tearoom came about."

"Well, that doesn't sound too bad," Jan said.

He grinned. "Great. Shall we say tomorrow morning? I believe you open at ten?"

"Yes," Elaine said.

"I could come at 9:30 to talk to you before you open."

"Perfect," Elaine said. They would have dropped off the twins by then.

"Okay! Thank you very much. I'll see you in the a.m." Garrett stood and shook both their hands again and breezed out into the hall.

"He seems like a nice young man," Jan said cautiously.

"Yes, he does, and Sadie's a sweetheart." Elaine stood. "Come on. We have investigating to do, and time is flying."

In Elaine's car, they drove to the chamber of commerce office. They both knew the woman manning the desk, Shannon Bryce, who was in her early thirties and had a little girl in the twins' VBS class.

"Hello," she said with a big smile when the cousins walked in the door. "What brings you two here today?"

Elaine stepped forward. "We want to look up some events the chamber of commerce took part in back in the 1940s."

"Oh, that's a long time ago," Shannon said. "You might have to go to the library."

Jan said, "We were told some of the old records might be over there."

"Yeah, the library has some of it in their vertical file. What specifically did you want?"

"Anything to do with the lake monster," Elaine said.

Shannon blinked. "I'm sorry. Say that again?"

"The lake monster," Elaine said.

"They called it Chick," Jan added.

Shannon looked puzzled. "I've never heard of that. What exactly are we talking about?"

Elaine sighed. "Some of the older people in town remember a big fuss about a creature in the lake. Apparently the town decided to make it a draw for tourism. Will Trexler told us about it, and the man Macy Atherton bought her property from told her about it years ago."

"Beatrice Orwell remembers it too," Jan added.

"*Hmm*. When was this? The 1940s?"

"Yes," Jan said. "After the war—'46 to '48, we think. Maybe longer than that."

"Okay, let me take a look in our files."

"If it helps, the I Scream stand was called Chick's Ice Cream Stand for a while." Elaine held out the copied document Mark had given them.

Shannon put on her reading glasses and scanned the paper. "Wow. The Anderson family owned it. Okay, 1947." She sat down at her computer and clicked some keys.

Jan and Elaine waited quietly. After a minute, Shannon turned her chair toward them.

"Yeah, looks like it kept that name three or four years, then changed hands again. The stand burned in 1952, and a different owner rebuilt it in '55. It was called Dairy Treet then. I'm not sure when it became I Scream, but I could probably find out."

"That's okay," Jan said.

Shannon scanned her computer screen. "I don't see anything else about a monster named Chick."

"Maybe we should head on over to the library." Elaine looked at Jan.

"Sure."

"Tell Priscilla what you want. If they've got it, she'll find it," Shannon assured them.

"Yeah, she's terrific," Jan said.

They spent an hour at the library with Priscilla Gates, the librarian. She was friends with the cousins, and their mission intrigued her. "You two come in with the most fascinating requests," she told them as she led them to a drawer full of filed documents and articles.

Jan laughed. "And you can usually help us find what we need. Thanks!"

Elaine and Jan carefully went through the files Priscilla recommended, pulling out ones they thought might give them some pertinent information.

"It seems to have really taken off in 1947," Elaine said after browsing several items.

"That's the year the town had the Chick float in the parade," Jan noted.

"Yes. And the chamber of commerce seems to have collaborated on that. They had a brochure that year with a cute little sea monster on it, along with a loon swimming on the lake. But the next year's materials just have a drawing of the lake with pine trees and a canoe."

Jan frowned. "I think the craze was still going on then."

"Yes, but maybe not such a frenzy," Elaine said. "And Dana Austin established Green Glade Cottages in '47. At least, that's the first year Mr. Austin was a member of the chamber."

Jan looked at her watch. "Oh, it's time to pick up the boys."

"Why don't you go get them?" Elaine suggested. "I've got a few more things I want to look at."

"Okay." Jan neatly stacked the folders she'd been using and stood. "We'll see you at home."

Elaine read through the remaining documents in her stack and took a few notes. She was sure a couple of the people from the chamber of commerce at the height of the Chick phenomenon were still living in Lancaster. They would be very old, but she thought she might be able to turn up a few. Most of the businesses from that era were gone, but some were still run by family members of the original owners. They might have some old records that told what their families did during that time.

Finally she put away her pen and notes and reported back to Priscilla.

"Find some good stuff?" Priscilla asked.

"Some hints," Elaine said. "Thanks a lot."

She walked out into the sunshine and looked across the street. The tearoom's parking area was only half full, which was normal around lunchtime. On a whim, she turned right and peered in the windows of the shop called Gift Me.

Elaine hadn't had time to visit the Main Street shops for a while. The Maine-made items in the window appealed to her, but she really wanted to talk to Fiona Latimore, who owned Oldies But Goodies, a little way down the street, so she walked on.

Fiona's shop smelled spicy and a little like old books. Elaine loved the eclectic merchandise Fiona stocked—small antiques and new treasures from around the world.

Bree, a college student who was Fiona's summer assistant, glanced at her from behind the counter and smiled. She was rolling some fragile items in tissue paper for a customer.

Elaine returned the smile and waved at her. She ambled down an aisle, gazing at old tins and composition dolls. She paused to admire some Chinese lacquerware.

One wall held shelves of old boxes, samplers, and signs, and she scanned them, then froze. High on the wall, between an Old Town Canoe sign and a vintage Moxie crate, was a hand-painted wooden signboard with the words "Chick of Chickadee Lake" emblazoned on it. Swimming gaily past the letters was a smiling creature that could only be the lake monster. It looked a bit like dragon sketches Elaine had seen in children's books. The green animal sat on the water, with a plump body well above the surface, triangular plates along its spine, and a long, snakelike neck topped by a cheerfully smiling face and red eyes.

She gazed up at it for several seconds, studying the shape and colors. Then she walked back toward the counter, hoping Fiona was there, but the sixty-something owner was nowhere in sight.

The previous customer was just walking out the door, leaving Bree free to turn to her.

"May I help you, Elaine?"

"Yes. I was wondering about the sign on the shelves back there—the one that says 'Chick of Chickadee Lake.'"

"Oh, that." Bree smiled. "Isn't it whimsical?"

"Yes, it certainly is. Do you know how old it is?"

Bree shrugged. "No, I don't. You'd have to ask Fiona. I think it's been in the back room for quite a while."

"Oh? She just put it on sale recently?" Elaine asked.

"Yes. We don't change those high shelves very often, but once in a while someone wants to buy something displayed there, and one of us has to climb up. Fiona had me switch out some things for that shelf a week or so ago, and we put out that sign."

Elaine nodded. "So…how long is a while? Do you know how long she's had it?"

"Goodness, I don't. But Fiona is pretty good about keeping records of where she gets stuff. She could probably tell you."

"Is she here?"

Bree shook her head. "She's off on a buying trip in Bangor. She'll be here tomorrow, though."

"Do you know the price?"

Bree grimaced. "Sorry, I don't. I can check for you, but I'll have to get the ladder."

The bell over the door rang, and four women entered, chatting and exclaiming over some of the wares.

"Don't bother. But could you ask Fiona to call me? I'll talk to her about it."

"Sure." Bree stepped toward the new customers.

Elaine left feeling a bit unsettled. That signboard was tangible evidence of the old legend. She hoped Fiona would be able to tell her where and who it came from.

She wished she'd offered to buy it on the spot, but then Bree would have had to get a ladder and climb up there. Oh well. She'd phone Fiona later if she didn't hear from her. And it was something to tell Jan about.

JAN LOOKED UP from putting a Band-Aid on Max's knee when Elaine came into the kitchen.

"Oh good, you're back."

"What's happening?" Elaine asked.

Jan stood and tossed the bandage wrapper in the wastebasket. "Did you forget we're having lunch with Bob and Nathan at the Hearthside at one?"

Elaine clapped a hand to her mouth. "I completely forgot. I'm sorry." She looked at the clock. "We can still make it."

"Barely," Jan said.

"Who's watching the boys?"

"Dori Richardson. She's got Riley upstairs. If you're ready, we can go right now."

"Okay." Elaine felt disheveled and unprepared, but Nathan would understand.

"Go on up," Jan said to Max. "And you be good for Dori."

"We will," Max said and jogged toward the stairs.

Jan smiled. He had included his twin in his reply, even though Riley wasn't even in the same room. She grabbed her purse off the counter. "Let's go, then."

The restaurant wasn't far, just past the Bookworm, across the street, and a half block out the Pine Ridge Road. They walked briskly, and Elaine told Jan about her stroll through Oldies But Goodies and the sign she'd seen.

"Odd that it turned up now," Jan said. "Do you think it's old?"

"I couldn't really tell. It was about four feet out of my reach. Fiona wasn't there, and Bree had other customers, so I didn't get close enough to really look it over."

"We'll have to talk to Fiona about that for sure," Jan said. They walked into the Hearthside Restaurant's parking area. Nathan's car and Bob's were both there.

"Oh, we're late," Elaine said. "I'm sorry."

Jan checked her watch. "No, we're not. The guys are just early."

Bob and Nathan were sitting at a table near the empty flagstone fireplace, but stood and smiled when they saw the two women enter. Jan and Elaine made their way between the tables. The dining room was nearly full.

"Hi!" Bob kissed Jan's cheek and pulled out a chair for her. Nathan greeted Elaine with a kiss too, and they all sat down.

"Bob was just telling me about this lake monster thing," Nathan said. "There's never a dull moment on Chickadee Lake, is there?"

Elaine laughed. "Apparently there's more excitement than we ever knew about. Neither of us remembers hearing about Chick when we were kids, but some of the town's eldest residents remember snippets about it."

The waiter came to the table, and they discussed what to order. When they had decided and the waiter left them, Jan said, "We've done a little research—haven't had time for much—but we've established that the first stories about it surfaced in the mid-1940s."

"In 1946, to be exact," Elaine said. "That was the first reference we've found to it so far. And by the next year, the whole town was quite enamored of their mascot. The ice-cream stand's name was changed to Chick's Ice Cream, and the town sponsored a float depicting Chick in the Fourth of July parade."

Nathan laughed. "That's a riot."

Jan said, "Yeah, it seems it was a big deal back then. Tourists came from all over to look for the creature, and new businesses sprang up. That's when the Green Glade Cottages were built, and the boat launch area was improved."

"See what I mean?" Bob grinned at Nathan. "These two will dig up every bit of information about those doings. But the question is, what's going on now? Are people really seeing something on the lake, or is it the power of suggestion?"

"I'd be inclined to vote for that theory," Nathan said. "Hyperactive imaginations."

"Well, I'm certainly not convinced it's real," Elaine said. "Not now or in the post-World-War-II boom. But I saw something odd today." She told them about the painted sign she'd seen in Oldies But Goodies.

"Was it a business sign?" Bob asked.

"I'm not sure. It wasn't very large. Maybe two feet square, if that."

"I'd like to see it," Nathan said.

"Fiona isn't in today," Elaine told him. "Could you come back tomorrow, and we'll go in and look at it?"

"Sure. She gets some interesting things in that shop. I'd be happy to go in with you."

"That's fine," Jan said, "but I wish we could do something about the current gossip. It's scaring my grandsons."

"I doubt you can stop it, sweetheart," Bob said. "You might just have to roll with the punches. Make light of it."

Nathan nodded. "Sure. Tell them it's not real, but it's like a fairy tale or something."

"You can't prove it's *not* there," Bob said. "But maybe we can encourage people to try to prove that it is."

Elaine cocked her head to one side. "Do you think anything *is* going on, Bob? Two boaters have said they saw something they vaguely described. It could have been a submerged log, for all we know."

"I guess you haven't heard the latest story," Bob said.

"What's that?" Jan asked.

"I had breakfast at Kate's Diner. A guy came in there who said he'd gone out fishing this morning. He saw something— an animal, he said—at least twenty feet long. Longer than his motorboat."

"Near the outlet from the bog?" Elaine asked.

"I'm not sure exactly where, but he said it was either a very large fish or some kind of reptile."

Jan's brow furrowed. "Not a log?"

"He said it was swimming under the water. *Swimming.*"

Jan looked across the table at Elaine. "Maybe there really is something."

Elaine shook her head. "That's impossible."

"Is it?" Nathan shrugged. "I tend to agree with you. The lake is too shallow for anything that big. But something's going on."

"Are these witnesses credible?" Jan asked.

Bob chuckled. "Spoken like a lawyer. The man at the diner seemed sober, but he was agitated. I didn't speak to the others personally."

"I was there when Clifton docked and made the first report," Elaine said. "He was definitely sober—on his way to a meeting. And I would consider him credible."

"Absolutely," Jan said.

"But neither of us has talked to Chad Prentice about his sighting," Elaine added.

"True," Jan said. "He might be suggestible, and it was around dusk, wasn't it?"

Elaine nodded. "I wouldn't call Clifton gullible, but I don't know about the other two."

Bob sat forward. "So, what we need is either another sighting, preferably a firm one, or a means to debunk this whole thing and put it to rest, once and for all."

"How do you suggest we get that?" Elaine asked.

"Yeah," Jan said. "We don't want to encourage people to perpetrate hoaxes."

"No, but if the local papers ran a feature about the sightings, maybe the next person who saw it would be prepared to snap a picture or something." Bob smiled at her. "I think challenging these folks to prove their claims might be worthwhile. If no one comes up with convincing proof that there's a creature in the lake, it'll fizzle out."

"Yes," Nathan said. "And if there is something, maybe some publicity would uncover the truth. But I don't for a second think it's a sea monster."

"Or a lake monster." Bob grinned. "I'm sure you can get some free publicity out of it for the town. And that's probably what the town officials and the chamber of commerce decided back in the '40s. Why not? What will it hurt?"

"It might scare some little children I know," Jan said.

Nathan shrugged. "You can tell them it's all in fun. They're smart kids."

Bob looked hopefully at Jan. "It might bring in more folks for the firemen's muster and raise more money for the fire department. Making a bigger deal of it might smoke out the truth. And if it's just a case of some fishermen getting spooked by shadows, what's the harm?"

Jan gazed across the table at Elaine. "What do you think?"

Elaine pulled in a deep breath. "I tend to trust these guys' judgment. I suppose a little publicity wouldn't hurt. And it would certainly help Diane draw in patrons for her play. The ticket money from that is going to the fire department."

Bob grinned. "Great. Who's the reporter you like at the *Courier*? Candace?"

Jan nodded. "Candace Huang."

"Talk to the *Sentinel* too," Nathan said. "They have a wider audience. Maybe even the *Kennebec Journal*."

"Why not?" Bob wrote gleefully on his paper napkin. "If there's anything out there, I want someone to stand up and prove it."

JAN TUCKED THE twins in at eight o'clock. She was behind in her baking, and she hadn't really done much that day, but she was beat. She went out into the upstairs living room, where Elaine was Skyping with her son, Jared, and his family in Ohio.

"Lucy and Micah want to know if they can Skype with the twins tomorrow," she told Jan.

"Sure," Jan said. "That will give them something to do between lunch and their swim time. Tell them 1:30."

The boys wanted to swim every single day. Elaine had taken over the lifeguard duties that afternoon so Jan could make Wednesday morning's muffins, but she still had cookies and scones to do in the morning. She'd planned on danish pastries, but decided she didn't have time. They were labor-intensive, requiring that she roll out the dough multiple times.

"I think I'll turn in early tonight," Jan said when Elaine signed off with her grandchildren.

"Okay. Nathan's coming here around eight in the morning, before he goes to the auction house. He'll have breakfast with me, and then we'll check out Oldies But Goodies."

"Fiona doesn't open until nine, right?"

"Right. Nathan wants to be there when she unlocks the door, so he doesn't lose too much time out of his business day." Elaine smiled. "You know, if he thinks that sign is vintage—"

Across the hall, one of the little boys screamed.

CHAPTER NINE

Elaine and Jan ran to the doorway. The light from the hall spilled in, revealing Riley sitting bolt upright on the near side of the queen bed, screaming. Jan dashed to him.

On the other side, Max sat up, blinking and muttering. Elaine hurried around the bed and sat down on the edge.

"It's okay, Max. Your brother's just having a bad dream."

Jan, meanwhile, was hugging Riley. "*Shh. Shh.* It's okay. It's only a dream."

Riley dissolved into heart-wrenching sobs for a couple of minutes and then subsided into hiccups.

"You're okay." Jan still held him, stroking his head and shoulders. "Grandma's here."

"What happened?" Max demanded.

"Riley had a nightmare," Jan said.

"How come?"

"It just happens sometimes."

Elaine said, "Some of our dreams are happy, and some are sad, and some are kind of scary."

"What was the dream about?" Max turned to his twin.

Elaine had a theory that talking about dreams made them easier to remember in the morning. "That's not important," she said.

But Riley was already talking. "I saw the slimy monster."

"Oh, come on, now." Jan pulled him close. "You know the monster isn't real."

"Caleb Ryder says it is."

Elaine caught Jan's eye and raised her eyebrows. Caleb was the pastor's younger son. He was ten now, and he might think it was funny to tell a couple of seven-year-olds a tall tale. Still, she couldn't imagine him being malicious about it.

"It was all black and ucky." Riley sniffed.

"Oh, honey, it was just a dream," Jan said.

Max looked up at Elaine. "Why do they call it a nightmare?"

"I don't know. Maybe we could look it up tomorrow and find out."

Max frowned. "I want a drink of water."

"Please?" Elaine said.

"Please."

"Okay." Elaine stood. "How about you, Riley? Would you like a drink?"

He nodded vigorously, wiping a tear on his cheek.

Elaine went to her bathroom and filled two small paper cups with cold water. When she got back to the guest room, Jan had turned on the lamp and was sitting between the two boys on the bed, reading to them from *Dr. Seuss's Sleep Book*.

Elaine gave each twin one of the little cups and waited while they drank the water. They passed the cups back to her and cuddled up on each side of Jan as she read. Max already had his eyes closed. Elaine smiled and tiptoed out.

NATHAN WAS PUNCTUAL the next morning, and Elaine sat down with him and the boys for breakfast in the dining room. Elaine's goal was to keep the twins out of the kitchen so Jan could get on with her work.

She had the table all set up, and she brought in juice, milk, muffins, scones, bacon, yogurt, and scrambled eggs. Nathan filled his plate and helped the boys choose what they wanted.

"I don't usually eat like this in the morning," he said. "I just grab coffee and maybe a piece of toast."

"It's nice to have a big breakfast once in a while." Elaine reached over to tuck Riley's napkin into his collar so he wouldn't spill anything on his fresh T-shirt.

Nathan sipped his juice and looked up at the gilt-and-crystal chandelier. The fixture came from a beautiful old lakeside house that had fallen into disrepair. "Did you find out any more about that?"

Elaine followed his gaze. "Not much. We've been really busy. I told you about Denny Gray, who owns the house we think it was in."

"Yeah, but you said that wasn't the name of a real person."

"Right. Well, a real person by the name of *Dennis* Gray owned the house for a short time, ages ago, from what I understand. It wasn't easy, but I found a Denny Gray LLC online, and recently discovered that it was based in Boston. The man who seems to be the 'face' of the corporation turned out to be a model. I found him in stock photos."

"So, he's sort of the human face for the corporation?"

"I think maybe," Elaine said. "We want to find out what was going on with the Dubois house and the chandelier, but I don't think this is the week to do it."

"Well, if it helps, I'm going to Boston soon," Nathan said. "If you want me to do a little poking around, let me know."

"I may take you up on that, if you have time. Let me think about it." Elaine would love to go down there and dig into it herself, but she'd need to set aside a couple of days if she included travel time. With the twins visiting and the firemen's field day coming up, she didn't think she'd be able to get away. Besides, this was the tearoom's busiest season.

"Can I have a muffin, please?" Max asked.

"Sure you can."

She held out the basket, and Max chose a large apple-cinnamon muffin.

Riley looked solemnly at Nathan. "I had a bad dream last night, Mr. Culvert."

Nathan suppressed a smile, but Elaine said, "Culver, honey."

"It's okay. I'm sorry to hear you had a bad dream, Riley." Nathan cocked an eyebrow at Elaine.

"That's right, but it wasn't real," she said soothingly.

Nathan opened his mouth and then closed it. Elaine was glad he hadn't asked what the dream was about, but apparently Riley was eager to tell it anyway.

"A big monster came up out of the water," he said.

"Really?" Nathan glanced at Elaine, then wriggled his eyebrows at the boys. "Was it a...tickle monster?"

Max giggled, but Riley said sternly, "No. It was the lake monster."

"I see," said Nathan. "You know the lake monster isn't really a monster, right?"

"That's what Grandma said," Riley admitted, but he didn't look convinced.

"I think it would be fun to see the monster," Max said. "We could tell Caleb, and he would be so jealous."

Jan popped her head in the doorway before Elaine could say anything. "Boys, finish up now. I'll take you over to the church in about fifteen minutes."

Nathan looked at his watch. "We could drop them over there before we go to Fiona's."

"Sure," Elaine said.

"Oh, well...that would be helpful," Jan said. "Are you sure?"

"No problem," Nathan said.

"I was going to try to speak to the pastor for a minute," Jan said.

Elaine said, "Oh, about...that thing we discussed?" She meant the monster, but didn't want to mention it again in front of Riley.

"Yeah. But I guess I could call him this afternoon."

"Would you like me to say something if the opportunity comes up?" Elaine asked.

"If you want. I just—" Jan broke off and glanced at the boys. "Use your own judgment."

"Okay, I will. And don't forget that filmmaker, Garrett, is coming at nine thirty. He may want to get some footage of you baking."

Jan sighed. "If he insists."

"You'll be fine," Nathan said. "Just give him a cup of tea and one of these muffins."

When they dropped the twins off at the church, all the children were lining up with their class groups before the front steps. Elaine got out of the car, and the boys unbuckled and climbed from the backseat.

"Have fun, guys," Nathan said.

"You too," Max told him soberly.

"Bye, Mr. Culvert," Riley said.

Nathan chuckled. "You know what? You can just call me Nathan, okay?"

Riley looked cautiously up at Elaine.

"It's all right, since he told you to," she assured Riley. "And I'll tell your grandma."

"Okay." Riley flashed Nathan a smile and ran toward the church.

Elaine walked over to where Kit Edmonds was marshaling her students.

"Hi, Elaine!" Kit called. "Thanks for bringing the boys."

Elaine let Riley and Max jostle into Kit's line with their friends and walked over to stand beside Sarah Ryder, the pastor's wife.

"Hi. Is Pastor Mike around?"

Sarah glanced about. "I guess he's inside at the moment. Do you need him?"

Elaine lowered her voice. "Well, I suppose you've heard this lake-monster talk."

"Oh yes," Sarah said. "The kids think it's super cool."

"We were a little concerned about the boys. I was going to ask the pastor if there was a way to calm them a little during Bible school—assure them it's not real at the very least."

Sarah nodded. "The kids in my class have been vocal about it. In fact, Mike spoke to Caleb about it last night."

"Riley had a nightmare," Elaine said softly.

"Oh dear. I'm so sorry. I will definitely talk to my class about it."

"It might be better not to unless they bring it up," Elaine said.

Sarah shook her head. "No, they're talking about it during game time too. Some of the older kids are egging on the little ones, I'm afraid."

"It's not going away, so I'm trying to think of ways to make it fun, not scary. Maybe I'll make up a funny story about a friendly lake monster."

"I'm sure they'd like that. I'll tell Mike about your concerns."

"Thanks," Elaine said. She went to join Nathan at his car, and they drove around the corner to Oldies But Goodies.

"Looks like she's open," Nathan said. He parked in front of the store, and they went inside. They were greeted by the faint smells of cloves, cinnamon, and old wood.

"I love this store," Elaine said.

Nathan looked around. "Yeah, I do too. Fiona does a lot of importing."

"Yes, she's traveled all over, and she has international contacts."

He leaned close to a glassed-in case and peered at a pair of mixed-metal vases.

Fiona came from deeper within the shop and smiled at them.

"Elaine, how nice to see you this morning."

"Hi, Fiona." Elaine looked back at Nathan, and he stepped up beside her. "Do you know Nathan Culver?"

"Of course. Culver Auctions." Fiona extended her hand.

"Hi," Nathan said. "We've met a few times."

"Yes. I always enjoy your sales." Fiona's gaze flicked to Elaine. "Bree said you came in yesterday."

"Yes. I'm interested in an old sign you have on a shelf. Chick of Chickadee Lake?"

Fiona laughed. "Isn't that marvelous? So whimsical."

She turned and led them to the spot where Elaine had stood the previous afternoon, gazing up at it. The sign was still there, and Nathan spotted it.

"Oh yes. That has local appeal for sure. What's the story behind it?"

Fiona furrowed her brow. "Let's see, I think I got that last spring in a batch of stuff. I'll have to check my records. I went to a couple of large sales in late May. It might have come from one of those."

"Can you give us a price on it?" Elaine asked.

"Sure. Just a minute." Fiona went to the checkout to look it up in her computerized inventory.

"I'd like to see it up close," Nathan said to Elaine. "It's a primitive style, but it can't be older than your 1947 events."

"I agree," Elaine said, "and it might be much newer."

Fiona came back smiling. "I put $39.50 on it."

"Thanks," Nathan said. "Do you have a ladder handy? I'd like to get it down and look at it more closely."

"Of course. I'll get it."

"Just show me where," he said. "I can bring it in."

"Oh, thank you. I'd feel so lucky if I didn't have to climb up there after it."

"No problem," Nathan said, following Fiona toward the back of the shop.

Elaine stayed and browsed the treasures in the nearby displays while they got the tall stepladder. Nathan carried it back and set it up below the high shelves. Meanwhile, several more shoppers drifted in.

"You go ahead and get it," Fiona said. "Just be careful. I'll go see if I can help these folks."

Elaine held the bottom of the ladder steady as Nathan cautiously climbed up to where he could reach the signboard. He lifted it gingerly off the shelf, tucked it under his arm, and made his way down.

"Should we put the ladder away?" Elaine whispered. "It's blocking the aisle."

"Well, we might have to put this back up there if we don't buy it." Nathan handed her the sign and collapsed the ladder, then leaned it against the nearest wall, out of the way.

Elaine held up the painted board. "What do you think?"

"It's cute. I like the subject." He turned it over and put on a pair of reading glasses. "The paint could be the right era. It's not anything as modern as acrylics." He studied the edges of the board and the places where the paint met bare wood on the back.

"What is it?" Elaine asked.

"I think it's regular enamel, and the board is actually three pieces fastened together, not one wide board."

He turned it to the front side again.

"It doesn't seem to be for a particular business or event," Elaine mused.

"No. Just a celebration of Chick. Unless there was more to it." He set it on edge, with the bottom edge up. Two small holes penetrated the wood. "I think there was another part to this, hanging from the bottom of the sign. Maybe a smaller board they could change out with prices or times or something like that."

"What would it be for?" Elaine asked.

"Anything. Boat rides for a dollar. Barbecue noon to two. Coffee and a doughnut, two bits."

"*Hmm.* You're thinking it had to do with some sort of community event?"

Nathan nodded. "You mentioned a parade with a Chick float."

"Yeah, Fourth of July, 1947."

"There you go. There were probably several promotions that day taking advantage of the monster craze."

Fiona came over, smiling. "What do you think?"

"We'll take it," Nathan said.

Elaine arched her eyebrows at him. She still wasn't sure a dubious piece of memorabilia was worth it. They still didn't have proof the signboard had been painted seventy-odd years ago.

"It would look cute out on the side porch, I guess, where Clifton told us about his sighting," she said.

Fiona looked sharply at her. "I heard something about that, and other sightings, supposedly. Is the scuttlebutt serious, or some sort of joke?"

"I don't think there's anything large in the lake, if that's what you mean," Elaine said, "but there are rumors going around."

"If you don't want it, I'll buy it," Nathan said. "If this new interest takes off and becomes a frenzy, anything from the original craze will go up in value."

Fiona frowned, and Elaine wondered if she wished she had priced the sign higher. After a moment, she laughed. "Hey, either you're getting a forty-dollar piece of whimsy, or you're getting a good investment. Either way, you can't lose."

"I agree." Nathan reached for his wallet.

"Oh no, I'll buy it," Elaine said. "I guess it doesn't really matter all that much if it's genuine."

"I think it is," Nathan told her. "Let me buy it for you as a gift."

"No—" Elaine looked up into his warm blue eyes, so like the color of the lake in the afternoon sun. That smile, combined with his loving gaze, was very hard to resist. "Okay. Thanks."

His smiled widened. "Thanks for letting me." He quickly made the transaction.

"Want that wrapped?" Fiona asked.

Elaine shrugged. "It's only down the street."

"Please do wrap it," Nathan said. "I don't want to take a chance of chipping that vintage paint."

Elaine gave him a little chuckle. "Spoken like an auctioneer."

A few minutes later, they arrived back at the tearoom. Half a dozen cars were parked out front, and the Open sign was out.

"Did we take that long?" Elaine glanced at her watch. "Sure enough, open for business ten minutes ago."

"Well, putting the ladder back took some time," Nathan said amiably. He got out of the car and lifted the newspaper-wrapped signboard from the backseat. "Now, where do you want this until it's hung?"

"On the back porch, I guess. I'd like to get it up right away."

Nathan carried it in, and they went to the kitchen doorway. Elaine stopped short.

Garrett Wolfe was standing in the middle of the room with a hand-held video camera pointed at the work island. His friend Adrian sat at the table watching, with a cup of tea and a plate of scones before him. Jan leaned over the granite surface, rolling out cookie dough.

"Great," Garrett said. "That's great. Now, can you cut out some cookies?"

"I'm not done rolling," Jan said. "It's still too thick."

"Sorry."

Elaine looked up at Nathan and smiled.

"Quiet on the set," she whispered. "Maybe we should leave it in my office for now."

Nathan carried the sign in for her and set it down, leaning it against a wall. "I'd better get to work, but that was fun."

"Thanks. I always enjoy being with you."

Nathan bent and kissed her lightly. "I'll call you later."

CHAPTER TEN

L ater that day, Jan looked up as Rose entered the kitchen with her order pad in hand.

"Hi," Jan said. "What do you need?"

"A pot of green tea with two cups, and I'll get the cookies. Thanks. And Pastor Ryder is out front. Do you have time to talk to him now?"

Jan glanced toward the oven. She'd just put a sheet of mini cream puffs in to bake. Elaine was at the library story hour with the twins, who had refused to enter the water that afternoon.

"Can he come in here?" Jan asked as she got down a teapot for Rose's patrons. "I got a little behind on my baking this morning, what with all the excitement with Garrett."

Rose grinned. "I'll tell Pastor you need to stay in the kitchen and send him back."

"Thanks. Tell him he can have all the cookies he can eat."

Rose finished fixing her tray and went out with it. Jan had only spent twenty minutes with Garrett, but he had lingered at the tearoom, videotaping and interviewing customers, for more than an hour, and nothing had gone according to routine while he was on the premises. It was good for business, she supposed.

A moment later, Pastor Mike came to the doorway and looked in hesitantly.

"Hi, Jan."

"Oh, hi." She wiped her hands on her apron and went to take his hand. "Sit right down and I'll get you something to drink. How can I help you?"

"Thanks, but I just ate a late lunch. VBS week is always hectic at our house."

"It's been kind of crazy here too," she admitted. The timer rang, and she grabbed her oven mitts. "Just let me take these cream puffs out, and we can have a nice chat."

He watched her work with great interest. "Do you bake all day?"

"Some days," Jan said. "Usually just in the morning, but it depends on what's going on and how much food we need to prepare. I've been doing extra cookies for VBS, and I had a few special orders this week. Then Sadie Taylor's cousin asked if he could come film here for a while." She shook her head. "I should have said no, but he says it's great footage. He's documenting a lot of small-town entrepreneurs, or something like that."

"Sounds exciting. So, how's it going with the twins? Sarah said they're a little wound up about the lake monster rumors."

Jan sighed and stood for a moment with the spatula in her hand. "They're having a great time, and they love VBS, but I think they're a little worried."

"I'm sorry to hear that."

She slid the last few cream puffs off the sheet onto a cooling rack. "Riley had a nightmare last night."

"Poor little guy."

Jan nodded. "He said the kids in his class are talking a lot about the monster. Older kids too."

"I'm afraid my Caleb is guilty," Pastor Mike said. "I spoke to him this morning about how it could frighten the younger children. He thought it was funny at first, but I reminded him of how scared he's been in the past when things have happened that upset the family. It sounds as though it might be time for me to speak to all the children as a group."

"That might help," Jan said, "but we're trying to help them see the lighter side of it. I don't want them to be scared of stuff like that. Of course, it's not just kids that are talking about it. More people in town keep claiming they've seen it, and gossip runs through the tearoom pretty quickly, I'm afraid."

"*Hmm.* Well, maybe I can tie it in with our Noah's ark theme, though I'll have to make it very clear that we're not talking about a real animal."

"How would you do that?" Jan asked. "Max asked the other day about dinosaurs on the ark."

"Yes, and the kids have wondered about the whales and the seals, animals that spend all or a big part of their lives in the water. One of the teens even asked about freshwater fish, and how they could survive if the ocean covered everything."

Jan smiled. "There's a thinker for you. What did you say?"

"I've been reading up on this topic to prepare for VBS, and there are actually several theories out there, one being that the ocean wasn't as salty then, and all the new water that was added was freshwater. Of course, it's all speculation. And animals like seals and polar bears have to spend some time on land, so I think they were included in the ark. Or maybe they found icebergs to rest on, I don't know. But anyway, when it comes to octopuses and lobsters, I don't think Noah had to have any on board. Now, sea monsters are another whole category."

Jan smiled. "Elaine said she told Max they might have taken baby dinosaurs or dinosaur eggs on the ark. But I'm pretty sure they didn't take any monsters."

"Right. And that's what I'll tell the kids. There are no sea—or lake—monsters, so Noah didn't have to worry about them."

Jan frowned. "The twins will go back to their parents this weekend, but I don't think Chick is going away anytime soon. It's too catchy an advertising theme."

Pastor Mike's eyebrows shot up. "Really?"

"Yeah. Back in the 1940s, the town went wild over the idea and used it to promote the tourism. They named businesses after the monster and had parade floats that were shaped like one—sort of like the Loch Ness Monster."

"The older kids have heard about that one, of course," Pastor Mike said. "I suppose it lends more credence to the tales."

"And there's apparently one in Lake Champlain too. Elaine and I have been reading up on that one. Champ, they call it, and they've even passed laws to protect it. It's all publicity, I think, but it's working for them, so some of the Lancaster people think it could work here."

"You think someone's feeding these rumors for gain?"

Jan shrugged. "I don't know what to think. And I'm not sure it's such a horrible thing, if it's all in good fun. But I don't want children to be scared by it. My grandsons love playing in the water, but they wouldn't go in today."

"I'm sorry, Jan." Pastor Mike stood. "My kids had seen the Narnia film *The Voyage of the Dawn Treader,* so Caleb thought he was pretty well versed in sea monsters."

"I don't know if the twins have seen that or not. I'm guessing not. It would be a little scary for them, I think. I know my older grandchildren love it."

"And I'm not saying they should see it," Pastor Mike said. "Just that there's a lot out there in the culture. They'll run into it sooner or later."

"I know. Elaine and I were just going to try to keep them from hearing about it, but that backfired. Everyone's talking about it. So now we've decided to try to make it more like a fairy tale, but not too scary," Jan said.

Pastor Mike made a face. "Some of those old fairy tales were downright gory. But I think you're right—they'll be exposed to it one way or another, so you might as well help them think of it as a made-up creature—like Smokey the Bear or Pegasus. I'll definitely work on something this afternoon to tell the kids at VBS tomorrow, and I'll make sure Caleb soft-pedals the stories."

"Thanks," Jan said.

"It's a legitimate concern. I think our teachers can help us a lot on this. If their students mention Chick, maybe they can use it as a springboard to discuss not only cryptozoology, but how to show Christ's love by not scaring the little ones."

Jan smiled. "Thanks, Pastor. I knew you would understand."

ELAINE AND THE twins returned to the tearoom with several new library books in hand. Jan sat down with them for a snack, and the boys were full of chatter about story hour and Bible school, but they didn't mention the lake monster once. Elaine was dying to show Jan the sign she and Nathan had bought, but she thought it best to hold off on that.

When they finished their snack, Jan looked at the twins. "So, do you want to hunt for more turtles today?"

"Yeah," Riley said.

"Can we swim, Grandma?" Max asked.

"Sure. I can come down to the dock and watch you for a while. I'd better not go in though. I need to do some more work later, and I don't want to have to change."

Elaine eyed her questioningly.

"I can take my laptop down there," Jan said.

Elaine nodded. She must be planning more lake monster research—at least, something she didn't want to speak plainly about in front of the boys.

"I don't want to swim," Riley said, scowling.

"Okay," Jan said quickly. "You can both put your suits on and hunt turtles, and I'll be there in case you decide to get wet. Fair enough, Max?"

Max scowled at his brother. "Oh, come on. That monster won't come to Grandma's beach."

Riley made a stubborn little sound in his throat and turned away.

"Now, Max," Jan said, "Riley doesn't have to swim if he doesn't want to."

While the boys raced upstairs to change into their swimsuits, Elaine took Jan into her office.

"Here, I want you to see this. Nathan thinks it's probably from the 1940s." She undid Fiona's tape and pulled the newspapers off the signboard.

Jan stared at it for several seconds. "Well! It's kind of cute. And it's green—not at all like the slimy black thing in Riley's nightmare. It looks more like Cecil the Seasick Sea Monster."

Elaine laughed. "I don't think many people remember *Beany and Cecil*, Jan. Maybe if they had a show like that now, the boys would think Chick was cute."

"Maybe we should show the boys this."

Elaine eyed her keenly. "Do you think so?"

"Yes. This picture isn't at all scary. It might give them a better image to think of." She told Elaine about her conversation with the pastor.

"You may be right. If they can forget the 'monster' part, they might think of it as a fun fictional character."

Jan looked at the price tag on the signboard. "Well, I'd say you got a bargain. I wonder who painted this."

"Who knows? It's not great art, but I figure it might come in handy if they make Chick the theme of the muster."

"Yes. Do you want me to bring the boys in now?"

"That's up to you," Elaine said.

Jan shrugged. "I suppose it's normal for a lakeside community to have a wacky legend like this. Let's show it to them."

"Okay."

When the boys came downstairs, Jan called to them. "Come into the office, guys! We have something funny to show you."

When they entered, Elaine held the sign up on top of her desk. "What do you think of this?"

"Wow," Max said.

"Is it real?" Riley asked.

"It's a real sign," Elaine told him. "But the animal isn't real."

"That sign is really old," Jan said. "Older than I am."

"That's really old." Riley reached out to touch the board.

"It's from way back, about seventy years ago, when people first made up stories about there being a big critter in the lake," Elaine said. "They named it Chick, like Chickadee Lake, but it was just pretend."

"See how it looks like a cartoon?" Jan asked. "It was just a fun story they told to make people want to come and stay at the lake."

Max looked at her solemnly. "How big was it?"

"It wasn't big at all," Jan said. "It wasn't real. People just pretended it was."

"It kind of looks like a dinosaur," Riley said.

"A *make-believe* dinosaur," Elaine replied. "It was kind of an advertising animal, like the squirrel on your breakfast cereal box. He's not real, either."

"Now, are you ready to catch more turtles?" Jan asked.

"Yeah!" Riley and Max ran for the door.

Elaine chuckled and rewrapped the board. "While you and the twins enjoy your beach time, I thought I'd walk over to the fire station and see what the firefighters are up to. If they have refined their plans for the field day beyond the muster and a barbecue, we may have some ideas on what we can do that day."

She watched Jan and the boys head down to the shore carrying sunscreen, a small fishing net, and face masks, though Riley still insisted he didn't want to swim. Elaine checked with Rose and Archie to make sure they didn't have more customers than they could handle and then slipped out through the garage.

At the fire station, she found Tag, Caden, and Jason washing the tanker truck on the pavement outside the building.

"Well, hi, Tag," she called as she approached. "I'm surprised you're over here in the middle of the day."

"Hi," Tag said with a grin. He flipped his too-long brown hair back from his forehead, revealing his attractive blue eyes. "Business has been slow, so I hung a sign that says "At the Firehouse" on the door and came over here to get some stuff done."

"I guess the motorcycle- and snowmobile-repair business has its busy times and its lulls, like the tearoom," Elaine said.

"Like most any business, I guess. What can I do for you, Elaine?"

"I wondered if you'd made any more progress on your plans for the field day. Jan and I would like to participate."

"Yeah, you mentioned making special cookies or something?"

"We'd like to do more than that," Elaine said. "We were thinking maybe we'd set up a game of some sort on the lawn, if the weather's good."

"Actually, the auxiliary is going to run games for the kids all day long." Tag scrubbed away at the truck's headlights. "We're setting up vendor booths at the school grounds. You can use one if you want."

"Great. We can run a booth with cookies and cold drinks. Let me know if there's anything else we can help with."

"Maybe come up with something that has to do with the lake monster," Caden said.

"You're not serious." Elaine looked from Caden to Tag.

"As a matter of fact, Rachel and Alicia are over at the town office right now, talking to Mark Payson about it," Tag said. "Seems there's been another sighting, and we're starting to think Macy may have called this one right. It could draw in a lot of people."

"And there's the woman who owns Computer Gal," Jason said, looking at his brother.

Caden nodded. "Right, Diane Blanchett. She's writing a play about it."

"She mentioned that to me." Elaine frowned. "She's going ahead with it, then?"

Tag nodded. "Sounds like it will be quite a production. They're putting it on at the Old Grange Hall right after the muster ends. She said they'll sell tickets and give the money to the fire department."

"We'll certainly buy tickets," Elaine said. "I think Jan told her we'd help backstage too. I'll have to talk to her again."

"Hey, you want to see our sign for the barbecue?" Tag asked.

"You've got it ready?"

"We're using the banner from the last one, but we changed the dates," Caden said. "And Rachel and Elsa painted a new piece of canvas to stitch over the picture on one end. Guess what's on the new part."

Elaine thought for a moment. "I'm guessing it's not a fire truck."

Tag laughed and tossed his sponge into a bucket of soapy water. "Come on in and take a look."

Inside the firehouse, the twenty-foot banner was rolled up and lying on a folding table. Tag grasped one end while Caden held the roll steady. He pulled out the first six feet of the canvas, and Elaine gasped. A four-foot-high, six-foot-long likeness of Chick the Lake Monster nearly dazzled her in its bright-green, red, and black acrylic paint. Rather than the cartoonish figure she had expected, the creature seemed almost lifelike.

"Wow. That will get some attention."

"We'll hang it across Main Street, so all the cars drive under it," Tag said. "And the *Courier* and *Sentinel* are both giving us some space in their community events columns."

"Yeah, and that gal from the *Courier* said she might be able to get a picture in for us," Caden said with a grin. "Think we should use this for the picture?"

"I don't know," Elaine said. "Maybe it would be better to have one of you in full turnout gear. Focus on the muster."

Tag gazed at the garish banner. "I don't know, I kind of like Chick myself."

"Maybe she'll take a picture of you guys hanging up the banner," Jason suggested.

Tag laughed. "Maybe so. I like that idea. Well, come on, guys. We need to rinse off the truck, in case we get a call."

Elaine walked slowly back to the tearoom, mulling over Tag's words. To her surprise, Jan was in the kitchen, stirring a bowl of batter studded with chocolate chips.

"What's up?"

Jan paused in her stirring. "Rue Maxwell called with an emergency muffin order. The B&B got unexpected guests for overnight—a family of six—and she needs extra for tomorrow's breakfast."

"Oh. Where are the boys?" Elaine asked.

"Down on the shore. I left them turtle hunting, with strict orders not to get in the water. Would you be willing to check on them?"

"Sure." Elaine went to the back porch and looked down toward the dock. Riley and Max were crouched beside their turtle tub. She went back inside. "They're okay."

"Thanks. They're good kids." Jan reached into the cupboard for her muffin tins.

"They sure are." Elaine eyed her for a moment, then spoke her mind. "Do you think Tag King could be behind the monster stories?"

Jan stood for a moment with two muffin pans in her hands. "Why do you say that?"

"He's got a new sign on his street banner for the barbecue—a giant picture of Chick."

"I didn't know Tag was artistic," Jan said.

"Rachel Leon did it, and apparently she got Elsa in on the project, so you know it's going to be eye-catching."

"She's a good artist," Jan said. "Her work isn't always to my taste, but she does have talent."

Elaine smiled. "I wonder if she'll cast a statue of Chick for the sculpture garden. But seriously, Tag is getting into this. I have to wonder if maybe he heard about the old stories and decided to put it out there again to add a little spice to the fund-raising campaign."

"I doubt it. But even if he did, there's nothing wrong with that, is there? I just didn't like to see children frightened. But I think the boys are doing much better now. We talked a little more about that sign board, and I think it's growing on them." Jan glanced toward the back door. "Speaking of the boys..."

"Right." Elaine walked out on the porch again, just as Max let out a yelp.

She threw the back door open. Max was pounding up the steps from the deck below.

"Grandma! Come quick!"

Elaine looked beyond him, her heart in her throat, but Riley, too, was running toward the house with a small box turtle clutched in one hand.

"Max, what is it?" Elaine hurried down to meet him on the steps.

Behind her, Jan said, "What on earth?"

"We saw it, Grandma! We saw the big green monster!" Riley seemed more excited than frightened, but as he jumped up onto the deck, he tripped over one of the cast iron chairs, and thudded to the ground. He lay there moaning.

"Here." Elaine took Max's arm and pulled him past her, to Jan. She hurried down to the deck between the house and wharf and gathered Riley into her arms. "What is it, buddy? What happened?"

Riley looked up at her, his eyes huge and teary marks streaking his dirty face.

"My foot! My foot!" Riley shoved the turtle into Elaine's hand and grabbed his left foot.

Elaine held the turtle carefully and looked down. Riley's big toe was bleeding.

"Oh, honey, you stubbed your toe on the chair. Come on, I'll put a bandage on it."

He got up and hobbled beside her up the steps toward Jan and Max.

"So what happened?" Jan was saying. "Why were you yelling?"

Max's eyes were as round as Riley's.

"The monster, Grandma! We saw the monster."

CHAPTER ELEVEN

Elaine looked sharply at Riley. "Did you see something in the water?"

Riley nodded vigorously. "A great, big, green monster."

"Green?" Jan asked.

"Yeah." Max swiped a hand across his face, leaving a muddy streak. "We went over into the weeds looking for more turtles, and it jumped up out of the water."

"Where?" Jan looked toward the shore.

Riley and Max both pointed. Between their waterfront and Sylvia's, a small point of land jutted out. In the curve of the shore, a little cove sprouted tall weeds. The bottom was mucky over there, and Jan had told the boys not to go into it without their water shoes, as leeches might lurk in the mud. But the turtles loved that area.

"I wanted you to see it, Grandma," Max said.

"I can't see anything now." Jan looked skeptically at Elaine.

Elaine shrugged. "I wouldn't think it was deep enough over there for anything large."

"It was really big," Max insisted.

"Okay." Elaine looked at Riley. "Well, mister, you need a bandage. Let's fix your toe, and then maybe you and Max can show us exactly where you saw this...whatever you saw."

Leaving the hapless turtle to find his way off the deck, she hauled Riley up into her arms and carried him up the steps. Jan hustled Max before them, through the back porch to the kitchen.

Archie was in there, preparing a pot of tea. "Thought I heard some yowling," he said.

Jan nodded. "Riley needs a Band-Aid. I'll get it." She hurried out into the hall.

"What happened?" Archie asked.

"Stubbed his toe pretty hard," Elaine said, settling the little boy on a stool near the work island.

"We saw the lake monster," Max said loudly.

Elaine winced and hoped none of the customers had heard him. If Macy Atherton was out there, she would spread it all over town.

"Indeed?" Archie stooped to Max's eye level. "What did it look like?"

"It was green all over, and it had red eyes."

Elaine frowned. "Red eyes?" That matched the monster on the signboard she had bought from Fiona. Was he adjusting what he'd seen to the picture on the sign?

Riley nodded his head up and down. "Red eyes. Like fire."

"Wow." She couldn't think of anything more lucid.

"Now, this red-eyed green monster," Archie began, "where exactly did you see it?"

"In the turtle weeds," Max said.

"Turtle weeds." Archie glanced at Elaine.

"Between here and Sylvia's beach," Elaine said. "It's a weedy little cove where they hunt turtles."

"I see."

"Elaine, where's my turtle?" Riley asked.

Jan came in carrying the compact first aid kit they kept in the hall bathroom near the door to the garage.

"All right, Riley, let me see that toe."

Elaine straightened and moved out of her way. "I left your turtle down on the deck, Riley. Do you want me to go put him back in the water if I can find him, or should I escort him to your turtle tub?"

"In the tub, please." His grubby little face was so sweet that she couldn't refuse him.

"All right, but I'll check the water temperature first." She hoped they could keep those poor turtles healthy until the end of the week, when she and Jan had agreed they should all be set free.

She went down to the deck, leaving Jan to bind Riley's wound and Archie to help cheer the boys. When she reached the platform with the white iron table and chairs, she looked around. The little box turtle was nowhere to be seen.

"Now, Elaine, don't panic," she told herself. "He's probably headed for the water."

She climbed carefully down into the tall grass beside the stairs and studied the foliage. The tiniest of movements drew her attention.

"There you are!" She scooped up the turtle and walked down to the small beach and over to the shaded tub. The boys' turtle ark had fallen in, and the stones and leaves were scattered, but five turtles of various sizes were still in the tub. Two were sitting on stones the twins had provided, sunning themselves. They others were partly submerged in the water, and one was munching placidly on a lettuce leaf.

Elaine really thought the tub population had reached its maximum, but what would Riley say if she turned his new acquisition loose? She decided to have a chat with him after his toe was bandaged and they had discussed the supposed monster thoroughly.

She looked over toward the cove and the little point of land. The weeds grew even thicker on Sylvia's side of the land, and trees and bushes crowded right down to the shore there. The thick growth provided privacy between their two swimming areas, but it also shaded that section, and the murky water harbored leeches, freshwater clams, and crawfish.

She walked carefully along the water's edge. There was no path, but the boys had trampled the grass and weeds in places. As she stepped out onto the point, she pushed through taller grass and bushes. She couldn't see any evidence that the boys had gone this far or crossed the narrow point. The grass looked undisturbed.

A tree on Sylvia's property leaned toward the lake, with a few branches overhanging the water. Sylvia's tiny beach was several yards beyond. She had no boat, and as far as Elaine knew, Sylvia swam rarely, if ever. No dock jutted out into the water, and no deck chairs sat near the shore.

She gazed out at the lake. A hundred yards out, a rowboat pulled away from her, headed in the direction of Green Glade Cottages. Probably one of Macy's guests.

On impulse, Elaine pulled her phone from the pocket of her capris and zoomed in on the boat. She still couldn't tell who was rowing. It appeared to be a man, but she couldn't be sure. He wore a pale-blue shirt and a wide-brimmed hat. She snapped a picture. Maybe Macy could identify the boat later.

She took a step and almost slipped into the water. Flailing, she grabbed one of the maple branches overhead and pulled herself back. The branch she'd seized was about an inch thick where her hand met it. She gazed at it thoughtfully and then looked down.

The water on Sylvia's side of the point was even muddier than on the tearoom side. In fact, it looked as though the muck had been stirred up recently. Some of the water plants looked mangled, and a few that had been pulled up or broken off floated on the surface. Elaine crouched and pulled a clump toward her.

"Hey!"

She stood and looked back toward the tearoom dock and beach. Jan and the twins stood on the shore near the turtle tub and abandoned ark. Elaine waved.

"What are you doing?" Jan yelled.

"Just looking." Elaine took a few cautious steps toward them. When she was out of the tall grass and weeds, she bent over and brushed off her pant legs. Then she walked back to where Jan and the boys stood.

Jan eyed her closely but didn't ask if she'd found anything. Elaine was certain they would have plenty to talk over later.

JAN AND ELAINE helped the boys change the water in the turtle tub and introduced the new box turtle to the older residents.

"It's getting pretty full," Elaine said. "Maybe you should let a couple of them go."

"No," Riley said. "We need them all."

"What for?" Jan asked. "They only took two on the ark."

"I think we should keep two each," Max said.

Riley folded his arms. "No."

Jan sighed and looked at Elaine.

"Maybe we can get another tub from somebody," Elaine looked questioningly to Jan.

"Maybe. But, guys, you know we can't keep them after you go home Saturday."

"I want to take mine with me," Max said.

"Well, you'll have to talk to your mom and dad about that," Jan said firmly. She looked at her watch. "I think you two need to have a shower and get the mud off you, and then we'll have a snack. How about that?"

"Can we go to the playground?" Riley asked.

"I guess so." The elementary school was closed for the summer, but the school officials didn't make a fuss if residents accompanied their children there to play, so long as the kids weren't left unattended.

Jan sent the twins upstairs to take turns in the shower. When they were gone, she turned to Elaine. "Okay, spill it. What were you doing in the weeds?"

"Looking to see if anyone else had been over there. And I think someone had."

"Someone?" Jan asked. "Or some*thing*?"

"The water on Sylvia's side of that point was all muddied, and the water weeds looked like something had churned them up."

"But a huge green monster with red eyes?"

Elaine sighed. "That I couldn't say. But something was there. I don't think the boys stirred up the muck or chewed up the weeds, and I didn't think the grass was trampled from our side to Sylvia's, which might mean the boys didn't go that far."

"Unless they went farther inland and then out to the other side of the point."

"I don't think they'd go out of sight of our house, do you?"

"No."

"And I did see someone rowing away, but he was quite a ways out, and I don't know for sure that he'd been there, or even that he'd touched shore on this end of the lake."

As she spoke, Elaine browsed on her phone and brought up the picture. "He was about midway between here and Green Glade. I thought maybe Macy could tell us if it's one of their boats."

Jan took the phone and squinted at the photo. The boat was too far away, and the person rowing wore a hat shading his eyes. "I don't recognize that guy, but it's a bad angle. Yeah, let's ask the Athertons. Maybe you could do that while I take the boys to the playground."

"Good idea." Elaine took her phone back and gazed at the picture. "You know, Riley said that the monster was black in his nightmare. But whatever they saw today was green. They both agreed on it."

"I noticed that," Jan said. "I asked them again, after you went down to the shore. They said it jumped up in front of them, and it was green, with red eyes."

"Like my signboard."

Jan nodded. "I'd think they made it up, but you found evidence of activity over there...?"

"I think we have a trickster on our hands," Elaine said.

Jan nodded. "I can't explain it, so you could be right. I think they both saw *something*."

"At least they didn't seem scared to death."

"You don't think Sylvia had anything to do with it?" Jan asked.

"Sylvia? No, why would she?"

"I don't know, but that little point is right on the boundary line."

"I'll stop in and talk to her when I go to the Athertons', but no, I don't think she's the type who would deliberately try to scare a couple of seven-year-olds."

Jan let out a deep breath. "Okay. I agree."

"I'll check in with Rose and Archie," Elaine said. "I'm pretty sure they're all set, and if they don't need anything I'll take this photo and talk to Sylvia and someone at Green Glade. Did you get your baking done?"

Jan nodded. "I'm okay until tomorrow morning."

"Well, relax and enjoy your time with the boys, if you can."

"I'll do my best."

MACY WASN'T HOME when Elaine arrived at the cottages, but her son, Shane, was in the office. As Elaine entered, he looked up from the paperwork spread before him on the desk.

"Hi, Shane," Elaine said with a smile. "Have you got a minute?"

"Sure. Although I need to have a boat ready for Mr. Townes at four." He glanced at the clock on the wall. "I guess there's plenty of time."

"This won't take long." Elaine retrieved her phone from her pocket. "I was down at the shore earlier, and I saw someone rowing a boat, heading this way. I wondered if you could tell me—is this one of yours?"

Shane took the phone from her and studied the picture. "Huh. Nope, it's not our boat. I'm not sure whose it is. You might want to ask at the marina."

"Thanks, I'll do that," Elaine said. "So, I guess that's not one of your guests, either?"

Shane looked at it again. "I don't think so, but it's kind of hard to tell. I don't recall anyone who's here now wearing a hat like that."

"Thanks." Elaine took the phone from him and hesitated. "I was kind of hoping to talk to your mother about the so-called lake monster."

Shane grinned. "Oh yeah, she was talking about it last night."

"Is this the first time you've heard of it?" Elaine asked.

"No, I've heard her tell it before. Apparently it was a big deal back before Mom bought this place."

Elaine nodded. "I heard that a lot more tourists started coming to Chickadee Lake in the late '40s because of the monster stories."

Shane pushed back his chair and stood. "It was all before my day. Mom's gone to Augusta this afternoon, but if you come by tomorrow, she'd probably love to talk about it."

"But people didn't actually believe in the monster, did they?" Elaine persisted.

"You'd have to ask Mom. I tend to think it was all sort of a wink-and-nod thing, like they all pretended they believed it."

"For the town's image?"

"Maybe. I don't know. Well, I'd better go get that boat ready."

"Sure. Thank you, Shane."

Elaine walked out to the parking area and watched him hurry down the path to the T-shaped dock, where three small boats were tied up. Two middle-aged men came out of one of the cottages carrying fishing rods and tackle boxes and headed for the waterfront.

She drove back to the tearoom and remembered after she'd driven in that she hadn't talked to Sylvia, so she walked over to the vintage shop next door.

Sylvia was waiting on a customer. Elaine browsed the summer fashions while she waited.

"Hi, Elaine," her friend said brightly a couple of minutes later.

"Hi." Elaine turned toward her with a woven straw purse in her hand. "I can't leave your store without this bag."

Sylvia laughed. "Great."

They walked to the checkout, and Sylvia rang up her purchase. "Now, what really brought you here?"

"Am I that transparent?" Elaine asked.

"In the middle of the day? Yes. And you have that—shall we say, 'air of mystery'?—about you."

"Aha. Well, here's the thing."

She told Sylvia quickly about the twins' sighting. Sylvia's face grew troubled.

"On *my* property?"

"Right down at the little point of land between your beach and ours."

Sylvia shook her head. "That water's too shallow for anything large."

"I agree," Elaine said. "But the boys said it jumped up at them. And when I looked a few minutes later, the water on your side was all muddy. So I think *something* was there."

"Well, I assure you, I had nothing to do with it. Do you think I should call Dan Benson?"

"*Hmm.* I'm not sure it's a matter for the police."

"Trespassing?" Sylvia asked.

"I suppose, although we have no proof any people were there. Maybe we ought to tell Jack."

"The game warden?"

"Yeah. Jack's gone out once or twice looking for evidence of this creature fishermen have claimed to see. He might find this interesting. Of course, the water has probably settled by now." Elaine sighed. "Jan and I should have called him right away, I guess."

Two women came through the front door, and the customer who'd been in the shop since Elaine's arrival came toward the counter with a dress over her arm.

"Would you mind calling him?" Sylvia whispered.

"Sure, I can do that," Elaine said.

Sylvia nodded. "If he's coming out, give me a buzz, and if I'm not busy, I'll dash out the back door and talk to him. Or he can come tell me afterward if he finds anything. I want to know if somebody was trespassing on my land."

CHAPTER TWELVE

Jack looked down at the painted signboard on the kitchen island.

"And the twins say they saw something like this today?"

"Well, keep an open mind," Jan said. "We didn't want to press them too hard about it, because of Riley's nightmare."

"Oh no—poor little guy."

"We also thought it would be better for you if the boys hadn't gone over it several times before you heard it."

"Thanks. Where are they now?" Jack looked toward the parlors. The tearoom had just closed for the day, and Archie was out in the entry, cashing up the day's receipts.

"Elaine offered to go up to the third floor and play with them for a while. We did show them the signboard, because we thought it might help them not to be scared if they saw an image of it that looked friendly. And today was the first time they described the monster as being green. After the nightmare, Riley was saying it was black and slimy. And they said today it had red eyes. That was new too."

"You said the other kids at VBS have talked about the creature though."

"True. Some of the older kids could have described it like this."

Jack nodded, studying the old sign. "Especially if their grandparents or great-grandparents remember when it was a popular story. I'd like to talk to the boys and ask them to take me to the spot where they saw the monster. If it's the same place Elaine told me about..."

"I'm sure it is," Jan said.

"Okay. I just want to hear it from them."

Jan nodded toward the pot of tea steeping on the counter. "Help yourself to tea, Jack, and there are scones in that white container. I'll go up and get the boys. I'll just be a couple of minutes."

She carried the sign into the office and hurried to the stairs. She climbed the two flights quickly, glad she'd been walking a lot for exercise lately. She could hear the boys' delighted squeals long before she reached the tower room. She mounted the last few steps and paused in the doorway. Elaine was throwing soft foam balls at the twins, who screeched as they dodged them, then gathered them up to pelt Elaine in return.

"Hey, guys!" she called, and they all stopped in midmotion and looked toward her. "Jack Weston wants to talk to you."

"Where is he?" Max asked.

"Down in the kitchen, eating scones."

"Can we show him the turtles?" Riley asked.

"Of course you can. But if he tells you that tub is overcrowded, be ready to let a few go, okay?"

Riley frowned. "Okay."

"Jack knows about things like that," Jan said. "Come on." She took Riley's hand and walked down the narrow stairs with him. Elaine followed with Max.

When they got to the kitchen, Jack popped the last bite of a scone into his mouth and brushed off his hands.

"Hi, Jack," Max said.

Jack grinned and swallowed. "Hi, fellas."

"Did you see our turtles?" Max asked.

"Not yet. Want to show them to me?"

"Yeah!" Max dashed for the back door, with Riley right behind him.

Jack smiled at Jan and Elaine. "Wish I had half that energy."

He followed the twins outside and down the steps to the deck. They had jumped off the side and tore across the grass to the tree line near the property boundary, where the turtle tub sat under the low branches of a fir tree.

Jack ambled toward the boys, and Elaine and Jan followed slowly, to give the boys time to show off their pets.

When they reached the tub, Jack was holding up one of the larger turtles and inspecting the yellowish markings on its shell and spots on its face and legs.

"That is a fine box turtle, Riley."

"Thanks!" Riley wiggled all over. "I'm going to see if my mom will let me take him home."

"Well, if you do that, you make sure you have a good place for him to live. See, turtles like to have a lot of space to swim in."

The boys' faces sobered.

"They really do better in the wild," Jack said.

"What about mine?" Max held up a slightly smaller turtle, mostly black with bits of red decorating the edges of its shell.

"Now that's pretty," Jack said. "Do you know what kind it is?"

"Grandma says it's a painted turtle."

"That's right," Jack said. "And if he ever pokes his head out, you might see that he has stripes on his face, where Riley's has spots."

"Yeah, they're cousins," Max said.

Jack nodded soberly. "Probably so." He looked down at the tub. "You've got a lot of turtles in your habitat, boys,"

"What's that?" Max asked.

"A habitat is where they live. Maybe you ought to pick one or two each that you like the absolute best, and let the rest go free."

Jan caught Elaine's eye and nodded in approval. Trust Jack to put the boys straight where wildlife was concerned. Elaine smiled and winked at her.

"Weeeell…" Riley looked at Max.

"I want to keep my painted turtle," Max said.

"I want one of each." Riley looked pleadingly up at Jack.

"That sounds good," Jack said. "Why don't we put these guys back in the habitat and take out the others? We can walk over to the point, over there, and release them into the wild. That's what we call it when we let wild animals go back to their natural surroundings."

"Yeah," Max said. "I'm releasing these two." He put his painted turtle gently into the tub and scooped out two small box turtles.

Jack put the one he'd been holding into Riley's grasp. "There you go, buddy. Put him where he'll be safe."

The turtle waggled its feet, and Riley carefully set it down on a rock inside the tub.

"Have you checked the water temperature lately?" Jack asked.

"We did," Jan said. "I make sure they check it at least twice a day."

Jack nodded.

Riley came away from the tub holding two small turtles. "I guess we can release these guys."

"Good," Jack said. "That's what a wildlife rehabilitator would do."

Max was already trotting along the shore toward the point.

"I don't want to go over there," Riley said.

Jack crouched and looked him in the eye. "Why not?"

"That's where we saw the monster."

"Uh-huh." Jack glanced at Jan and Elaine. "Tell you what, you don't have to go over there. You can release your turtles under the dock, in the shade. How about that?"

Riley nodded and headed stolidly toward the shore end of the dock.

Jack stood and grinned at the cousins. "Great boys."

"Aren't they?" Jan said. "I thought he wasn't scared anymore, but maybe I was wrong."

He nodded. "Maybe you can stay here with Riley, and Elaine and I can go over to the point and get Max to show us where they had their sighting."

"I think that's a good idea," Jan said. She was very curious about it herself, but she wouldn't force Riley to go over there. She'd had enough of nightmares, thank you.

"So, you were standing right here?" Jack asked Max.

Elaine watched as the little boy nodded. Jack crouched beside him, so he was eye level with Max. "What happened when you first saw it?"

"We yelled and ran."

Jack smiled. "I would too, buddy. But I mean, where did it come from? And did it make any noise?"

"Not really. It just kind of..." Max raised both arms slowly before him and then jerked them toward himself. *"Whoosh!"*

"So, it came toward you?"

Max nodded.

"Was it in the water?"

"I...I think so. It was over there." He pointed across the point of land. "It jumped up high, so we saw it."

Elaine looked back at the dock and the deck near the house. Jan was sitting in one of the wrought iron chairs on the deck, holding Riley on her lap.

"But it came toward you," Jack said.

Again the nod from Max.

"But you can't really see the water on the other side of this land, can you? The grass is pretty tall here." Jack waved his arm, encompassing the small area that made up the point.

"It came up out of the water." Max turned to face Jack as if challenging him. "It flew up out of the water."

"It flew."

"Yeah."

Jack cocked his head to one side. "Did it have wings?"

Max was quiet for a moment, then shook his head. "It had legs and red eyes and a big mouth."

"Was its mouth open?"

"Yeah. I think."

"Did it have teeth?"

Max shook his head. "I'm not sure. It was smiling."

"Smiling?" Jack crouched beside him. "The critter you saw was smiling?"

Max's lips twitched. "Yeah. I was scared at first, because we didn't know anything was there, and Riley yelled. But when I looked back, it looked kind of...I don't know. Kind of like the picture Elaine showed us."

"Oh yes, I saw that. But it didn't touch you."

"No. We ran fast."

"Where were you when you looked back?"

"Like halfway to the dock."

Jack frowned. "Was it still up in the air?"

Max shook his head slowly. "It stayed there for a second, and then it kind of floated down. And then it was gone."

"It didn't follow you?"

"No. I think it was down behind the bushes after that."

Jack stood and gazed toward the spot where Max insisted the monster had been. "How big was it?"

"Really big," Max said.

"Bigger than me?"

"Yeah. Like five times as big."

"Anything else you remember?" Jack asked.

"No."

"Did you see any boats around?"

Max shook his head.

"Okay," Jack said. "That's pretty good. You want to go back and play with Riley now?"

"Yeah."

"Go ahead. And thanks for showing me."

Max darted toward the water and ran around the edge of the shore until he reached the deck. Jan gave him a hand up, and she started up the steps toward the house with the boys.

Elaine looked at Jack. "So, what do you think?"

"So far, I'm keeping an open mind."

"Jan told you about the boat I saw?"

"Yes. That's why I asked Max about boats. Do you have the picture with you?"

Elaine took out her phone, pulled up the photo, and showed it to him.

"*Hmm.* Looks like an aluminum boat with a small motor, but the guy's rowing."

"Maybe so no one would hear him?" Elaine hazarded.

Jack nodded. "If the kids heard a boat motor, that wouldn't exactly fit with a monster, would it?"

"There's something else," Elaine said.

Jack raised his eyebrows expectantly.

"When Max said it flew, that made me think of something I saw earlier." She pointed. "See those maple branches overhanging the water?"

Jack nodded.

"Wouldn't you say that's over the spot where the monster would have been when the boys saw it?"

"Pretty close, I guess." Jack squinted at the branches. "What are you thinking?"

"Look closely at them," Elaine said. "Tell me if you see anything."

Jack took a step closer and pulled the lowest branch toward him. "*Hmm.* A twig with a few leaves is broken off." He looked down and scanned the shore and nearby water. "Maple leaves floating over there." He nodded, and Elaine followed his gaze.

"I see them," she said. "What else?"

Jack scrutinized the branch closely and then looked at the next higher one.

"Hello! The bark is scrubbed there." He reached for the limb and drew it down to his eye level, as Elaine had done earlier.

"What do you make of it?" she asked.

"I'm not sure. It's almost as if..." He looked out over the calm lake. "As if someone tossed a line over this branch and then pulled on it, and it dug into the bark here."

"My thoughts precisely." Elaine put her hand on Jack's shoulder. "Now tell me, if you wanted to make a monster fly up out of the water and scare a couple of children, how would you do it?"

"Yeah, I see what you mean. It would have to be very light though. This branch isn't very big. Anything heavy would break it."

Elaine thought for a moment. "How about a balloon monster? Like one of those big parade balloons?"

"Maybe. I'm thinking it wasn't as huge as Max thinks it was. When you're little and you're scared, the scary thing tends to seem bigger than it really is. And they said it didn't make noise, right?"

"Right. But how would you get rid of it afterward quickly?"

Jack surveyed the water and the shore on each side. "And how could you be sure nobody would see it from the cottages or the marina?"

"You couldn't," Elaine said. "I think he had to pick his moment carefully. Or she. If it was light, it could have been staged by a woman."

"Why not 'they'?" Jack asked. "Seems to me it would take more than one person to rig that up and take it down in a hurry."

"Well, the boat I saw leaving only had one person in it."

"That's true. But there wasn't a monster in the boat with him."

Elaine took her phone out. "I have no explanation for that. For any of it, really." She turned so her phone was shaded. "I'm going to transfer this picture to my computer so we can enlarge it and get a better look."

"I'd like to see it when you do."

She nodded. "Come inside, Jack. If you've got another minute, that is. It won't take long."

"This is business," he said. "My time is yours."

Elaine led Jack back around the shore, past the turtle tub, and up the steps into the house. Jan and the twins were nowhere in sight, but Rose was in the kitchen, filling the hot water reservoir for brewing tea.

"Hi, Jack," she said with a smile.

"Hello, Rose. I don't suppose you've seen the monster?"

"No, but a lot of my customers are talking about it."

"Really? Any new sightings?"

"Emily Liston said her son saw something this morning on this end of the lake, but she didn't think it was anything."

"I'll check it out," Jack said.

Rose looked at Elaine. "Jan asked me to tell you she and the boys went over to the apple orchard."

"Okay, that's good," Elaine said. "Maybe it will distract them from this whole business." She was sure Amy and Van would call that evening to check in on the twins, and she hoped that by then they would have calmed down.

She took Jack into her office, where she quickly emailed the photo to herself from her phone. She opened her email on her computer, then transferred the boat picture to a photo editing program. She brought it up full screen, and Jack leaned in over her shoulder.

"Can you crop that and make it even bigger? Just the part with the boat, I mean?"

"I can, but the detail won't get any finer."

"That's okay. I was wondering about this." He pointed to a tiny splotch of color showing over the aluminum boat's gunwale.

"It's green," Elaine said.

"Yeah. But what is it?"

"Good question."

"That boat must have registration numbers on the bow," Jack said. "Too bad it was heading away from you, so we can't see them."

"And there's no name on the stern."

"No, but if you print me a close-up of the motor and one of the whole thing, I might be able to find someone who can identify it."

"Somebody on this lake must own it," Elaine said, clicking rapidly on the mouse to focus on the part he had requested.

"Well, anyone can put in at the town boat landing, or over at the one in Penzance."

"You're saying it could be some out-of-stater who just came up here to fish for a day?"

Jack shrugged. "It's possible, but I'm betting it's someone local, or at least staying in the area."

The picture Elaine was working on came into focus, cropped and enlarged.

"Huh." Jack squinted at the screen.

"Like you said, it's green." Elaine stared at the green hump sticking up over the side of the boat.

"Would you call that grass green?" Jack asked.

"New grass, maybe. Chartreuse?"

"Or maybe John Deere green?"

Elaine laughed. "Maybe so. You think someone's been getting artistic with tractor paint?"

"Nothing would surprise me in this case."

"So you're taking it seriously? This is a case?"

"Oh yeah." Jack straightened. "I've got work to do. I'll let you know if I find out anything."

THAT EVENING, AFTER Elaine talked briefly with Sasha on the phone—she was still spending most of her free time unpacking her apartment—Jan and Elaine huddled over their laptops in the living room upstairs. The boys had settled down quickly after FaceTiming with their parents and were asleep at Jan's last check.

"I'd like to make a list of people we think might be involved in spreading the rumors about Chick," Jan said. She had a legal pad handy, and she put her laptop aside in favor of that. Something about writing names on paper sometimes helped things gel in her brain.

"Okay," Elaine said readily. "When Jack phoned, he said the inquiries he made about the boat didn't turn up anything."

"I really hoped someone at the marina would recognize the boat."

"Me too, but Jack said they didn't." Elaine tapped her chin. "What about Tag? I think you should put him at the top."

Jan wrote down the fire chief's name in block letters. "I'd love to see the fire department raise a lot of money, but not by scaring people."

"I'm sure that most people would see it as a fun, wholesome thing—a legend the town could embrace," Elaine said. "But today's episode..."

"I know what you mean," Jan said. "Still, whoever made that thing could have made it a lot scarier looking. Instead, it's almost likc they deliberately made it look fake. Cartoonish."

"Maybe they don't want to scare people. Maybe they just want to keep folks interested and talking about it. They might have picked the boys to surprise because they wouldn't realize immediately it was a fake, like a grownup would."

"It's possible," Jan said. "What the boys saw might be totally different from what Clifton and Chad thought they saw in the water. So who else might have something to do with the thing the boys saw?"

"Fiona?" Elaine asked doubtfully.

"You said she didn't know much about the sign."

"True. How about old chamber of commerce members?"

"Wait a minute," Jan said. "They might have been in cahoots the first time, but I'm talking about now. Who scared the boys today?"

"Okay." Elaine settled back in her chair. "I guess I was thinking along the lines of descendants. Anyone in the 1947 chamber of commerce would be too old to do anything physical today."

"Yes. But I'm thinking Macy is a good candidate. The man she bought her place from was in on the first round of publicity. She could have gotten ideas from what he did back then."

"Yes, but that wasn't Macy rowing the boat," Elaine said. "I'm sure of that."

"No, but it could be someone working with her. In fact, I think we should look hard at Shane and Zale too. They're certainly athletic. Maybe the whole Atherton family is in on this."

"But would they try to scare little kids?"

Jan chewed the end of her pen. "Probably not. At least, not Zale."

"I'm not sure Shane would either."

"Okay, so who else?" Jan asked.

"*Hmm.* Who has boats?"

"The marina. I'm putting down John Tuttle and his wife, even though they said they didn't recognize the boat in the picture. And that brawny guy who works for them—Eddie."

"Yeah, and Derek Jameson is helping them with the boats this summer," Elaine said.

"Oh right. I saw him over there the other day," Jan said. "I'm putting him on the list, along with Chad Prentice, Diane Blanchett, and Clifton Young."

"So many?"

Jan shrugged. "Any one of them—or a combination of several—could have thought this thing up."

"Well, Diane's certainly creative enough, and Clifton's very smart. And the Leon sisters painted the monster on the banner. They could have created the one the boys saw." Elaine sat back and sighed. There were just too many possibilities. "I could go talk to the folks at the marina tomorrow," she said.

"Good. And if I can get away from the kitchen for a while, I'd like to talk to Candace Huang. Maybe she can find something in the *Courier's* archives."

CHAPTER THIRTEEN

The day's edition of the *Penzance Courier* was on the door-step when Elaine got up Thursday morning, and she and Jan browsed it while they ate breakfast.

"Looks like Candace followed through on Bob's suggestion for a story," Elaine said.

"Oh, let me see."

Elaine passed the section to Jan and pointed to the story midway down page three.

"*Lawyer Seeks Proof of Lake Monster.* That's a catchy headline." Jan scanned the short article. "Candace seems to be playing it straight. She quotes Bob as saying no one can prove there's anything abnormal in that lake, and anyone who thinks they can should step forward."

Elaine took a sip of her tea and met Jan's gaze. "Let's hope whoever made that—that floating, flying *thing* does step up. Do you want me to take the twins to VBS?"

"I'll take them," Jan said. "You can go ahead to the marina if you want. I'll drop the boys and run over to Penzance."

"Sounds good." Elaine heard footsteps on the carpeted stairs. "Oh, here come the troops. Got their breakfast ready?"

"I sure do." Jan jumped up as the twins pounded through the door.

"Good morning," Elaine said.

"Hi, Elaine." Riley looked a lot happier than he had the previous afternoon.

"Oops, you've got your shirt on backward." Elaine helped him pull his arms in and slide the T-shirt around so the dump truck design showed on the front. "Hi, Max."

"Hi." He pulled out a chair and plopped into it.

"Here's a banana," Jan said, passing one to each boy. "Eat that while I get your eggs and sausage."

"Yum," Riley said.

"Is it the link kind or the patty kind?" Max asked, frowning.

"Which kind do you like?" Jan asked cautiously.

"Oh, I like 'em both, but my dad likes the patties."

"Well, your dad isn't here." Jan put a plate of scrambled eggs and link sausage in front of him. She paused, waiting pointedly.

"Thank you," Max said.

"You're welcome. And here's yours, Riley."

"Thanks, Grandma."

ELAINE WALKED OVER to the marina after Jan and the boys had left for the church. John Tuttle and one of his employees were down on the dock, working on a rental boat. Elaine went into the store and found Linda Tuttle behind the counter.

"Good morning, Elaine," she said with a bright smile.

"Hi. Looks busy in here." Elaine glanced around. At least half a dozen people—mostly men—were browsing the fishing tackle and boating equipment.

"Yeah, people want to get out on the lake and fish or water ski—whatever takes their fancy."

Elaine smiled. "We're having such beautiful weather for it. I wondered if you or John could help me out. Jan and I are curious about these lake monster stories we keep hearing."

Linda laughed. "I've heard them too. John said we ought to make something out of them to bring more people in. I do think it's increasing our boat rentals."

"Really?"

"Yes, we've had several go out this morning already, and calls for three more this afternoon, including the pontoon boat."

"That's great," Elaine said. "I'm glad things are going well. We've been busy at the tearoom too. Listen, I saw a boat I didn't recognize yesterday, and I wondered if you or John could tell me if it's one of yours." Elaine took out her phone and brought up the photo. "What do you think?"

"*Hmm,* hard to tell. We have several aluminum fifteen-footers like that, but I can't see the number. I guess you'll have to ask John. He's down at the dock right now."

"Thanks."

Elaine walked to the back door of the store, passing a couple headed for the checkout laden with lifejackets, a bait can, and several items of fishing tackle. She followed the boardwalk and steps down to the marina's dock.

John Tuttle's white hair contrasted with eighteen-year-old Derek Jameson's brown locks as they bent over the fifty-horse-power outboard motor on the stern of a cabin cruiser. Derek looked up as Elaine came onto the pier.

"Hi, Mrs. Cook."

"Well, hello, Elaine," John said.

"Hi, fellas. John, I've got a little mystery you may be able to help me solve. Linda said you might be the man to identify a boat I snapped a picture of yesterday."

"Oh? I'll take a look." John wiped his hands on a rag and reached for the phone Elaine held out to him.

"Jack Weston showed me that photo yesterday. It's not one of my boats."

"How can you be sure?"

"Everything of mine that size has a Johnson motor on it. That's an Evinrude."

"Oh." Elaine couldn't argue with that.

Derek leaned over to see the photo, and John passed him the phone.

"Who's that rowing it?" John asked.

"I was hoping it was a customer of yours," Elaine replied.

He shook his head. "Could be someone with a cottage down the lake, I guess."

"Maybe."

Derek handed the phone back carefully. "I don't recognize him either."

"Well, thanks," Elaine said. "Now, John, you've heard the stories going around about a lake monster?"

He wiped a hand across his brow, leaving a small smear of motor oil. "Well, sure. But I don't put much store in 'em. Why're you asking?"

"Jan's little grandsons thought they saw something yesterday, between our waterfront and Sylvia Flood's. They've been hearing other kids talk about the lake creature, and we thought at first they were just wound up from the stories. But now I'm not so sure."

"You think they really saw it?"

"I think they really saw *something*. Whether or not it was a living creature, I have my doubts."

John sat back a little and studied her face. "Does this fella in the boat have something to do with it?"

"I'm not sure. I took that picture just minutes after the twins came running and saying they'd seen the monster."

"Well, I'll keep my eyes and ears open," John said. "If I see or hear anything along those lines, I'll let you know."

"Thanks." Elaine hesitated, then asked, "Did your father have something to do with publicizing the lake creature back in the 1940s?"

John laughed. "Oh, you mean Chick?"

"Yes. Isn't that what we're talking about?"

"I don't know. Is it?"

"Well, some people are connecting these new sightings with the ones back then. But I'd almost concluded that the 1940s monster was a creative publicity stunt to draw in tourists."

"Almost?" John eyed her keenly.

"Well, there's no proof that it was real, but there's quite a bit of evidence that merchants in town played on the commotion it caused to grow their businesses."

"Including my folks," John said.

"Well, yes. And I don't fault them for that."

He smiled. "You're just wondering if I dug it up to do the same thing all over again."

"Is that out of the question?"

"I suppose it makes sense for you to think that." John stood and grabbed the edge of the dock. "Hold on, and I'll show you something."

"I didn't mean to interrupt your work," Elaine said.

"That's okay." John stepped up onto the dock and looked back at Derek. "You go ahead and clean that carburetor. I'll be back in a few minutes."

"Yes, sir." Derek picked up a small can of gasoline and an oily motor part.

John led Elaine along the dock to shore and toward a large storage building. "My dad kept a little souvenir that you might enjoy seeing."

"John, I wasn't accusing you or your father of anything shady," Elaine said. "I just don't want the boys to be frightened or get hurt."

"Oh, I know. But I also know you've got a nose for this kind of thing."

Elaine wasn't sure whether to be offended or not. She decided to take it as a compliment. "It's true, Jan and I do enjoy puzzles and mysteries."

"Well, this is a little piece of memorabilia." He unlocked the storage building and rolled back the wooden door.

In the dim building, several boats sat on trailers or staging. One was a large wooden hull that appeared to be still under construction or extensive renovation. Elaine followed John inside and around it, past several smaller boats, from old wooden rowboats to a small fiberglass catamaran. The walls were hung with oars, old lifejackets, spars, and other boating gear, much of it outdated.

"You've got a regular museum in here," she said.

John laughed. "That's the truth." He stopped in a shadowy corner and threw back a tarp, revealing several handmade signboards. "These are ones we can hang on the sign out front. A lot of them are really old. I've painted over some of the ones that weren't relevant anymore, but somehow I couldn't bring myself to paint over this."

He reached behind several other boards and lifted out a sign about four feet long and eighteen inches high. He turned and set it up on the edge of a workbench, so Elaine could see it.

"Chickadee Lake, Home of Chick, the Friendly Lake Monster," she read. On each end was a hand-painted version of the creature on the sign she had purchased from Fiona. "I love it!"

"You do? I thought you hated Chick."

"Good grief, no. I'm just concerned about the children and someone possibly being injured. Max or Riley Kincaid might have fallen into the water and hurt themselves when they got scared yesterday."

"Well, I don't know anything about that," John said. "But I did see the notice in the paper about people needing to fess up if they're behind all this."

Elaine smiled. "Bob Claybrook isn't really upset, but he thought a news story might help root out whoever's behind it. We're interested. We don't necessarily want to stop it. We just want to make sure there's nothing malicious behind it." Elaine stooped and looked closer at one of the depictions of Chick on John's sign. "I've got a smaller sign that's a lot like this. I bought it from Fiona Latimore, and the monster on it looks very much like this guy. Do you know who painted this sign?"

John shook his head. "Could have been my mother, I suppose. My dad wasn't very artistic."

"Could I bring my sign over and compare them? I honestly suspect the same artist may have created both of them."

He shrugged. "Sure. I've got to get that motor running though. Tell you what, why don't I have Derek lug this over to your place?"

"You wouldn't mind?"

"Nope. It's not worth anything beyond sentimental value."

"You might be surprised," Elaine said. "I paid forty dollars for my little one. You might get a few hundred for this, especially since you know the provenance and can guarantee it's sixty or seventy years old."

"Is that right? Well, I don't want to sell it. It's part of the Tuttle Marina history, you know?"

"Yes, I understand perfectly. If you really don't mind, I'd love to borrow it for a day or two."

"I'll tell Derek to wash his hands real good and bring it over." John set the sign down on the floor, leaning it against the leg of the workbench.

"Maybe we should wrap it, so people don't see him carrying it down the sidewalk," Elaine said. "I don't want to start a Chick frenzy."

John laughed. "I think you're a little late. But there's a piece of canvas here. I'll tell him."

"Thank you, John. I'll leave the garage door open. Ask him to set it in there, please."

They walked out into the bright sunlight. Elaine gazed out over the sparkling lake. Was there really a large creature swimming beneath the gentle waves, or was it all a practical joke? She hoped there wasn't anything more sinister behind the sightings, or a creator who had a nefarious motive.

JAN WALKED WITH the twins across the church lawn, to where Kit Edmonds was gathering her class.

"Good morning, Max!" Kit called to the boy in the lead.

"I'm Riley."

"Oh, I'm sorry. Good morning, Riley." Kit looked at his brother. "And good morning, Max."

"Hi," Max said. "We saw the monster."

Kit's eyes widened. "You did?"

"Uh-huh."

Riley nodded in confirmation.

Kit looked anxiously toward Jan.

"Well, they saw *something*," Jan said. "We're looking into it. I'm sorry, and I hope it won't cause a disruption to your class." She looked sternly at the twins. "Now, boys, you know what I told you. Don't be jabbering away in class about what you saw."

"Okay, Grandma," Riley said.

"Can I go tell Caleb?" Max asked.

"Why don't you leave that for snack time?" Kit asked. "I'm sure he'd like to hear your story. And so would I."

Jan patted Riley's shoulder and nodded to Max. "Be good, both of you. I'll see you later."

She walked to her car with some misgivings and pulled slowly out of the parking lot. She had complained about her grandsons being upset by the other children's chatter. Were they going to be the guilty ones today? She sighed and headed for Penzance.

She parked in front of the bakery on the charming main street and walked a few yards to the brick building that housed the *Courier*. Inside, the office retained the old-fashioned charm of the aging building, with old hardwood floors and exposed brick on the walls. The desks, however, held sleek computers and modern phones.

"Hello, Cookie," she said to the receptionist.

"Well, hi, Jan. How may I help you today?" Cookie asked.

"I'm here to see if you have anything in the archives about the lake monster."

Cookie grinned. "I suspected that might be it, seeing how your boyfriend was in a couple of days ago about that very topic. You saw today's piece?"

"Yes, and the number of sightings is growing."

"People see what they want to see."

"Some people, yes."

Cookie rose and walked with her between the desks. River White looked up. When he saw Jan, he leaped to his feet.

"Jan. How're things in Lancaster?"

"Just fine, River."

"I was thinking of riding out there today, after I interview the first selectman about Penzance's summer road projects."

"You're welcome anytime," Jan said.

"Have you seen the lake monster?"

Jan stopped walking and turned to face him. "I haven't seen it myself. I have to wonder if it's just a case of overactive imaginations. What do you think, River?"

"I don't know, but it's what other people think that's interesting."

"River White!" Cookie scowled at him. "Candace is all over that story, so you leave it alone. You saw her article this morning."

River frowned and plopped down in his chair. "Yeah, well, Candace isn't here. I didn't want her to miss something when one of Lancaster's lakefront property owners walks into the office."

"Thanks for your concern," Jan said. She and Cookie continued on to the room where file cabinets lined the wall—their morgue. The files held thousands of clippings from the *Courier* in the days before they had entered the computer world.

"I know Candace has been looking at this too," Cookie said, "so she may have some of the files out. But I suggest you look under 'Chick' and 'monster' first, or maybe 'lake monster.' If you find something, you might want to browse old papers from around the dates the articles were published. And do check with Candace."

"I will," Jan said. "Thanks."

She set to work, keeping an eye on the time. She wanted to be back at the church in time to get the boys when VBS let out. An hour later, she was quite discouraged. She had found only a couple of articles mentioning Chick. One was in the minutes of a chamber of commerce meeting, where the merchants had discussed incorporating the lake monster as the theme of the July 4, 1947, parade and festival. The other was a brief mention in August of that year that three boys reported a sighting, but their fathers had determined that what they'd seen was the prow of a canoe protruding from a weeded area near the bog.

Jan made copies of the two articles and replaced the clippings in the files. She gathered up her printouts and her purse and turned to the door.

Candace stepped into sight, but paused and smiled when she saw Jan.

"Hi. Cookie told me you were in here."

"Yeah." Jan walked toward her. "I was looking for material on the lake monster, but all I found were these." She held out her copies.

Candace glanced at them. "Yes, not very helpful. I've got the good stuff here." She held out a folder to Jan. "We can make you some copies if you want them. I haven't dared leave this folder in the office when I went out for fear River would riffle my desk while I was gone."

Jan opened the folder. Staring up at her, on top of several other clipped articles, was one with a murky, fuzzy black-and-white photo of...something.

"What's this?"

"The only known surviving photograph of Chick."

"Really? It's not one of the Lake Champlain critter or something like that?"

Candace shook her head. "Notice how the foreground and the monster—if it is a monster—are out of focus?"

"Yeah."

"But look at the house in the background, on the far lakeshore."

"That looks familiar," Jan said.

"It ought to. It's the house Clifton Young owns now."

CHAPTER FOURTEEN

Jan stared at her. "Clifton was the first person to report seeing something in the water this year."

"That's right." Candace had a rather smug smile. "I put that together myself."

Jan looked down at the picture. "Do you know who took this photo?"

"Read the cutline."

Jan pushed her glasses up and read aloud, "Is it real? This photo was snapped July 1 on Chickadee Lake, not far from the Lancaster town boat landing, by Harold McCullough."

"Read the story that goes with it." Candace took the folder and walked toward the copier. "He said at the time that he was so nervous he almost dropped his camera in the lake. It's the only picture he got before the thing dove underwater. Apparently there was another shot of the churning water after it submerged, but I haven't found any existing copies of that one."

Candace ran copies of the half dozen articles from her folder, stacked them and tapped them on the top of the copier to straighten them, then handed the pile to Jan.

"Have fun."

"Are you following up on this?"

"Of course. If Lancaster's going to make a big deal of Chick for its fire department's field day—not to mention you've got a lawyer asking for proof of life—well, hey, you can't stop me from following up on something like that."

"Proof of life," Jan said slowly. "Did Bob say that?"

"No, actually he said proof that the lake monster is real. I suppose if someone killed it, or if a dead one washed up on shore, he'd accept that."

"What if someone proved it was real, but it wasn't a monster?"

"You mean a hoax?"

"Yeah."

"I guess you'd have to ask your boyfriend about that."

Jan smiled. "Oh, I will. Trust me on that."

Cookie called from the doorway, "Candace, there's a structure fire on Town Farm Road. You need to get out there. Matt's going out to get some pictures, but it sounds like a big one on the scanner. Lancaster and Smithfield are both sending mutual aid."

"Okay, I'm on it." Candace looked at Jan. "Sounds like I won't have time to do anything on that topic today. If you and Elaine find anything, keep me in the loop."

"We will," Jan said. Candace was being generous with her files, and if something did come of their research, Jan wanted her to be the one to break the story.

As Jan walked through the newsroom, Candace was already striding to the front door. Jan nodded to Cookie and made her way to her car, her mind spinning.

The blurry photo published in the *Penzance Courier* decades ago was taken by a man named Harold McCullough. She had gone to school with several McCullough children, and she was pretty sure some of the family members still lived in Lancaster.

ELAINE HEARD JAN'S car pull into the garage and left her desk to go and meet her.

Jan hadn't come into the house, but stood in the garage, staring at John Tuttle's sign. It stood on end against the wall beside the steps that led into the house.

"Hi," Elaine said. "What do you think of that?"

"Where'd you get it?"

"Out of John Tuttle's storage barn. I'm not keeping it, but he let me borrow it so I can compare it to the one I got at Fiona's."

"Yeah. The monster looks a lot like yours."

"I haven't put them side by side yet," Elaine said.

Jan nodded slowly. "What's the story on that?"

"John thinks maybe his mother made it, back in the day." Elaine draped the tarp over it and tucked the edges in. "So, did you find anything at the *Courier*?"

Jan smiled and held up a folder. "Wait till you see what Candace gave me."

They went into Elaine's office and closed the door. Jan handed Elaine the folder, and she sat down at her desk and opened it. The top sheet held a copied news article with a very indistinct photo of…something. Something in the water.

"Oh my. That's supposed to be Chick?"

"Yep." Jan grinned. "That was my reaction when I saw that picture. It was a little clearer in the original newspaper she copied it from, but not much. Candace said there may be other pictures, but that's the only one she found. So what now?"

Elaine squinted at the fine print. "Harold McCullough."

"There are still McCulloughs living in Lancaster, aren't there?" Jan asked.

Elaine nodded. "Unless I'm mistaken, there's still a *Harold* McCullough."

"Not the same person who took the picture?"

"I met a woman named Grace McCullough. Where was it? Not here." Elaine frowned. "Anyway, she's older than we are, and I'm sure she mentioned that her father-in-law lives with her and her husband." She snapped her fingers. "It was at the diner the day I went over and had breakfast with Lydia so we could talk over our ad copy for the *Wave*."

As she spoke, Elaine took a phone book out of her desk drawer. She leafed through it.

"There are a couple of McCulloughs listed, but no Harold or Grace."

"You could ask Lydia," Jan said.

"Good thought."

Jan nodded. "Well, I'm going to check in with Rose and Archie. I might have time to bake a batch of muffins before I go get the boys."

Elaine picked up the receiver of her desk phone and called the diner. A woman answered cheerfully. "Kate's Diner. This is Patti speaking."

"Hi, Patti. It's Elaine. Does your sister happen to be there?" Kate Pierce's two daughters, Patti and Lydia, helped her run the business.

"Nope, she went into town. Try her cell."

"Okay, thanks." Elaine guessed that "into town" meant Waterville, the nearest small city with a variety of shopping options. She located Lydia's cell phone number and called it, half expecting that she would need to leave a message. To her surprise, Lydia answered on the second ring.

"Hi, Elaine. What's up?" Lydia asked, upbeat as always.

"Hi. Sorry to bother you."

"It's okay. I'm waiting for a prescription for Mom."

"Maybe I'll give you a diversion then. I wondered if you could tell me about the McCullough family. I met Grace at the diner a week or two ago."

"Yes, she's a nice person," Lydia said.

"I think she said her father-in-law lives with her and her husband?"

"Yes, that would be James."

"Oh. I was hoping you'd say Harold."

"No, Harold is his brother. I think he's in assisted living."

"He's still alive then?"

"Yes. Very sharp for someone his age."

"Wonderful. Can you tell me how to reach him?"

"Well, you could call Grace," Lydia suggested. "She and her husband are in the book, I think."

"I looked, and I didn't see a Grace."

"Try Eugene. That's hubby's name."

"Thanks. Enjoy your outing." Elaine hung up and looked up the name. Sure enough, Eugene McCullough was listed, living on Pine Ridge Road. She called the number and soon learned that Eugene's uncle Harold lived at an assisted-living home on the outer fringes of Lancaster, almost at the Penzance town line.

Elaine hurried to the kitchen. Jan was thumbing through one of her recipe files but hadn't started baking yet.

"Got time to pay a little visit to Mr. McCullough?"

Jan gaped at her. "The photographer?"

"Yup. He's at the Birches assisted-living facility. It's only about five miles away."

Jan glanced at the clock and fumbled with her apron strings. "Let's go."

As they walked through the hall, Rose came from the entry. "I hope you don't mind, but Diane Blanchett asked if we'd sell tickets for the *Chick of Chickadee Lake* play here, and I took a dozen to sell at the counter."

"That okay with you?" Jan asked, looking at Elaine.

"Sure. It's for a good cause."

"Great," Rose said. "If we sell them all, she'll bring us more."

"We're going out for a little visit," Jan told her. "We won't be gone long."

Elaine drove, and they were walking in the front door of the Birches in less than ten minutes. They stopped at the front desk.

"Hello," Elaine said to the receptionist. "We would like to visit Mr. Harold McCullough if possible."

The woman smiled at them. "I'm sure Harold would love to see some friends. Let me call his room and see if he's in. What are your names?"

"I'm Elaine Cook, and this is my cousin Jan Blake."

The woman made a note and picked up her receiver. Elaine glanced at Jan. What if Mr. McCullough told her he didn't know them and refused to see them? Jan seemed to read her concern in her face, and she shrugged.

A moment later the receptionist smiled at them. "Mr. McCullough said he's always happy to have company. He's in room 113." She directed them down a hallway.

Jan and Elaine found the room easily, and Elaine knocked.

"Come in."

She opened the door and they went in. A man with snowy white hair sat in a wing chair near the window, across from a settee.

"Hello, Mr. McCullough," Elaine said, walking toward him. "Thanks for agreeing to see me and my cousin."

"Welcome," he said, smiling as he shook their hands and repeated their names. "What brings you ladies out? Are you with the social service?"

"No," Elaine said, settling on the settee. "Jan and I wanted to ask you some questions about the past."

"Oh, you're with the historical society."

Jan laughed. "No, we're not that either. We're just a couple of gals who own a tearoom on the lake, and we're curious about some things that happened back in the 1940s."

"Around the time of the war, you mean?"

"After the war, "Elaine said. "Do you remember in the late '40s, when people said there was a monster in Chickadee Lake?"

"Why sure I do. It almost swamped my canoe once."

"Really?" Elaine shot Jan a glance. He certainly sounded as if he believed in the creature. "Can you tell us about that?"

"Well, I was out in a canoe I'd made and hoping to catch a lake trout for supper. I got down near the outlet to the bog, because sometimes the fish would bite good down there at sunset. And all of a sudden this huge thing pops up out of the water. Had a head the size of a pie plate, and it snapped at me like a big old snapping turtle."

Elaine stared at him.

"Could it have been a snapping turtle?" Jan asked.

"Not unless snappers can fly," Harold said. "It rose up about four feet out of the water. Its head, I mean. Scared the living daylights out of me."

"Is that when you took the picture?" Elaine asked.

"Picture?" Harold asked. "No, no. Not that night. I hit at it with my canoe paddle, like you would with a baseball bat. It ducked under the water, and my canoe rocked. I thought I was going under and that thing would have me for his supper."

"What did you do?" Elaine asked.

"Soon's I could breathe again, which was a while, I paddled on out of there. Went straight to the marina, and I told John Tuttle what I saw. He thought I was crazy."

"John who's there now, or his father?" Jan asked.

"Oh, his daddy. I misdoubt young John was even born yet."

"How old were you then?" Elaine asked.

"I was eighteen or so. John and his wife were just starting out with the business then, catering to the tourists who came to fish. I guess they did all right." Harold shook his head. "Nobody would believe I'd really seen something. Or at least not the way I told it. They all said I must have been drunk."

"Were you?" Jan asked without cracking a smile.

Elaine caught her breath. That seemed a little rude.

"I assure you, I was not," Harold said. "So I decided to go back the next day and either shoot the thing with my shotgun or shoot it with a camera. Took my friend Andrew Rogers with me, so's I'd have a witness."

"What happened?" Elaine asked.

"We didn't find it. But a couple of nights later, we went out again. Andrew and I decided to go into the bog and prove there was something living in there. We thought we'd either get eaten alive or come out heroes." He laughed.

"So...?" Jan prompted.

"Oh, we found it."

"You did?" Elaine was stunned.

"And it didn't eat you, obviously," Jan said.

Harold smiled. "I was so hoping I could prove to everybody what I'd seen. But it didn't turn out exactly the way I expected. It took a friend's help and a bit of time. And in the meanwhile, other people started seeing odd things on the lake, and some folks started to believe there really was something to my story."

"But you were the first to see it?" Elaine asked.

"I believe so. People would claim to see things in different parts of the lake. Then, along about the end of June, Andrew and I went out one evening determined to find it."

Elaine eyed him carefully. "What did you find?"

Harold chuckled. "Way back in the bog, we found a big old beaver lodge. That wasn't too surprising, really, because now and then folks would see beavers out swimming in the lake. But we got a little too close, I guess. Just as I was setting up to take a picture of the lodge, up out of the water beside us—as close as I am to you—jumps this monster of a beaver. I mean huge! Big and black and fussing at us with the big ol' teeth a-going." He shook his head. "Scared us big-time, I'll tell you."

"What did you do?" Jan asked.

"Funny thing." He chuckled. "At least, Andrew and I thought it was funny afterward. After we'd calmed down a bit, Andrew asks, 'Did you see that?' I says, 'I sure did.' He says, 'I'll bet that's the monster you saw.' But I didn't want to admit it."

"Why not?" Elaine asked.

"Well, I was so sure it was a dinosaur or a sea monster, something like that. It was hard to give up the notion, but the more I thought about it, the more I guessed Andrew was right. That beaver was so big, and he took me by surprise, so close to the boat and everything—I didn't remember him slapping the water with his tail or nothing, but he sure did jump up high out of the water. I'm telling you, that thing was a giant."

"But you couldn't get pictures of it?" Jan asked.

"We did better than that." Harold laughed again. "Andrew and I talked about it, and we decided we *would* get a picture of the monster. Not the beaver, but the lake monster I *thought* I saw."

"You faked the picture," Elaine said.

Jan had brought her folder with her, and she opened it and took out the copied news story with the photo.

"I got this from the archives at the *Penzance Courier,* Mr. McCullough. Is that the picture you took?"

He took it and squinted at it. "Eh, I guess so. It's a bad copy though." He smiled, thinking about it. "Folks were so stirred up about it by then, we decided we'd give 'em what they wanted. We made a monster out of a couple of old sacks, and I stuffed part of an inner tube to make the neck. We took it out in a rowboat one cloudy evening when nobody was at the boat landing, and we set it up in the water, and I took a picture. I made sure it was out of focus, though, so's you couldn't really tell what it was, just a shape."

Elaine looked at the photo. It could be that. It could be just about anything.

"We told people we'd put the boat in at the boat launch, and all of a sudden, there it was, about ten yards away from me, poking up out of the water. I grabbed my camera, but I was shaking so bad, that was the best shot I could get before it submerged."

Elaine couldn't help smiling. "Did it scare a lot of people?"

"Maybe a few, but the town got more good out of it than anything else. Why, the whole chamber of commerce and the selectmen all got on the bandwagon—or in the rowboat, it you will. They made Chick the town's mascot and had him in parades and everything."

"How long did this go on?" Elaine asked. "Because we grew up here, but we never heard anything about it until this summer."

"Oh, it didn't last too long. Five or ten years, at the most, and the sightings stopped. Of course, Andrew going off to school and me joining the Coast Guard might have had something to do with that." He laughed, then looked sharply at Elaine. "You're not going to turn me in, are you? It was a prank. I can't see getting in trouble over it after all these years."

Elaine smiled. "I don't think anyone's going to arrest you, Harold. Besides, what you did wasn't against the law, was it?"

"I don't know for sure. But I wasn't the one who got the whole town making signs and naming their guest cottages after the monster."

"Do you remember when the ice cream stand was named Chick's Ice Cream?" Jan asked.

"I sure do. I thought it was funny. I mean, I may have had the first sighting, which turned out to be a beaver, but by the time I found out what it really was, half the people in Lancaster claimed they'd seen it. And the monster they talked about didn't look like a beaver."

"No, it looked more like the Loch Ness Monster," Elaine said. "Only it was green, with red eyes."

Harold shook his head. "That sounds about right. Some of the pictures had rickrack down the back of the thing, like a stegosaurus. But it was all made up."

"Are you saying people other than you made up sightings?" Elaine asked.

"I think some did, just to get attention or to draw in business. If there were two or three sightings every year, the people would come. Everyone wanted to rent boats and go looking for the monster. This lake isn't huge, but it's big enough to feed a legend like that."

"Do you still have the original photo you and Andrew took of the creature?" Jan asked.

"No, I gave it to one of my grandchildren a long time ago. I didn't have room for a lot of stuff when I moved in here, and Brenda seemed like the one who cared most about family history, so I let her have it."

"Does she still live in Lancaster?" Elaine asked. "Maybe she'd let us see it."

He shook his head. "She lives in California now."

"Oh." Elaine looked as disappointed as Jan felt.

"Candace Huang, the reporter, told me you also had another picture, besides this one that they printed," Jan said.

"Yes, the one where it supposedly dove underwater. Mostly it's bubbles and ripples. But you might be able to make out a dark shape underneath the water. It might be around here somewhere."

He got up slowly and reached for his walker. Elaine almost told him not to trouble himself, but she really wanted to see that picture, so she kept quiet. She got up and followed Harold to a bookcase at one side of the room. He pulled out a photo album and put it in her hands.

"It'd be in that one or this one." He chose another album from the shelf and turned toward her.

"Here, let me carry them," Elaine said.

He moved slowly to his chair and sat down. Elaine moved his walker to one side and gave him the album he'd chosen first.

"May I look in this other one?"

"Sure," he said. "Look for a picture of water."

Elaine laughed. "I can handle that." She sat beside Jan on the settee and leafed slowly through the album. The old photos intrigued her. She supposed most were of McCullough family members. She wanted to ask a lot of questions, but Jan checked her watch, and Elaine remembered they'd have to leave soon to pick up the twins. But someday she'd love to return and ask Harold about the black-and-white photos of a man on an old tractor, and one of a young fellow she was almost certain was him walking beside a team of oxen. Another showed a young woman in loose pants with her foot on the running board of an antique car—antique now, that is. Elaine supposed it might have been new when the picture was taken.

"Here you go," Harold said. He leaned forward and passed her the open album.

Jan sidled over and held one side of the album. They both scanned the photos mounted on the two pages. Jan spotted it first and pointed.

"Oh yeah." Elaine bent closer. The gunwale of a wooden boat was prominent in the foreground. Beyond it, turbulent water looked as though it churned, and beneath the surface, a dark blob was visible. She stared at it for several seconds, trying to make the shape into some sort of animal.

"That's your fake monster?" Jan asked at last.

"Yup. We sank it just for the picture."

Elaine remembered the twins' insistence that the creature they had seen had red eyes. If someone had recreated the legendary creature of Chickadee Lake, they hadn't followed the color scheme.

"Your masterpiece wasn't green, was it?"

"Oh no. It was very crude. Dark brown or black, and as I told you, the neck was black." Harold smiled ruefully. "It's been a long time, ladies. More than seventy years. I don't think you answered my question though. You're not going to rat me out, are you?"

Elaine looked at Jan. "I don't think we need to, do you?"

"Well, this doesn't prove that the new sightings were bogus," Jan said.

"True." Elaine eyed Harold. "Would it hurt you if we exposed your hoax? I don't want to make trouble for you, but I would like people to know the truth. And if they know the 1940s monster was fake, maybe it would help us find out who is behind the new commotion."

Harold sighed. "I suppose it's time for me to confess."

"What about your friend, Andrew?" Jan asked.

"Oh, he's gone. Passed away about ten years ago. I miss him."

"I'm sorry," Elaine said. She thought it might have gone over well as an amusing feature story—written by Candace, of course—about the two "boys" who confessed many years later to stirring up the frenzy in their youth. "Let us think about it. It may not be necessary."

"Would you mind if we borrowed this picture?" Jan asked. "I promise we'd be careful with it and bring it back to you."

"Sure, why not?" He waved a hand.

"Thank you," Elaine said, though she wasn't sure what Jan wanted with it. She glanced at her. "Anything else?"

"We brought you some cookies," Jan said.

"What, cookies? I like cookies." Harold's eyes lit up.

Elaine was glad Jan had remembered. Jan gave her the album and opened her tote bag. While she got out the bag of oatmeal cookies and cheesecake bars she'd brought Harold, Elaine carefully worked the photograph loose from its mounting corners. She put it between the pages of the small notebook she carried in her purse, so it wouldn't get bent.

"Well, thank you, ladies," Harold said, eyeing the cookies through the plastic bag with anticipation. "I didn't know I was getting paid for conversation today."

Elaine laughed. "You earned it. May I come back sometime and talk to you about the other pictures in your albums? I'd love to hear some of the stories behind them."

"Anytime," Harold said. "And if you think you have to break the news about my encounter with the giant beaver, I won't deny it. I guess I've had a pretty good run with the monster story, eh?"

"You sure have," Jan said.

CHAPTER FIFTEEN

Friday was the last day of Vacation Bible School, and Jan made sure the boys had spotless clothes, combed hair, and clean hands and faces.

"Now remember," she said at the breakfast table, "tonight's the closing program. We'll all go over together after supper. Great-great-aunt Virginia and Bob and Nathan are coming too. We all want to see what you've learned this week."

Riley gave her an angelic grin. "We get to bring home our handwork tonight. Mrs. Ryder said so."

"Yeah," Jan said. "You've been so mysterious about it all week! What did you make?"

"It's a secret," Max said, shooting a warning glance at Riley. "We made something for you and something for Mommy and Daddy and Elaine."

"Oh, how nice," Jan said. "I can hardly wait to see them. Anybody want more milk?"

"I do." Riley held up his empty glass.

Max fiddled with the last bite of his scone. "Can I feed this to the turtles?"

"*Hmm*, I think it would be better if you stuck to the turtle food," Jan said. "The two you've kept have done so well all week, and you don't want to accidentally make them sick now."

"I sure hope Mommy and Daddy let us take them home," Riley said.

"Well, if they don't, you know they'll be here in the lake, waiting for your next visit," Jan assured him.

"If the monster doesn't eat them," Max said darkly.

"Now, that's enough about the monster. We told you, somebody made that thing you saw just for fun. It isn't real."

"We need to feed the turtles," Riley said.

"Oh, you should have done that before you got into your good clothes."

"In my pajamas?" Riley gave her a look of mock astonishment.

She laughed. "All right, let's get the turtle food and go give them a little."

They picked up the container on the back porch, and she opened the back door.

"Hey!" Max yelled. "Bad kitty! You get away from there!"

Riley scooted out the door after him and down the steps yelling, "No, Earl Grey! Bad, bad cat!"

Jan looked over at the shady spot where the turtle tub sat. Sure enough, Earl Grey was poking his inquisitive nose over the edge of the galvanized washtub. Jan hurried down the steps to the deck, hoping the cat hadn't harmed the turtles.

Earl Grey scampered off into the tall weeds as the boys approached and disappeared into the brush on Sylvia's property. To Jan's relief, she found both boys talking to their very healthy pets when she reached the turtle tub.

"Would Earl Grey eat them?" Max asked anxiously. "I don't want him to eat Pokey."

"I don't think so," Jan said, "but maybe it would be wise to cover their tub overnight."

"Yeah," Riley said, picking up his pet, Shelly, and examining it closely. "We don't want them to get eaten before Mommy and Daddy say if we can take them home."

"You go ahead and feed them," Jan said. "We'll think of a way to keep them safe." She hadn't even considered up until that moment that other predators—raccoons, for instance— might find the captive turtles a succulent snack.

The boys sprinkled a little food in the tub, and then went back to the deck. As they stepped up beside the wrought iron chairs and table there, Rose's boat nosed in beside the dock.

"It's Rose!" Riley yelled and charged down the steps to the dock below.

"Yeah, Rose!" Max was right behind him.

"Boys!" Jan looked at her watch. There was no danger yet of them being late for the last day of VBS, so she decided to let them greet Rose.

As the waitress tied her boat securely and climbed out onto the dock, the twins regaled her with a lurid tale of Earl Grey's suspicious behavior.

"An' he looked real guilty when he saw us," Riley said.

"Uh-huh," Max added. "He snuck off into the bushes, right over there." He pointed.

Rose took one hand of each twin and headed up the steps with them. "Well, maybe Archie can find an old screen or something we can use for a roof on the tub."

Jan nodded. "That's a good idea, Rose. Could you ask Archie about it? I've got to get these two over to the church."

"Sure," Rose said with a smile.

"Oh, and good morning," Jan said.

Rose laughed. "Hi." She bent down and looked into the boys' eyes. "You guys have fun today, okay? Brent and I are coming to your program tonight, and we're bringing his daughter, Emma. She's about your age."

"She'll like our play," Max said confidently.

"Oh, you're in a play?" Rose asked with exaggerated surprise.

"*Mmm-hmm*. Noah's Ark."

"Oh. What part do you play?"

"We're twin horses," Max said.

Riley whinnied with impressive realism and pranced about on the steps.

"Hey, don't go falling off the stairs and breaking a pastern," Jan said.

"What's that?" Riley asked.

Max frowned. "I thought the pastor was the boss of the church."

"Not pastor, pastern. Come on. I'll explain in the car." Jan herded the boys in through the back door.

"Grandma, can we have money for the missionary project?" Riley asked.

"I'm not sure. Where would a horse keep his offering money?"

"In our saddlebags!" Max shouted.

"Well, you've got me there," Jan said. "Let me find my purse."

WHILE JAN TOOK the twins to the church, Elaine went to see if Rose and Archie needed any help. Rose was in the kitchen, setting out the cups, saucers, and small plates she would need during the morning rush.

"So guess what? My dad said Russell Edmonds said he saw something swimming away into the bog as he passed by there this morning."

Elaine had to laugh at the hearsay of it all. "Something large and green, by any chance?"

"How did you guess?" Rose gave her a grim smile. "Elaine, you don't think there's anything to this monster business, do you? I mean, how could something that large live in the lake without anyone seeing it until last week? And then, all of a sudden, it pops up several times."

"Yes, it did pop up, didn't?" Elaine thought of the way the boys said it jumped up at them.

"Russell seemed to think it was a fake, but he was too far away to get a good look. Dad told me I could bring the boat, but not to go near the bog. He was going to call Jack when I left."

"I hope we can find out what's behind all this soon."

"Me too." Rose looked up at the clock. "I'd better go unlock the front door. Want to make sure we have plenty of hot water ready?"

"Sure." Elaine puttered about in the kitchen. She heard voices, and the front door opened and closed several times.

When she felt everything was ready for the first orders, she went out to the entry. Linda Tuttle stood near the checkout, talking to Rose. She smiled as she saw Elaine approaching.

"Oh good, you're here! John asked me to give you these." Linda held out a manila envelope. "He said you were interested in the Chick memorabilia."

"Chick memorabilia?" Rose asked.

Elaine smiled. "I think she means Chick the Lake Monster."

"Yes," Linda said.

"Oh, that Chick." Rose shook her head. "I guess that makes sense."

Linda laughed. "He also hopes I can bring back some muffins for him and the boys for their coffee break."

"Of course you can," Elaine said. "Come on into the kitchen and I'll get you some."

She led Linda out to the room that was the heart of Tea for Two. They kept a supply of flattened boxes in a cupboard for takeout orders, and she took out one that would hold a dozen muffins.

"We have blueberry, lemon poppy seed, and apple cinnamon today. Do you have a preference?" Elaine folded the box as she spoke.

Linda smiled. "Those guys will eat any flavor. I guarantee it."

Elaine set out to fill the box.

"Oh, half a dozen is plenty," Linda protested as Elaine reached for muffin number seven.

"Nope. This is on us," Elaine said. "You and John have been wonderful about sharing what you know about Chick.

Derek too, and I think you've got a couple of other guys over there working."

"We do. This time of year, we need extra help with the boat rentals and the motor repairs, not to mention sales." She watched Elaine fill the box without further protest. "Thank you so much."

Elaine closed the box and put it in her hands. "Please tell John I sent a big thank-you to all of you."

"I'll do that. Bye now."

When Linda had gone out, Elaine sat on a stool at the island and opened the envelope. Inside she found several snapshots and clippings of display ads cut from newspapers. The ads were for the marina and featured little clip-art silhouettes of what the Tuttles had imagined Chick looked like. To Elaine's way of thinking, they resembled cheerful dinosaurs.

The snapshots included one of the sign she had borrowed, out in front of the business, and three of a pontoon party boat. Along the sides of the boat, plywood cutouts had been mounted. The brightly painted figures portrayed the green lake monster of the signs, only much larger.

Chick's body was a bright grass green with yellow highlights, and his eyes were a vivid red. Along his spine, black triangular plates marched, all the way to the arrow-point tip of his tail, which curved gracefully upward at the stern of the boat. In two of the pictures, customers were enjoying their excursions on the Chick boat. In the third one, the boat was mounted on a trailer. Elaine surmised that one was taken shortly after the cutouts were added to the boat. The paint looked fresh and bright, and the whole vessel invited guests for a fun outing on the lake.

She was still looking at the pictures when Archie came into the kitchen.

"Hi, Archie. Can I help you with anything?" she asked.

"Thanks, but I've got it." He took a teapot from a shelf and set his customers' choice of teas to brew, then began laying out the cups and utensils. He glanced over at the photos Elaine had spread on the table. "What have you got there?"

"Tuttle family pictures from the old days, when Chick the Lake Monster was all the rage."

Archie stepped closer and looked down at them. "Well now, that's not so scary, is it?"

"No, it looks like a lot of fun," Elaine said.

"*Hmm.* Green creature with red eyes, like the boys said they saw."

"Yes. If they saw this boat, I don't think they'd be scared, do you?"

"Doesn't seem likely."

"John said the lake monster brought his parents prosperity. Other people in town too."

"I don't doubt it," Archie said. "Maybe it will do the same again." He set the teapot on the tray and picked it up.

Jan came in a moment later, flushed but smiling.

"Everything going well at the church?" Elaine asked.

"Yes. The kids are so excited about the program. And Garrett Wolfe was over there, videoing the kids as they went inside."

"Why?"

"Small-town life, slower pace, simpler lifestyle." Jan shrugged and looked down at Elaine's papers. "What's this?"

"John Tuttle sent it over. Ads for the marina with Chick on them, and pictures of the party boat his father fixed up to look like Chick."

"It's cute."

"Yes, if you can call a twenty-four-foot pontoon boat cute."

"With those pictures on the sides? It's adorable. I wonder if seeing those would help Max and Riley." Jan arched an eyebrow at Elaine.

"Because it's a nonscary image of something like what they saw, with the same color scheme?"

"Something like that."

"Maybe." Elaine gathered the photos and clippings and slid them back into the envelope. "We've got the whole family coming for supper before the VBS program. Think we'll be ready?"

"I sure do," Jan said. "Tara's bringing Jack, and Sasha's even tearing herself away from the moving boxes, and bringing Brody along, and Brian's whole family is in, plus your mom. Not to mention Bob and Nathan."

"Sounds like we need to use the east parlor," Elaine said. "A crowd that big wouldn't fit in the dining room."

"How would you like to be in charge of the setup, salad, and breadsticks?"

"I'd love to." Elaine went to fetch an apron.

AFTER LUNCH, THE twins begged to have one last swim in the lake. The day had turned out to be hot, and even Riley wanted to swim, if they could do it on the Bookworm side of the dock, away from Sylvia's property and the point where they had seen the monster.

Jan and Elaine swapped off watching them while they played in the water and on the shore. The boys gave the turtles some cool water and took them out of the confining tub for a while. However, the turtles didn't seem to want to race that day, so Max and Riley lost interest and put them back in their tub.

Elaine came down to the shore at two o'clock to relieve Jan.

"Diane called," she said as she sat down in one of the chairs on the deck. "She wanted to know if we could give her three dozen cookies for the first play rehearsal. I told her we could."

"Sure," Jan said. "Does she want us to do anything else?"

"Not yet, unless we want to try out for the play. She's casting this weekend."

"I don't think so," Jan said. "We've got so much going on. But go ahead if you want to."

Elaine shook her head. "I'm with you. I told her I'd help with props and things backstage if she needed extra people, but I think I have enough projects going right now."

"I'd like to spend some more time figuring out who made that pop-up thing the twins saw," Jan said. "That may be easier to dig into after they've gone home though."

"Yes." Elaine looked down to the shore. Riley was piling up rocks at the edge of the water, and Max was splashing him, trying to get his attention. "It seems to me that if somebody really wanted to scare them, they'd have made the monster look scarier. But why would they choose the boys to try it out on, anyway?"

"Good question." Jan looked at her watch. "I'd better go start getting things ready for supper."

CHAPTER SIXTEEN

W hy can't Mommy and Daddy come see us?" Riley asked as his grandmother flattened his cowlick with a wet comb. "Everybody else is coming."

"They're not back from their trip yet, honey. They're still in Nantucket. But I'm going to video your class when you sing, so they can see it later, okay? Just be good when you're on stage, and do your best. They plan to come back tomorrow evening. We can show it to them then."

Riley was agreeable to the plan, and Jan turned to Max. His hair was more cooperative, but he had already spilled something on his clean shirt.

"Oh boy, let me sponge that." Jan hauled him closer to the bathroom sink.

"I'm sorry, Grandma."

He sounded a little tired. Jan wondered if the weeklong stay was a bit much for the boys, or if he was just tired from all his activity. In addition to swimming that afternoon, they had walked to the ice cream stand for treats, and then Elaine had taken them for a ride in Rose's boat and tried fishing with hand lines. Max had caught a sunfish, much to his delight. He was very disappointed when Elaine told him he had to throw it back in the water because sunfish weren't good eating and there was no way his grandma would cook it for supper. Unfortunately, no edible fish took the boys' bait, so they had putted on home. After they'd washed, Elaine had set the tables with the twins' help.

Their great-great-aunt Virginia, Elaine's mother, arrived for supper, followed almost immediately by Bob and Nathan.

"Bob!" Max cried, running to meet him in the entry. "I caught a fish, but Elaine wouldn't let me keep it."

Jan allowed him two minutes to tell his fishing story while she made sure that everything was ready in the kitchen. As Elaine and her mother greeted Nathan, Jack and Tara arrived, and Elaine gave them an abbreviated version of the fishing expedition. Soon Sasha came in with Brody, and Brian arrived with his family.

When they all sat down to the meal, the east parlor rang with their happy voices. Jan looked over the group and sighed with contentment. Bob reached for her hand and squeezed it.

"Happy, sweetheart?"

"You know I am." She smiled at him, marveling again at the way God had brought them together and blessed her large, boisterous family.

Everyone enjoyed hearing about the boys' adventures throughout the week and updates on the Chick sightings.

"Grandma, you'd better have some kind of lake monster alarm on your dock, in case it comes too close," Kelly said.

Jan laughed. "Now that's a novel idea." She stood up. "Well, we'd better get going, or we might not all get seats."

Elaine glanced at the clock. "You're right. The dishes will have to wait."

BOB TOOK JAN and the twins in his car, and Nathan drove Elaine and her mother. The others sorted out their own carpooling arrangements.

When they reached the church, the pews were filling rapidly. Nearly a hundred children had attended the Bible school. Many of them lived in Lancaster and Penzance but did not regularly attend Lancaster Community Church. Their parents and friends had come out to see them perform, swelling the audience.

While Jan escorted the twins to their classroom to prepare, Elaine and Nathan found seats with enough room for Virginia to join them.

"I'll find another spot for me and Jan," Bob said and moved quickly down the aisle. "The others may have to sit on the folding chairs they put at the back."

Elaine found herself next to Charlotte Benson, the wife of State Trooper Dan Benson.

"Your daughter must be in the same class as Jan's twin grandsons," Elaine said.

"Yes, she's told us all about Riley and Max, and she was so excited when she found out she could tell them apart yesterday because Riley had a bandage on his knee."

Elaine laughed and looked beyond Charlotte at her husband. "Hi, Dan."

"Hello, Elaine," he said. "Are things staying calm at the tearoom?"

"Not with Amy's twins visiting. Say, have you heard much about the lake monster sightings? Our boys claim they saw it yesterday."

"Yes, I did hear about that. I hope they weren't too traumatized."

"I think they were more startled than scared, although Riley was a bit unsettled."

Dan frowned. "I spoke to Jack Weston about it this afternoon. He said Russ Edmonds reported another sighting this morning."

"I heard about it too. Rose Young told me."

"I guess Russell was in the mail boat, which is a bit large to take into the bog. He didn't get a very good look—just glimpsed it going out of sight."

"Something weird is going on, Dan," Elaine said.

"Yeah, Jack and I think someone's rigged something up in the bog."

Elaine leaned toward him and said softly, "Not just the bog. When the twins saw it, that thing was near our beach, on the side toward Sylvia Flood's property."

"That close?"

"Yes. Unfortunately, Jan and I were both inside at the time, so neither of us actually saw it. Jack came over later, and he and I agree there was *something* there, but we're not sure what."

"Well, I'll keep in touch with Jack, but unless we get a complaint or evidence of a crime, it's not really my business. Keep me posted, though."

Elaine nodded. "Thanks, Dan, If I hear anything concrete, I'll do that." She saw the rest of her and Jan's family enter the auditorium and shuffle for seats together in the overflow section.

"Here they come," Virginia whispered as the auditorium lights dimmed. "Aren't the boys just adorable?"

The children filed out by class, and the preschoolers and kindergarteners performed first. Then it was time for the twins' class. Kit Edmonds prompted the children to recite the Bible verses they had learned that week. Afterward, they sang a song about the animals Noah gathered into the ark. Different children sang lines about various animals. Max and Riley stole the show by singing a verse about the two horses that went aboard. They pranced about in unison and gave an impressive neigh, in stereo, at the end of their lyrics.

When all of the classes had presented their parts, Pastor Mike let the children go and sit in the audience with their families while he presented a few awards and recapped the lessons the children had learned during the week. Then he asked one of the deacons to offer prayer and excused the throng. The guests could visit each classroom to view the children's handwork and go into the fellowship hall for refreshments.

Elaine's mother found several old friends among the guests, and she stayed with them while Elaine and Nathan wandered through the classrooms and enjoyed the exhibits. They met up with Jan, Bob, and the twins in the boys' classroom.

"With all the excitement, I forgot to tell you all at dinner," Bob said with a grin. "I've had several calls about the article in the *Courier.*"

"Really? Anyone come up with anything solid?" Nathan asked.

"Well, I'm not sure. Most were just vague feelings or thinking something moved in the shadows. There's one I need to look into. The receptionist at the clinic says she knows who started the legend back in the 1940s, but she has no idea who or what is behind the new commotion. But I've been so busy at the office, I haven't had a chance to pursue it."

Elaine wondered if Jan had told him all the details of their interview with Harold McCullough. They'd have to discuss it later.

Nathan smiled. "I've got a big auction tomorrow, but maybe Elaine and Jan would have some time to check it out when the twins leave."

Elaine looked at her cousin. "Are you game?"

"Why not?" Jan said. "It's not like we have a business to run or anything like that."

Bob laughed. "I know you two. You'll find time." He reached inside his sport jacket and took out a small notebook. "Here we go. The receptionist's name is Bree Dickerson."

"We know her," Elaine said. "She's awfully young to know about this stuff, isn't she?"

"She told me her grandfather told her about it." Bob leafed through his notebook. "The way she tells it, there was a single woman who was the town clerk for a few years, and she was Bree's grandfather's cousin. She had something to do with it."

He tore out a leaf and gave it to Jan. "Maybe if you talk to her, she can remember more than she told me."

"Okay, we'll do that," Jan said. "Thanks."

Riley and Max ran over, and Riley held up two little turtles made from cardboard cups cut from an egg carton. "Look, Grandma. We made animals, and I made these."

Jan took the small items and held them up. "Why, those look a lot like Pokey and Shelly."

"Uh-huh," Riley said. "I painted them to look like our turtles."

"That's clever," Jan said.

"You can keep them, Grandma. They're your present."

"Oh, thank you so much! I know just where I'll display them."

"I made porcupines." Max held up two creatures made from pinecones, with googly eyes and cutout feet and a tail glued on.

"How cute," Elaine said.

"They're for you."

Elaine stooped and kissed Max's cheek. "Thank you. I'll treasure these."

"We've got pictures and stuff too," Riley said.

"And our presents for Mommy and Daddy," Riley added.

"What did you make for them?" Jan asked.

Max took her hand and led them all to the table where woodworking projects were laid out.

"We didn't build them," Max explained, "but we sanded and painted them."

Riley picked up one of a pair of elephant-shaped bookends. It was painted with a background layer of light gray and decorated with slashes of red, pink, and purple.

"That's very colorful," Elaine said. "I'm sure your mom will like it."

Max picked up his set. These elephants were pale green, with spatters of blue, yellow, and orange all over them. "This is the boy elephant, and this is the girl." At Jan's blank look, he added, "For the ark."

"Oh, I see," Jan said. "Well, we need to think about how we're going to carry all this home safely."

One of the helpers brought them a box, and they carefully arranged all the twins' masterpieces in it. Bob took the box out to the car, and they all went to get refreshments. The boys got cupcakes and punch, and Jan made them sit down quietly to eat them with Avery and Kelly. Nathan poured himself a cup of coffee and brought Elaine some tea.

"Bob's leads about the monster didn't sound very promising," Elaine said.

"I know," Nathan said. "I wish they did. I know it's driving you crazy that you haven't found out what's going on."

ELAINE PAID A visit to Bree Dickerson on Saturday morning, since Jan wanted to spend the day with the twins. The clinic was not open on the weekend, so Elaine found Bree at home, working in her small garden. When Elaine explained her errand, Bree removed her gardening gloves and invited her in for a chat.

"I told Mr. Claybrook I don't know all that much," she confessed as they sat in her pleasant living room. Elaine caught a distant view of the lake through the patio door. "But I was doing some family history a few years ago, and my grandpa did tell me about his cousin, Madeline Buckley."

"That name sounds familiar," Elaine said. "Jan and I did some research on the town officers and chamber of commerce from the 1940s. I think I saw Madeline's name in a couple of documents we gathered."

"She was town clerk of Lancaster from 1946 to 1950," Bree said. "She was single at the time, in her fifties. As I understand it, she was good at the job. And she was very concerned about the men who returned from the war and didn't have employment."

"Yes." Elaine leaned back in her chair and thought for a moment. "That was the time when the boom began in Lancaster. New tourist businesses were built. The Tuttles expanded the marina. The cottages Macy Atherton owns now were built then."

"I think Will Trexler started working on his fly dope around that period too," Bree said. "All the people coming to fish and water ski complained about the mosquitoes, and that inspired him."

"You may be right." Elaine had talked to Will, and she really didn't think he was behind the original legend of Chick. "He would have been just a boy when all that started though."

"I guess you're right," Bree said. "The fly dope came a little later."

Elaine nodded. "I talked to him about the monster. He said he and his friends tried to find it, but they never saw it. Pearl said her father saw it once though. She believed his story."

"Well, I don't know what to tell you," Bree said. "Bob Claybrook said he wants information about what's going on now. But since he was interested, I thought I'd tell him what I knew about Madeline Buckley. She really promoted Chick, and through that, the town."

"I'm glad you told us," Elaine assured her. "I'll see if I can find out anything more."

"Good, and I hope you learn the story behind what's happening now."

Elaine thanked Bree and went home.

A light rain began to fall as she drove, and the wind whipped up whitecaps on the lake. Bad weather for water monsters, Elaine thought. There probably wouldn't be any new sightings today.

Jan and the boys had taken shelter in the upstairs living room when the rain started and were playing a game of Chinese checkers. Elaine joined them, and they spent a quiet hour together. Around four o'clock, Amy called her mother.

"Why don't you just leave the twins here tonight and get them tomorrow?" Jan suggested.

Elaine watched her cousin's face as she talked on the phone.

"Well, okay," Jan said. "I'll make sure they have everything packed up. You and Van plan to have supper with us."

She closed the conversation and turned to the boys. "That was Mommy. She and Daddy will be here in a couple of hours."

"Yay!" Riley cried, his eyes shining.

Max looked a little downcast. "Do we have to go home?"

Elaine smiled. Max, at least, hadn't had his fill of Grandma's house yet.

"I'm afraid so," Jan said. "Your mom and dad can't wait to see you again. You guys pick up the game, and then we'll get your clothes and things packed."

"Do you want me to start supper while you help them?" Elaine asked.

"If you wouldn't mind. Van and Amy just crossed into Maine, and I told Amy they ought to go home and get one night of good rest before they come for them."

"I heard. I guess she nixed that idea?"

"Yes, she misses the boys too much."

Elaine smiled. "She's tenderhearted, like her mom."

"Who, me?" Jan swatted a hand through the air. "I planned for extra people tonight, in case they decided to come. There's pot roast in the slow cooker, and of course, there's plenty of dessert."

"So, potatoes and a vegetable?"

"Sounds great. And believe it or not, I think we have some leftovers from last night." The twins had all of the marbles back in their containers, and Jan walked over to fold the board and close up the box. "Okay, guys. Did you leave anything up in the tower room?"

"Our trucks," Max said.

"Oh, you don't want to forget those," Jan said solemnly. "Let's go up and get them first, and we can look around in case anything else is up there that you're taking with you."

"Don't forget our turtles," Riley said.

"Are the turtles upstairs too?" Jan put on a shocked face.

Riley laughed. "No, they're outside, Grandma."

"I thought so. Let's get the tower room stuff first."

"Okay," Riley said.

Elaine headed for the kitchen.

By the time Van and Amy arrived, the rain had slacked off, and the boys were able to tug them down to the shore to meet the turtles.

"Oh, sweetie, I don't know," Amy said doubtfully as Riley held up his pet, two inches from her face.

"Please," Riley said earnestly.

"Dad will let us," Max said confidently.

Van's eyebrows shot up. "Oh, Dad will, huh? Listen, Mommy's going to have a lot to do with the new baby coming and everything. I don't think she'll have time for extra pets."

"We'll take care of them," Max said.

Riley ran to his father's side. "Yeah, and turtles don't take much work. You don't have to walk them or brush them or—"

"Hold on," Van said, throwing Jan a questioning glance.

Jan stepped up and took the box turtle gently from Riley. "You know, honey, Jack told us the turtles would be happier if you let them go."

"But we let all the others go," Max reminded her.

"True, but these two have been shut up all week, and they must really itch to go swimming in the lake and—"

"The monster might get them." Riley's face was scrunched up as if he was about to cry.

"Monster?" Van asked. He glanced at Elaine, than at Amy.

"What are you talking about?" Amy bent to look Riley in the eye. "What monster?"

"The one in the lake." Riley buried his head in her maternity top, and Amy patted his back, looking helplessly at Jan.

Elaine stepped forward. "Maybe we should go in and wash and have supper. We can tell your mom and dad all about everything while we eat."

Riley sniffed. "Okay." He took his turtle from Jan and reluctantly put it back in the tub.

Max let go of his painted turtle too, and they trooped up the steps to the house.

Over the meal, Elaine and Jan explained about the odd sightings on the lake, and Riley and Max chimed in about what they had seen while they were playing on the shore.

"Do you think someone is doing this maliciously?" Van asked.

"What's that?" Max asked, frowning.

"*Maliciously* means intending to do harm to people," his father said. "Hurt them, or even just to scare them."

"I was scared," Riley said. "A little."

Jan reached over and patted his head. "You're okay though. And it wasn't a real monster. Elaine and I are sure of that."

"How do you know?" Max asked, his eyes wide.

"Yeah," Riley said. "We saw it."

"Because lake monsters aren't real. Or if they are real, they're not monsters. They're something else that people *think* are monsters." Jan looked around at all of them. "One man said that what he saw might have been a floating log. Another man said that he thought he saw a monster a long time ago, but it was just a big beaver."

"I'm scared of beavers," Riley said.

Elaine decided it was time to change the subject. "Hey, what about the presents you made for your mom and dad?"

"Oh yeah! Wait till you see them!" Max grabbed Riley's sleeve and tugged him toward the stairs. "Come on. Let's get them."

They came down again carrying the elephant-shaped bookends, and Amy and Van accepted them as though they were priceless treasures.

"These will be perfect on top of the bookshelf in the family room," Amy said.

Her husband examined each one with great care. "Yes, I think these will be a great addition to the décor."

Van also settled the turtle question once and for all after supper.

"Guys, the turtles would be lonely at our house. There are a lot here in the lake, and I'm sure they don't want to leave all their friends behind."

"But they have each other," Max said.

"Yeah, like me and Max." Riley had tears in his eyes.

Van crouched and laid a hand on each boy's shoulder. "But your turtles aren't twins. They aren't even the same species."

The boys looked sulky.

"Did you know that Mike and Jaden are home from summer camp?" Van asked.

Riley blinked hard, and Max's eyes lit. "Oh boy!"

"Yes, and they'll be wanting to play with you," Van continued. "See, they don't like to be away from their friends that long, even though they had fun at camp."

Riley nodded slowly.

"The turtles want to be with their friends too," Van said.

Max looked at Riley. "We have to let them go."

Riley's lip quivered. "Okay."

Van smiled. "Good boys."

Jan looked toward the window. "I actually see a little sunshine out there. Shall we go down and release the turtles into the wild?"

The whole family went back to the shore, and the boys said tearful goodbyes to their pets.

"Have fun in your wild habitat!" Riley called as the little box turtle ducked beneath the water.

"You'll come back next week for the field day, won't you?" Jan asked.

Amy smiled. "We wouldn't miss it."

"We all want to see the firemen's muster," Van assured her.

"The boys can say hi to their turtles then, and maybe we'll have some answers for them about the you-know-what," Elaine said. She truly hoped the mystery of the lake monster would be put to rest by then.

CHAPTER SEVENTEEN

Jan drove to church Sunday morning, and it felt odd not to have the twins in the car with her and Elaine. At least the boys had gone home happy. Amy had told them they had presents she and Van had bought on their trip awaiting them after they got home and unpacked the car. Both boys had hugged Jan and Elaine tight and asked if they could come back again soon. Jan felt slightly bereft this morning, but also very free. She had nothing more pressing on her agenda today than cleaning out the empty turtle tub.

After Sunday school, Jan went to the fellowship hall and got a cup of tea. She was debating whether or not to eat a doughnut when Lydia Pierce approached her.

Saved from temptation, Jan thought, and she turned away from the pastry table.

"Lydia, how are things going?"

"Everything's great at the diner," Lydia said with a smile. "I wanted to show you and Elaine something that came in for the *Wave*." Lydia published a small weekly newspaper in the summertime. Local business owners advertised in it, and people could pick it up free at more than a dozen locations in town.

"Sounds intriguing," Jan said, looking around the fellowship hall. She spotted Elaine talking to Pearl and Will Trexler. "There's Elaine. Let me get her."

A moment later, Lydia drew both cousins into an empty Sunday school room.

"Sorry about the cloak-and-dagger stuff, but I don't want anyone else to know about these yet, except maybe Jack Weston."

Elaine's eyes widened. "Oh. It's something to do with local wildlife, shall we say?"

"You got it." Lydia took an envelope from her tote bag. "When I opened the door this morning, these were on the porch." She handed each of them a photograph. "Left by an anonymous donor, of course."

"Of course," Jan agreed, gazing down at the slightly out-of-focus print. "Is that supposed to be the lake monster?" She saw an object floating in water. It might have been an alligator, except its green color was unnaturally bright. Both ends tapered. One was long and slender, suggesting a tail. The other end might be a head. Jan squinted and tried to consider it impartially. It might be a reptile. Or an inflatable toy.

"Well, these photos are better than Harold McCullough's," Jan said.

Elaine studied the one in her hand. "There's no way to tell how big it is. That could be a toy."

Lydia nodded. "True. No scale whatsoever. No location given—nothing."

Jan swapped pictures with Elaine. The second one was snapped from a slightly different angle and a bit farther away. She made out a small slash of red on the end that might be a head. The red eyes the boys insisted they'd seen? She wasn't convinced.

"This proves nothing."

Elaine looked up. "Does the photographer expect you to print these in the *Wave*?"

"That's what I'm thinking."

"Would you do that?" Jan asked.

Lydia shook her head. "Not until I know more. I think whoever left these at the house wants me to print them, but I'm not going with something this vague. I'd need to at least know who took the pictures and where and when."

"If someone got close enough to the thing to take pictures, why haven't we heard news of another sighting?" Jan asked.

Elaine's mouth morphed into a grimace. "I suppose this *could* be what the twins described to us after they saw it, but I don't know."

"So, you think the pictures were faked?" Lydia asked.

"Well, I certainly don't think it's a real, live, breathing lake monster." Elaine winced.

"Of course," Lydia said. "I'm skeptical myself. I don't see how it could be a real animal. Unless someone let an alligator loose in the bog. But aren't they tropical animals? I don't think one could survive a winter up here." She sighed. "Right now, I'd just like to get the scoop behind these pictures."

"They came to you as prints?" Jan asked. "People don't usually get prints nowadays." She turned over the one she held.

"I think they printed them out themselves, from a computer," Lydia said.

Jan recognized the faint text on the back of the picture. "Yeah, that's the name of a company that makes photo paper for home printers."

Elaine looked at hers. "I see it too. I guess this means anyone could have rigged up these photos with a digital camera, or even a cell phone, and then printed them out and left them for you to puzzle over."

Jan swapped pictures with Elaine again. "I have an idea. What if you printed something in this week's *Wave*, saying you received some photos purporting to be the lake creature, but you won't print them until you know who submitted them and get more information about the pictures."

"That might bring a response," Lydia said. "Why do you suppose they sent them to me, not to somebody at the *Courier* or the *Sentinel*?"

Elaine looked at Jan. "I don't know. Any thoughts?"

Jan hesitated. "Well, Candace Huang dug out the old picture the *Courier* had printed in 1947 for us. I wonder if the person who made these knew about that."

Lydia nodded slowly. "Maybe they think I'm more gullible, or that I'd jump at the chance to scoop the bigger papers."

"Or maybe they sent copies to the other papers too," Jan said.

Elaine frowned. "I'll call Candace later, just to make sure. It's an interesting thought. If she got copies, I think she'd tell me. Right now, we'd better get to the sanctuary."

"Wait a sec." Jan held out the picture she'd been studying. "What's that in the corner?"

Elaine took it. She and Lydia bent their heads over it.

"I don't know," Elaine admitted. "It looks like the edge of something..."

"Some structure?" Lydia asked.

"But it's in the water," Jan said.

"Not a boat," Lydia murmured.

"A dock?" Elaine lifted her gaze to meet Jan's.

"Let me see it again," Jan said. She took the picture and held it about a foot from her face. "That looks like rusty metal..."

"It's barrels," Elaine said. "That's a float."

Jan grinned, knowing at once that Elaine was right. "Yeah. A swim float, with empty fifty-five-gallon drums as the base."

The three women looked at each other, excitement gleaming in their eyes.

"So, maybe we can pinpoint where this photo was taken," Lydia said in a hushed tone.

Jan nodded. "Who has a float off their shore?"

"There are quite a few," Lydia said, "even if you don't go all the way down the lake to Penzance. Most of the cottage businesses have them, and the boys' camp, and quite a few of the private cottages."

"Maybe we should take a boat ride this afternoon," Jan said. "Not much of it shows in this picture, and it's not very clear—"

"But that part is more focused than the thing in the foreground," Elaine noted.

Lydia frowned. "I've got to go to Augusta this afternoon. It's a family thing. My mom would never forgive me if I skipped it."

"Would you mind if we went out and did some exploring?" Jan asked.

"Not at all," Lydia replied. "I just wish I could go with you."

Elaine looked at the picture again. "I'll bet we can find this spot. Maybe Rose will let us borrow her boat."

"I don't mind if you show Rose," Lydia said. "In fact, you might have to show those pictures to people you talk to. Just ask them to keep it quiet, okay? I guess that's all you can do."

"Of course," Elaine said.

Jan checked the time. "Come on, or we'll be late for the service."

ELAINE ENJOYED GETTING a view of Lancaster from the water during their Sunday afternoon outing. The sun on the water was a bit dazzling, and she and Jan had both donned sunglasses and floppy hats. Rose sat beside Elaine on the middle seat of the motorboat, with Jan in the bow, and Rose's boyfriend, Brent, manned the outboard motor in the stern.

"How about that one?" Jan yelled, pointing toward a float about fifteen yards out from the dock at the Heavenly Hill Cottages.

Elaine and Rose had both the photographs Lydia had loaned them in protective plastic coverings. They studied the pictures and compared them to the part of the float just above the water, and Brent slowed and idled the motor. Jan lifted binoculars to study the anchored float.

"No!" Elaine called. "The canvas on the deck of that one comes down over the sides. In the picture, we can see the wooden frame above the barrels."

Rose nodded. "I think you're right."

Jan turned around. "This isn't it."

They'd been down one side of Chickadee Lake and had headed back toward Lancaster, observing all the beaches and docks on the other side of the lake. Jan was making a list of all the floats they spotted, so they could discuss what they'd seen later or contact the owners if something came up.

Brent put the motor in gear, and they puttered toward the next float, which was positioned for swimming and diving off the boys' camp's waterfront.

A tall young man wearing khaki shorts, a T-shirt, and a baseball cap was working on the dock, closer in to shore. He looked up and waved as their boat approached.

"That's not the float in the picture," Jan said.

Elaine agreed, but she said, "Maybe we should speak to him. They might have seen something down here."

Brent eased the boat in to the dock and tossed the man the painter. He caught it and slipped the loop at the end of the rope over a piling.

"Hi," he said cheerfully. He had a string of small rubber buoys laid out on the dock. "I'm just fixing the rope for the crib area, while we don't have any kids here."

"Oh, there's no one at camp this weekend?" Jan asked.

"The last batch of campers left yesterday. We'll get a new bunch in tomorrow."

"Are you the director?" Elaine asked.

He smiled. "Just the waterfront director. I'm Ian. Can I help you?"

Elaine passed her photo to Jan, who was closest to the dock. Jan handed it to Ian. "We're looking for the float that shows at the edge of this picture. I'm pretty sure it's not yours." She nodded to the one a few yards out, waiting for campers to swarm it. "But I thought maybe you'd recognize it."

Ian glanced at the picture, and his eyes widened. "What's that thing?" He pointed to the supposed lake monster.

"We don't know," Jan said.

"Someone is claiming it's Chick, the monster of Chickadee Lake, but we're skeptical," Elaine said. "We thought if we could find the float near where the picture was taken, we might find out something about the rest of it."

"*Hmm.*" Ian looked thoughtful. "I'm not sure about the float. It could be the one that belongs to the Gowers, a couple of cottages down." He waved in the direction of Lancaster. "But that green thing in this picture reminds me of something."

"What?" Rose asked eagerly.

"A couple of days ago, we had a canoeing class. I had half a dozen boys out in one canoe, and a counselor called Uncle Dusty had about as many in another canoe. His canoe went quite a ways down the lake, and they beached to look for pine-cones for their crafts."

All the occupants of the boat waited in silence. Elaine had a feeling Ian knew something important.

"So when they came back, I asked Dusty what took them so long, and he showed me a soggy piece of cloth they'd found on the shore. It was like a heavy canvas, painted green, but then it had some bright yellow on it."

"Green and yellow?" Elaine asked.

"Yeah, but mostly green. I was thinking this thing in your picture might be something like that—see the lighter stripe?"

Elaine and Rose leaned in to look at the photo again. Though it was blurry, they could tell that a swath along what might be the monster's back looked lighter and yellower than the rest of the object.

"So, what happened to that cloth?" Jan asked.

"I think it might be in the shed over there." Ian pointed to the shore. "We keep equipment in there—lifejackets, paddles, things like that. And there's a barrel we use for trash. If you want to hang on, I can check and see if Dusty tossed it in there."

"If you wouldn't mind," Elaine said.

"Sure. Hold on." Ian gave the picture to Jan, then jogged off the dock toward a small shed on the shore.

"You think it could be something significant?" Brent asked.

Elaine shrugged. "Well, Lydia's pictures don't look like the earliest newspaper picture of the supposed monster, but it might have some resemblance to the drawings and paintings done later."

"They were cartoonish though," Jan said. "This thing looks flatter."

Elaine drew in a deep breath. "I agree, but that scrap of material sounds like it might match these photos—or what the twins saw."

A minute later, Ian returned with a rag in his hand. "Here you go. It was in the trash barrel, all right." He handed it down to Jan.

She smoothed out the material and looked at it keenly, then passed it to Elaine. Elaine and Rose both examined it. The stiff material had definitely been painted a flat green on one side, and a smear of yellow brightened one edge. The yellow might have been used to define the shape, or to add features. The ragged edges made it look as though it had been torn off something larger. Rose turned it over. The back was the grayish woven material people used to cover their floats or make sails.

Rose handed the foot-long scrap to Brent.

"Do you mind if we take it?" Elaine asked.

"Be my guest," Ian said.

"Thanks. And we'd appreciate it if you didn't spread it around that we've got these pictures."

"Okay."

"Where exactly did they find the piece of canvas?" Jan smiled up at him.

Ian pointed down the shore. "On this side of that float I was talking about. The camp owns quite a long piece of shore, but then you'll come to some private cottages. There's a little stretch of shore between them that's pretty rocky, and the woods come right down to the water. Lots of pine trees there, and the kids like to collect the cones."

"Thanks," Jan said.

Ian unhooked the rope and tossed it into the boat. Jan shoved off from the dock, and Brent started the motor again.

They cruised slowly along and passed a couple of fishermen. Soon they came to the wooded area Ian had mentioned.

"I don't think I want to land the boat there," Brent said. "It looks pretty rocky."

"That must be the float he meant!" Jan yelled, pointing ahead. She lifted her binoculars to her eyes.

Elaine turned to Brent. "Can you come in slow and quiet at the float?"

He eased up on the motor, and when they were within forty feet of the floating platform, he cut it completely. They drifted in alongside the outer edge of the float and bumped gently against it. The women compared what they saw with the pictures.

Elaine felt a glimmer of excitement. "I think this is it. If only a little bit more of it showed in the picture." She looked toward the shore. A shingled brown cottage sat above them, up a slope from the water. Rustic steps made from railroad ties were sunk into the hillside.

"See anybody?" Rose asked Jan.

Jan shook her head. "Looks like no one is home, but didn't Ian say this was the Gowers' place?"

"You mean Caden Gower, the fireman?" Elaine asked.

"Oh right," Rose said. "He was at the tearoom last week when Tag and the others were having that meeting."

Elaine nodded. "They sat out on the porch."

"Is he married?" Jan asked.

"Yes, I think so," Rose said. "I don't know them well, but I think the family has had this cottage for a while."

"I might give Caden a call later," Elaine said.

They continued slowly down the lake, but none of the other floats that were anchored in front of cottages could possibly be the one in the picture.

When they reached the tearoom's dock, they secured the boat and climbed the steps.

"I think this calls for tea all around," Jan said.

"Amen to that." Rose smiled at Brent. "If I know this place—and I do—we can probably find some pastries too."

"Sounds good," Brent said.

Elaine carried the bit of painted fabric. She looked over at the point between their property and Sylvia's. Could Lydia's pictures be snapshots of whatever had scared the boys? They had insisted on a green monster with red eyes. The green in the picture and on the canvas fit. But how did the monster appear to jump toward the boys? And why would someone do that? What was going on?

CHAPTER EIGHTEEN

"Do you think we should call Dan Benson?" Jan asked after Rose and Brent had left.

"I don't know," Elaine said. "We really don't have much to go on."

Jan frowned. "I suppose it's like he said before—there's no evidence of a crime."

"That's right. Even if someone made a fake monster to try to stir things up in town, is that a crime? Or is it just a prank?"

Jan shook her head. "I suppose you're right. But I'd still like to know who's doing it and why."

"I'm not sure how they can profit from it," Elaine said. "And if all they did was pull a fake sea monster around and leave photos on Lydia's front porch, I don't think that's illegal."

"I don't know about you," Jan said, "but I'm going to start thinking about the field day on Saturday. We need to make lots of cookies, and we promised to help with the play too."

"Oh, that's right." Elaine glanced at the clock. "We don't have to do anything tonight, but we'd better plan on spending every evening this week at the Old Grange Hall to help out at rehearsals."

"At least one of us every night," Jan agreed, "and we'd better both plan on being there tomorrow night, for the first full rehearsal. Now, what do you want to do for supper?"

"Let's eat out," Elaine said.

Jan smiled. "Great. I don't feel much like cooking tonight. The Hearthside or the Pine Tree Grill?"

"*Hmm*. I think I'd like some seafood. Let's go to the Hearthside. Do you want to invite Bob?"

"No, he was going down to his daughter's house this weekend."

Elaine shrugged. "And Nathan headed out for his buying trip to Boston this afternoon. Looks like we're on our own."

They both freshened up and left for the restaurant. Burk and Abby King owned the establishment, and they spent their winters in Florida, so the cousins could only enjoy their delicious menu in the warmer months.

When they walked in the door, Abby met them with a smile.

"Well, good evening. Good to see you."

"Thanks," Elaine said.

"Table for two?" Abby asked.

"Yes," Jan said, and the cousins followed her to a small table at one side of the room.

"Oh look," Elaine said, "Tag is here." She nodded toward a larger table, where four people sat.

"That shouldn't surprise you, since his parents own this place," Jan said. "But look who's with him—just the man you wanted to see."

"Caden Gower." Elaine sat down and took the menu from Abby with a smile.

"Do you know what you'd like to drink?" Abby asked.

"Ice water for me," Elaine said.

"Same here," Jan added.

"Okay, I'll be back in a minute." Abby walked toward the kitchen.

"They're pretty busy tonight," Jan observed.

"Yeah." Elaine looked toward Tag's table again.

"Is that Caden's wife with him?" Jan asked.

"I think so. And the other man is his brother. He was with Caden last week, when the firefighters met on our side porch. His name is Jason." Elaine arched her eyebrows at Jan. "Should we just go over and ask him about the monster?"

"I wish we'd brought the photos along," Jan said.

"I could dash home and get them."

Jan considered that. "It looks like they haven't eaten much yet."

"You put my order in," Elaine said, rising. "I'll have scallops and a baked potato and whatever is the vegetable of the day. I can be back in ten minutes."

"Really? Okay." Jan watched her scurry across the room and out the door and then looked at the menu.

Abby came back with their water glasses. "Need a minute?" she asked, glancing at Elaine's empty chair.

"No, I'll order," Jan said. She put in Elaine's request and ordered crab cakes for herself. She kept an eye on Tag and his friends as she waited, watching for Elaine. To her dismay, a short time later the diners turned down dessert. Caden, his wife, and Jason got up to leave.

"I'll see you at the station tomorrow!" Tag called after them as they left the table and headed toward the door.

Jan jumped up and hurried between the tables, intercepting them just before Caden stepped up to the checkout counter.

"Caden Gower?" she asked.

He stopped and looked at her curiously.

"I'm Jan Blake, from the tearoom."

"Oh sure," he said. "I've met your sister."

"Cousin," Jan said. "In fact, my cousin and I wanted to ask you something. After you're done here, would you mind speaking to me on the porch for a minute?"

"I guess not." Caden looked curious, and his wife gazed at Jan with a baffled look. Jason didn't seem to even notice her, but had stopped to have a word with someone at another table.

Jan stepped outside. Elaine's car pulled into the parking area, and she sighed. At least Elaine had returned in time, and with any luck, she had the visual aids with her.

"Hi!" Elaine strode across the pavement toward her.

"They're paying their bill," Jan said. "I'm glad you made it."

The door opened, and the Gowers came out.

"Hi, Caden," Elaine said cheerfully as she mounted the steps.

"Oh, hi, Elaine." The young fireman was about thirty, and he was dressed in khakis and a polo shirt. He held out a hand to Elaine. "Have you met my wife, Tanna?"

"Hi." Tanna smiled and shook hands. "You're from the tearoom?"

"Yes," Elaine said and introduced herself and Jan to the young woman.

"We were down near your house in the boat this afternoon," Jan said.

"You must mean the cottage," Caden said.

"Oh, so you don't live there?" Elaine asked.

"No, it was my folks' camp, and they gave it to Tanna and me for a wedding present. We actually live on the Bridge Road."

"Oh. But you go out there?"

"Sure," Caden said. "And we've spent a lot of time there this week, with my brother visiting." He nodded toward Jason.

Elaine smiled at him. "Hi, Jason."

"So, what did you want to ask?" Caden looked from her to Jan expectantly.

"It's about the lake monster," Jan said.

Caden's eyes widened.

"Lake monster?" Tanna said. "That's the silliest thing!"

"So you've heard the stories," Elaine said.

"Of course. How could anyone in town not hear them?" Tanna asked.

Elaine drew the plastic sheets from her tote bag. "Right. Well, someone sent these pictures to Lydia Pierce. She thinks they're supposed to be photos of the lake monster, but she won't print them in *The Wave* unless she finds out more. So this afternoon, we went looking for the location where these were taken, and we think that's the float at your cottage." She pointed to the floating object in the corner of one photo.

Caden took the sheet protector from her and stepped directly under a light and peered at the picture. Tanna squeezed in close to him and looked too.

"All right," Caden said after a long moment.

"Could I see?" Jason asked, and Caden put the picture in his brother's hand.

"That doesn't look like a monster to me," Tanna said.

"We don't think it's a real one," Jan replied. "But we'd like to know who took the picture."

"It's got to be a phony," Caden said. "Obviously. But it could be my float. There's really not enough of it showing in the picture to tell."

"We think there is," Elaine said. "We spent the entire afternoon inspecting floats on Chickadee Lake. I know the picture doesn't show much, but yours is the only one that matches it. We looked at the barrels, the wood frame, the canvas..."

"We're not saying you took the picture," Jan said quickly.

"But someone may have done it near your cottage," Elaine continued. "And there's more." She reached into her bag and pulled out the scrap of painted canvas.

"What's this?" Caden reached for the cloth.

Jason moved in closer, still holding the photo.

"We're not sure," Jan said, "but it could be a part of the make-believe monster."

"Where did you get it?" Jason asked.

"Some boys at the summer camp found it on shore not far from your beach," Elaine said. "They were down there picking up pinecones."

Caden's expression was puzzled. "So, you think maybe somebody put a fake monster out in the water near our float and took pictures and then...what? Lost part of it?"

"We don't know," Elaine said. "In fact, we don't even know that the piece of canvas has anything to do with it, but someone painted over a sheet of canvas, and I think it was part of something they built. We thought possibly the thing in these pictures was that object."

People going into the restaurant walked past them. Caden studied the photos again.

"Well, I think this whole thing is silly," Tanna said. "Let's go home."

Jan looked at Elaine and shrugged. "Our food is probably getting cold."

Elaine hesitated, then said, "Would you mind if we looked around your beach, Caden? We might find more debris, and maybe that would help us figure this thing out."

"Sure, knock yourselves out." Caden handed the scrap back to her. "But I don't see that it matters. We're still going to play up the stories to bring people in for the field day."

"Wait a minute," Tanna said. "You think the firefighters are doing this for publicity?"

"We don't think anything yet," Jan said quickly. "If they are, it's a pretty good advertising campaign. But that doesn't explain people like Clifton Young and—and—" She faltered, not wanting to name her grandsons.

"Chad Prentice," Elaine said. "And other people who claim they've seen something real this past week or two."

Jan nodded firmly. "Yes. We think there's something out there, and we don't like to see people scared. Somebody could get hurt."

"Aw, come on," Jason said. "A make-believe monster can't hurt anyone."

"That's true," Elaine replied, "but people can hurt themselves trying to get away from a make-believe monster."

Jan couldn't have said it better herself. "Well, have a nice evening." She collected the pictures, and Elaine put them and the piece of canvas back in her bag.

"Good night!" Elaine called, and the cousins went into the restaurant.

"There you are." Abby King stepped forward as they entered. "I had Burk put your plates under the warmer. I wasn't sure what had happened to you."

"Sorry," Jan said. "We're ready now."

Elaine nodded. "We sure are. Bring it on."

When they were seated again, Jan took a sip from her water glass and looked across the table at Elaine. "Wow."

"Yeah," said Elaine. "Did I sense a bit of tension there?"

"I don't think Tanna likes the idea that we might suspect the firefighters are behind this."

"Well, maybe it's not the whole fire department. Maybe it's just one fireman."

Jan nodded slowly. "Do you think Tag would level with us if he knew what was going on?"

"I don't know. He really wants his department to get that new equipment, and so do I. Thermal imaging cameras could save lives in this town."

Abby brought their entrees and smiled as she set them down. "Here we are. Enjoy!"

The crab cakes were good, but Jan couldn't stop thinking about the lake monster. She hoped that when the twins came back on Saturday for the field day, she had some real answers for them.

CHAPTER NINETEEN

About two dozen people turned out for the play rehearsal Monday evening, and Elaine listened carefully to Diane's instructions. The script sounded funny, full of clever lines and puns, with people trying to lure the lake monster out into the open. She jotted ideas for costumes on her note-pad. Meanwhile, Jan made a list of props that might enhance the production.

Diane had a few of the volunteers read various parts, and then announced, "Okay, I had certain actors in mind for some of the roles as I was writing this, and I think it's going to work well with Lydia Pierce as Myra, Russell Edmonds as Jake, and Des Murphy as the villain, Darius. Now, the Murphy twins have graciously agreed to portray Chick, the monster." Diane nod-ded and smiled at Des and Jo Murphy's teenaged sons, Nick and Chris. Nick waved, and they both grinned.

"That just leaves Hilda and Barney for main characters, and I've decided to put Chuck and Julie Yeaton in those slots." She looked around apologetically. "I hope the rest of you aren't too disappointed, because I need you all for the walk-ons. We'll need fishermen and tourists with small roles. Katelyn, I can see you as the woman who first spots Chick..."

While Diane talked, Elaine looked around at those who had volunteered for the production. Most of them were neighbors well known to her. She wondered if any of them might have had something to do with the reappearance of Lancaster's fictional monster.

Diane directed an initial read-through of the script and changed a few lines and stage directions.

"Great," she pronounced when they reached the end. "I expect the play will run about forty minutes. The parts aren't so large that they'll be hard to memorize this week. We're already selling tickets at Computer Gal, Tea for Two, the library, the Bookworm, the Hearthside, Tag's shop, Sylvia's Closet, A Little Something, and Sugar Plum. If you know of any more businesses that would like to take part in the ticket sales, let me know."

Des raised his hand, and she gave him a stack for Murphy's General Store.

"At last count, we've sold around sixty," Diane said, "and I'd like to fill up this theater for our show on Saturday."

"Give me a few, and I'll take them in to Gift Me," said retired state police detective Dutch Bigelow. He sold his bird carvings at the Gift Me shop, and Elaine was sure the owner, Marie Shenvi, would agree to offer the tickets to her customers.

"Thanks, Dutch," Diane said. "Now, Dutch is going to man the light board for us, and Jan and Elaine have agreed to work on costumes and props. Rachel Leon's doing makeup. Anything else?"

The troupe talked for a few more minutes, and then said good night and began to leave. Elaine leaned toward Jan.

"Time to have a little chat with Diane?"

"Fine with me," Jan said. It would be an opportunity to get some information from another one of the people on Jan's list of those who might be involved in the reappearance of Chick.

The cousins waited until Diane picked up her things and stepped into the aisle.

"Could we talk to you for a minute?" Elaine asked.

"Sure," Diane said. "Do you have some ideas for the props?"

"Well, yes, but we actually wanted to ask you about the monster. Not the onstage monster, but the one people think is out there in the lake."

Diane set her purse and tote bag on a chair. "What about it?"

Elaine looked at Jan.

Jan cleared her throat. "We're trying to find out who started the new stories about Chick."

"Does it matter?" Diane asked.

"Well, yes," Elaine said. "We think it might."

"Why?"

"We'd hate to see anyone scared by it and get hurt."

Diane laughed. "Who would be that scared of it? In real life, I mean. Of course, in my play, it's a real mania."

"Children," Jan said. "Somebody scared my little grandsons with a dummy monster. They weren't too badly traumatized, but one of them was slightly injured running away from it, and things could've turned out worse."

"I'm sorry about that," Diane said, "but I don't think anyone planned this phenomenon. It just started when someone said they saw something odd. Who was the first one to mention it? Wasn't it Clifton Young?"

"Yes, I think so," Elaine said. "At least, as far as I know. But he just made an innocent remark."

"But then other people remembered the old stories," Jan said.

"Well, I'll tell you what." Diane looked pointedly at Jan. "Bob Claybrook isn't helping the situation by being quoted in the newspaper about it. People are a lot more excited about it since that article ran. I'm just trying to capitalize on the mood to raise money for the fire department. I don't think the whole town is going to get hysterical over this."

"I do think it's mostly in good fun, with good intentions," Elaine said. "But you were one of the first to pick up on it and make something of it. We just wanted to check with you and be sure you didn't start the whole thing."

"Me? Absolutely not," Diane said. "And do you honestly see any harm in it? I'm sorry the kids were scared, but I had nothing to do with that, and as you said, it wasn't serious."

Jan realized she was taking the incident personally, because it was her little grandsons who had been affected. "I agree with you, and I didn't mean any offense, Diane. We're just checking with all the people who seem to have kept the stories going and might have a possible motive to do that. Yours is a good motive, I'm happy to say. And if that's all it is, then let's enjoy it."

Diane gazed at her uncertainly, then looked at Elaine. "Okay. Are we good?"

"Yes, we're fine," Elaine said. "Do you want us to rig up a costume for Chris and Nick that looks like the old drawings of Chick?"

"I haven't seen them, so I don't know."

"Well, drop by the tearoom tomorrow if you can," Elaine said. "I bought an old sign at Oldies But Goodies, and John Tuttle also loaned me an old sign the marina used in the late 1940s. Come look at them. I think it will give you an idea of what we're thinking—something not too scary."

"A friendly monster?" Diane asked.

"Sort of, yeah. That's what people portrayed it as back then, and we've got pictures of a pontoon boat that used Chick's silhouette. I do think it was one big lark for the town then, and it can be now."

"Sure." Diane looked earnestly at Jan. "I don't want anyone having a heart attack or falling off their dock because they're scared. I want to keep it light. But I honestly didn't start this. I only got the idea after I'd heard a couple of people had seen something in the water."

Jan reached out and squeezed her hand. "I believe you. Elaine and I will do everything we can to make the play a success."

Diane exhaled. "Thanks. Because we don't have a lot of time to prepare. I wish I'd thought of it sooner, but that would mean the monster stories started sooner, so I guess it's better to throw it together quickly."

"I'm sure it will be a lot of fun for everyone," Elaine said.

As they walked out to the car, she looked at Jan. "Did you mean what you said—let's just enjoy it?"

"Yes, I do. I think we need to stop worrying about it," Jan said. "Everyone else is having fun with it. Why shouldn't we?"

"SADIE TAYLOR PHONED," Jan told Elaine Wednesday afternoon. "She wanted to know if I could do eight dozen mini tarts and four plates of fancy cookies for the wedding reception on Sunday."

"Goodness, I thought she had a caterer and it was all set." Elaine was working on a green costume for Nick and Chris. Diane had approved her sketches the day before, and now it was just a matter of making it fit the boys and ensuring it looked cute.

"There was a problem," Jan said. "The caterer is sick. Anyway, Sadie couldn't get anyone else to serve a full meal at such short notice, so she's asking friends to make finger sandwiches and help provide side dishes and relishes. The cake is fine—it'll be delivered on time—but she wanted some other finger foods to fill in."

"Well, you're making all those frosted cookies for the field day on Saturday," Elaine said. "Do you think you can handle it?"

"Yes, I think so," Jan said.

"If you're sure."

"Well, I told her I would."

Elaine laughed. "Then I guess it's settled. Let me know if you need any help."

Nathan returned from his trip that day and called Elaine to ask her to meet him at the Pine Tree Grill for dinner. Jan had offered to handle all the props and costumes at the rehearsal alone that night so she could enjoy her time with Nathan, but Elaine was sure it would be too much.

"I really need to be there to do the fitting for the monster costume," she explained to Nathan.

"I guess I can go with you and help," Nathan said.

"No, you just got home. I'm sure you've got a lot of things to do."

"Is there someone else who could help Jan tonight?"

Elaine thought about it. "I can ask Jo Murphy. She can probably work with her boys better than anyone else. If she's not busy tonight, she'd probably be glad to."

"And what about Rose?" Nathan asked.

"You're right. There are people I could ask."

In the end, Jo agreed to help Jan that night, and Elaine entered the Pine Tree Grill guilt free.

Nathan was already seated, and Bianca Stadler, who co-owned the restaurant with her brother Mel, stood beside his table, chatting with him.

"Well, hi," Bianca said with a huge smile as Elaine approached.

Nathan sprang up to hold Elaine's chair.

"Hi. Thanks," Elaine said. "How are you, Bianca?"

"Great. Just great. Can I bring you something to drink?"

"Iced tea, please." When Bianca left the table, Elaine turned eagerly to Nathan. "So, how was Boston?"

"Much better than the last time I was there, when everything was frozen solid. New England cities definitely are at their best in summer."

Elaine smiled. "Find anything good for the auctions?"

"Did I ever. When can you come by and take a look?"

"Probably not until after the field day on Saturday. Jan and I will be pretty busy until the play is over."

"Oh, that's right," Nathan said. "Will I be in the way if I come hang around?"

"You don't have an auction that day?" Elaine asked.

"No. I've got one Friday night, and another on Sunday afternoon, but I'm free Saturday."

"I'd love to have you come," Elaine said. "The tearoom will be open that day, and Rose and Archie will handle it while Jan and I run a booth at the school."

"Well, put an apron on me," Nathan said with a laugh. "I can bus dishes or whatever you need."

"Thanks. Van and Amy are coming and bringing the twins, and Brian and Paula will be here too. In fact, Avery offered to help serve that day, and I think she's old enough now. Jan and I will close our booth as soon as the firemen's muster is over and go help get everyone into their costumes. You can come with us to the Old Grange Hall."

"Sounds like fun."

Bianca came back with their drinks, her bracelets jingling as she set down the glasses. "Are you ready to order?"

"Is your brother cooking tonight?" Nathan asked.

"Yes, Mel's out in the kitchen. What are you hankering for?"

"I think I'll have a steak. How about you, Elaine?"

"You know, I think I could eat one too right about now." They chose their side dishes, and Bianca left them again.

"You haven't asked me about Denny Gray," Nathan said with a teasing smile.

"I almost forgot about that," Elaine said. "Did you have time to do any snooping?"

"Yes, I did. You were right. Denny Gray is just the name of the company. However, it was chosen because the CEO and owner is the first Dennis Gray's great-grandson."

Elaine drew in a breath. "How about that? For some reason that pleases me. What's the current owner's name?"

"Dennis Clarkson. He's named for Dennis Gray."

"Well, that's interesting. And he owns the Dubois house now?"

"The company does, but they're planning to sell it, as you know. His new company specializes in real estate. He said that the Dubois house was one of their first purchases. He saw online that it was for sale last year and decided to buy it as an investment. He admits it was rather a whim, because of the family connection."

"Well, if he wants to sell many properties, he'd better make himself easier to get in touch with," Elaine said. "Do you think he would consider selling us the second chandelier for the tearoom?"

"You'll have to talk to him about that." Nathan pushed a business card across the table. "I didn't mention the chandelier, but he was a really nice guy and I'm sure he'd be happy to at least talk to you about the idea. I did say that you'd be interested in speaking with him and he assured me you'll be able to contact him here. The card and the number the workman you spoke to had was old, and he's just now getting a website built for the company—which I guess is why it was hard to find a presence for the company online. Contact him when you're ready." Nathan settled back in his chair. "So, tell me what you and Jan have found out about the lake monster. Bob called and told me you two have been working hard on it."

"We've mostly been going down a list of suspects Jan made."

"Suspects?"

"People who might have made a fake monster, for whatever reason—to draw in tourists, or to scare people—who knows. Anyway, we've tried to touch base with everyone who claimed to have seen something this month."

"And?" Nathan reached for his glass.

Elaine shrugged. "I think Clifton Young's statement was perfectly innocent. I'm not so sure about Chad Prentice. He may have been a little befuddled when he thought he saw something. Or maybe he really saw something—but didn't realize what it was."

"People see what they expect to see," Nathan said.

She nodded. "The other possibility is that he made it up and then created 'sightings' for other people."

"Who else was on your list?"

"Diane, only because the idea sparked her to write the play so quickly. But I don't see how she would have had time to create a fake monster." Elaine scrunched up her face. "She seemed a little hurt that Jan and I even asked about the possibility. Then there's Russell Edmonds. To me, he's a totally credible witness. But he didn't get a good look. What he saw going into the bog could have been a canoe or some other watercraft."

Bianca came back with their entrees, and Mel was with her. Each carried a tray with one of their steaks on a plate with a metal charger beneath it.

"Hi, y'all," Mel said. "Great to have you with us tonight."

"Thank you, Mel," Elaine said with a big smile.

"Good to see you too," Nathan added.

"Are you coming back to Trivia Night?" Mel asked. "We've got some great questions in the works for Friday."

"It's so much fun," Elaine said, "but Jan and I are working on the production at the Old Grange Hall for Saturday. Friday night is our dress rehearsal."

Bianca gave her an exaggerated frown. "Please don't tell me you're playing the part of the monster."

Elaine chuckled. "No, we're just helping everyone get the costumes and props they need."

"Well, good," Bianca said. "I can't see you or Jan portraying any kind of creature."

"Me neither," Mel said. "But if they had a part for a princess or a rodeo queen..."

Elaine's laugh grew louder, and Nathan winked at her.

"Now you're talking, Mel," he said.

"Can we bring you anything else?" Bianca asked.

"I think we're all set," Elaine replied.

"Well, enjoy your dinner." Bianca and Mel headed back toward the kitchen.

Elaine looked around. "They're doing well, aren't they? This place is busy every night, and on Fridays it's packed out."

"Great food and reasonable prices," Nathan said.

"And a lot of hard work." Elaine picked up her steak knife and fork. "One thing I can almost guarantee: whoever's behind these monster sightings has time on his hands."

"Right," Nathan said. "Nobody who works as hard as those two would put hours into something like that."

Elaine had to agree. While the Stadler siblings would probably throw in with other merchants to capitalize on the publicity Chick would bring, she seriously doubted they were behind it.

THURSDAY EVENING, AFTER Elaine and Jan had finished a dinner of chicken, apple, and walnut salad and shared a pitcher of iced chamomile on the porch, Jan headed to the sitting room to watch the news and put the finishing touches on the Murphy twins' costume. They had gotten a call that there were more than enough people to help with the play tonight so they weren't needed, so they decided that to stay home and working on costumes would be more productive than going to the Grange Hall to work on the play.

"I'll be right up," Elaine said. "First I want to try to reach Dennis Clarkson and see if we can find out more about the chandelier."

"Great idea," Jan said as she climbed the stairs, the ice in her still half-full glass of tea clinking.

Elaine settled into her desk chair, retrieved the business card Nathan had given her, and dialed the phone. It was after hours, so if she had to, she'd leave a message.

"Dennis Clarkson," a man answered a few rings in.

"Oh, hello!" Elaine said, startled. "I figured I would get your voice mail since it's so late."

"Well, you're in luck." Elaine could hear the smile in the man's voice. "I was just finishing up some paperwork before I head out for the evening. How can I help you?"

"My name is Elaine Cook, and I'm calling because I have a chandelier that used to belong to the Dubois house, and I was curious if you could tell me anything about it."

She heard an intake of breath in the receiver. "*You* have the chandelier?" he asked, sounding surprised.

"Why yes," Elaine said, now worried she'd made a mistake. "Is that...a problem?"

"Not at all—I'm glad it's in good hands, and we have recently decided to donate a lot of the items in the house to charity before we renovate it—but when did you...get it?"

"Oh, I found it here in Lancaster, a couple of months ago now, at the public works building, of all places. They were getting ready to throw it out, so I asked if I could have it."

"Of all places indeed," Dennis said, clearly confused. "That is just too strange for words. The house's groundskeeper reported it missing quite a long time ago."

Groundskeeper? "Do you mean Anthony Nichols?"

"Yes, that's the guy."

Elaine thought for a moment. She remembered specifically that Mr. Nichols, when she'd first met him on her trip to the mansion with Sasha, had said he didn't know anything about the house's chandeliers. Something didn't add up.

She wasn't sure what to say now, and she didn't want to make any accusations just yet, but she did have a hunch about what she should do next.

"Hello?" Dennis said.

"Oh, sorry," Elaine said, shaking her head. To cover her momentary silence, she changed the subject. "Well, if you're okay with the chandelier being in my possession, I'm wondering if you might also be interested in selling the other chandelier in the house to me."

"Oh, I can do even better than that. You can have it. It's nice to see someone so interested in it. And I'm glad it will be with its 'sister.'"

Elaine laughed. "That is way too kind of you, Mr. Clarkson, but I accept. We'll take great care of it, I promise."

"I have no doubt." Dennis said. In no time they'd made arrangements for the chandelier to be delivered to the tearoom.

"One more quick question," Elaine said. "I know this is strange, but I'd be curious if your groundskeeper knows anything about the, uh, maintenance and care of the chandelier. Do you think he would mind if you gave me his number?"

"Hmm," Dennis said. "I guess I can't think of what harm it could do. I haven't had much contact with him, but I should have his info here somewhere. Give me just a sec." His voice seemed to grow distant, and Elaine assumed he was scanning through the contacts on his phone. "Okay, here's the number," he said, and after Elaine had written it on a notepad in front of her, they exchanged pleasant goodbyes and she hung up.

Elaine tapped her pencil on the notepad. She felt like she was on to something. She dialed the number, and in a second stroke of good luck, the man answered.

"Mr. Nichols, hello, this is Elaine Cook. I met you a while ago when my daughter and I saw you on the Dubois property. I had asked you about a chandelier."

The man sounded tentative. "Hi," he said slowly. "I think I remember you. How can I help you?"

"Mr. Nichols, I don't want to assume anything"—she kept her voice warm—"but I have learned that you reported a chandelier missing, yet you had mentioned to me that you didn't know anything about the mansion's chandeliers. I'm wondering...is there more to this story?"

There was a long silence, and then he cleared his throat. "I suppose that was a bit of an untruth, what I told you, ma'am."

Elaine, her heart beginning to beat faster, tried to stay nonchalant. "How so?"

"Well, Mrs. Cook, I'm afraid I reported it missing because—well, I suppose there's no harm in telling you now—I took the chandelier myself."

Elaine was not surprised but still somehow couldn't believe her ears. "You did?" she asked.

"I'm afraid I did," he said. "I can tell you the story if you really want to hear it."

"I really, really do," Elaine said kindly.

"Well, see, at the time, my wife, Julia, had just been diagnosed with stage-four brain cancer, and she had only a very short time to live. She used to come along sometimes when I checked on the mansion and she always *oohed* and *ahhed* over the chandeliers. I figured nobody even lived there, nobody would care if it was missing. I would report it as if it had been stolen by someone else to protect my secret, and take it home to Julia." He paused a moment, sounding almost relieved to be telling the story. "I installed it in our home, and only a couple days later, my bride passed away."

"I'm so sorry," Elaine said, her heart filling with compassion.

"Me too, Mrs. Cook, me too," he said. "That was a while ago now, but time hasn't healed this wound as quickly as I hoped it would."

"I can totally understand," Elaine said, thinking of her beloved late husband, Ben. She inhaled. "So, then, how did the chandelier end up at the public works building if you'd installed it in your house?"

"Well, that's the strange part of the story," he said. "Only a week after she passed, I turned it on, and it started to spark. Before it could cause any damage, I turned it off, but I knew right then and there—those sparks were a message from my wife to return the chandelier."

Elaine didn't know what to make of that, but she did, of course, recall Roland Nance needing to rewire the chandelier when he reinstalled it above their dining room after it had sent off sparks. Mr. Nichols must have created a short somewhere during his own installation, which had caused the issue.

He continued, "So, I didn't want to bring it back to the Dubois house because of the sparks—you never know, they could have caused a fire, and I'm no electrical expert. I had a friend, Stan, in the public works office, and since he was an electrician, I thought I would get his advice. But when I pulled up to the office, I saw one of the contractors who worked at the Dubois house. I panicked, set the chandelier by the Dumpster behind the building, and drove off. I figured I'd come back later to get it."

"But you never did?"

"No, I did. I returned, but the chandelier was gone. I didn't know what happened to it. At that point, though, I figured it was out of my hands. No more sparks flew in my house after that, so I believed I had done right by my wife." Mr. Nichols was silent for a moment. "But I suppose now I need to do right by the owners of the house."

"Actually," Elaine said, "I'm not so sure. I think I can safely say that this secret can just be ours. Only a few minutes ago I spoke with the owner of the house, Dennis Clarkson, who allowed me to keep the chandelier, and in fact is giving me the second one. Since I'm now the owner of both the chandeliers, I have no problem dropping this whole thing, if you don't mind."

He sighed. "I don't mind at all," he said. "Thank you. To tell the truth, I feel like a weight has been lifted off my shoulders. I've been holding this story in for some time now. When you originally asked about the chandelier, I panicked, but I'm so glad you called me on it now."

Elaine smiled to herself. "Well, I'm glad you're glad. And if you ever want to visit the chandelier, it's installed safely, and no sparks are flying anymore. And who knows, your wife might like to know it's in a good home. Come by anytime for tea," she said.

"I might just do that," Mr. Nichols said, and shortly thereafter, hung up. Elaine stood up, took a deep breath, and headed up the stairs to tell Jan everything she'd just learned.

CHAPTER TWENTY

By Friday afternoon, Main Street was decorated with banners and signs depicting the lake monster and fire engines. The ball field at the school was set up for the first events of the firemen's muster, and the vendors' booths were in place around the edges of the playground. Excitement ran through the tearoom, and it seemed all the customers were talking about the next day's events.

Nathan and Bob took Elaine and Jan to a late dinner at the Pine Tree Grill after the dress rehearsal.

"Diane's nerves were jangling," Jan observed as she enjoyed her dessert.

"She'll be all right tomorrow," Elaine said. "I admit there were some loose ends, but it will all come together."

"Yeah, but it's our job to make sure the monster costume comes together." Jan rolled her eyes.

Elaine laughed and looked at Bob and Nathan. "The Murphy boys were having a little trouble keeping the front and the back halves of Chick together tonight. I had sewn it with snaps, but I think I'd better replace those with Velcro, to make sure they don't pop open during the rehearsal."

"Why don't you just sew them into it tomorrow?" Nathan asked, his eyes twinkling.

"Oh, they'd love that," Elaine said.

"Yep." Jan made a face. "I think Nick is a little claustrophobic already. He should have been the front half."

"You're coming tomorrow, right?" Elaine asked.

"I'll mosey over to help you," Nathan said.

Bob shrugged. "I'll come for the play, but you two will be tied up all day with your vendor booth, won't you?"

"Probably," Jan said. "And when it's over, we'll head to the Old Grange Hall to get ready for the performance."

Elaine sighed. "I guess you two won't see much of us at the play, since we'll be backstage the whole time."

"We can sit out front with your family and clap loud and whistle," Nathan said.

"Now, that's the spirit." Elaine regained her smile. "You can have dinner at our house afterward. It will be chaotic, but you seem to hold your own at our crazy family gatherings."

"I'm in." Nathan arched his eyebrows in Bob's direction. "How about it, Bob? Shall we cheer until we're hoarse and demand an extra curtain call, then join the mob at the tearoom for dinner?"

"Sounds like my kind of evening," Bob said, reaching for Jan's hand.

"Good evening, folks!"

Elaine couldn't see his face, but she knew it was Garrett Wolfe behind the video camera pointed at them. Sadie's cousin was getting to be a pest.

"All set for the big day tomorrow?"

"Yes, we are," Jan said.

"What will you be doing?" Garrett asked.

"We're selling cookies and lemonade and iced tea," Jan replied.

"And after the muster, Jan and I are helping backstage with the production of *Chick of Chickadee Lake*," Elaine added.

"And Nathan and I will be spectators," Bob said wryly.

Garrett lowered his camera for a moment and grinned at them. "Too bad you missed the trivia contest earlier."

"We came in just as it was ending," Elaine said.

"I've heard you four are past champions," Garrett said in smooth tones.

"We are," Bob admitted. "Did you film it tonight?"

"I sure did. Absolute small-town rivalry and fun."

"Who won?" Jan asked.

"A music teacher and a bookstore clerk."

"Oh, we know them," Elaine said. "That's Frank and Katelyn."

"We could have beat 'em," Nathan said.

"Yup, we have before." Bob winked at Jan.

Garrett laughed. "Enjoy." He moved on, swinging his camera toward the next table.

"Looks like all the advertising paid off," Jan said as she peeked out the front window, watching the crowd milling along Main Street on Saturday morning.

"It sure did," Elaine said.

"The advance article Tag got in the Waterville paper probably helped a lot," Jan said, "and of course, Candace's and Lydia's stories."

Fire crews from three other towns were coming to compete against the Lancaster Volunteer Fire Department in the muster, which would begin at ten o'clock.

"We'd better pack up our cookies and drinks and get over to our booth." Elaine walked quickly to the kitchen, where Rose was putting on water to heat for tea. Jan was right on her cousin's heels.

"Are you sure you and Archie can handle things here?" Jan asked.

"Oh yeah," Rose said. "Everyone will be over at the school grounds and we probably won't have many customers until the muster's over. We'll be fine."

"Okay, but call me if you need extra help," Jan said. "We'll send Paula and Avery over if you do. Sometimes people want a quiet place to take a load off their feet, and this is the perfect spot for that."

She had baked ahead all week for the event, as well as for Sadie's wedding, and had frozen her special firefighters' field day cookies. Elaine loved her dalmatians—dog-shaped ginger cookies frosted in white, with spots of chocolate icing. But Jan's favorites were the lake monster cookies. She'd come up with her own design for sugar cookies that included green icing and red cinnamon dots for the eyes. To tell the truth, they were pretty cute, if she did say so herself.

Archie helped carry insulated jugs of lemonade and iced tea out to Elaine's car.

"If Amy or Brian shows up here with their families, send them over to the school," Jan told him.

Tara, Jan's younger daughter, was already on the grounds when they arrived, setting up a display of her jewelry. Sasha and Brody had hoped to come later, but Sasha had texted to say she was tied up in a meeting with a potential client and would hopefully meet them later. Tara's booth was right next to Elaine and Jan's, and Nathan was helping her carry containers over from her car.

"Hi!" Tara came over and kissed them both. "There's already quite a crowd. Can I help you set up?"

"We're good, Tara," Elaine said. "Nathan can help us."

"Okay. People are already wandering around looking at merchandise," Tara said. "We're not even supposed to open for another half hour."

Jan smiled. "Guess we'd better get cracking."

Nathan helped them put up the sign that read Tea for Two.

"What now?" he asked.

"You can help Elaine," Jan said as she wiped down the booth's countertop. "She's getting the first batches of iced tea. Then you can hang up the price lists while I arrange the baked goods."

Tara kept an eye on her own booth while they worked, and within ten minutes the Tea for Two station was open for business. Almost immediately, a line formed to buy cold drinks and cookies. Faith Lanier, who carried some of Tara's jewelry at her gift shop, A Little Something, stopped by to see what new designs Tara had come up with for the field day, and soon other customers gathered to examine her pendants, bracelets, and earrings.

Amy, Van, and the twins arrived in the middle of the rush. Max and Riley ran into the booth and hugged Jan and Elaine.

"We're so glad to see you," Jan told the little boys, "but you guys are going to have to let us work."

"Do you need help?" Amy asked.

"I'll take the boys over to the playground if you want to stay here," Van said. The Fire Department Auxiliary was organizing children's games there.

"Maybe I should go with you, if Amy wants a turn here," Nathan said.

"We're going to be in a race," Riley said proudly.

"Great! I hope you win." Jan grinned as Van and Nathan led the boys away. "Good luck, Max!"

Amy pitched in to help serve the customers. As soon as the muster was announced, the crowd around the booths thinned. From where they were situated, the women could see some of the events. Most of the patrons drifted over to the ball field and playground to watch the hose roll contest and the bucket brigade. The ladder climb was especially exciting, as the firefighters raced to reach the top of a tall ladder extended from one of the Oakland Fire Department's trucks.

Just before noon, the midnight alarm event was announced over a loudspeaker.

"Oh, I'd love to see that," Tara said.

The crowd was now so dense they could see only part of the ball field, where the four fire departments would compete simultaneously in the event. Four firefighters from each team would begin by lying down at the starting line, as though asleep. When the alarm sounded, all would jump up and run twenty-five feet to don their turnout gear, then run another fifty feet to their fire trucks, then lay a hundred feet of hose as fast as they could.

"Go on," Elaine said to Tara. "We can watch your booth. Nobody's buying right now."

"I'll go with you," Amy said.

Tara and Amy hurried over to join the onlookers. Tempting smells reached them from the barbecue area, where the auxiliary members were beginning to serve lunch.

Tara returned twenty minutes later with her brother, Brian, and Paula and their two daughters.

"Look who I found at the ball field," Tara said.

Elaine and Jan greeted the family.

"So, Penzance won the midnight alarm?" Jan asked after hugs all around. She and Elaine had heard the announcement, but she was sure they would want to discuss the contest.

"Yeah, by like five seconds," Avery said.

Tara grinned. "You should have seen Tag yelling at the crew. He was hilarious."

They had a rush on iced drinks as the field was set up for the water barrel event, where teams would use their fire hoses to roll a plastic barrel the length of the playground. It was a favorite with the crowd, and the crews were almost guaranteed to soak each other after they reached the finish line.

"We'd better get over there if we want to see the excitement," Paula said. "We'll come back when this event is over."

"Why don't I just meet you at the barbecue?" Jan suggested. She and Elaine had agreed to swap off at lunchtime so that they could both eat the grilled chicken dinner in support of the fire department.

"Okay," Paula said. They ambled off, and Jan's stomach rumbled as the fragrance from the grills wafted over them.

Jan and Elaine managed to stagger their breaks to get lunch, with Nathan, Amy, Paula, and Avery helping man the booth in their absence, and then the cousins went back to work. Their supplies were dwindling fast.

"I'm going to run to Murphy's for extra ice," Elaine said when another event was announced and the crowd gathered around the edges of the playing field.

"Good," Jan said. "We'll need it, but couldn't Nathan do that?"

Elaine laughed. "He could, but he ran into some friends and wandered off with them. I'll go."

"Can you believe we sold over fifteen dozen cookies today?" Jan shook her head.

"Yes, I can. Should I go by the house and get more from the freezer?"

Jan took stock. "No, I think we're good. The muster will be over soon. We'll get another rush, but it won't last long. If we sell out, that's okay."

Elaine waved and headed for the car.

After the muster games finished and the awards were presented, Jan expected some people to hang around the grounds to play at the game booths and browse the merchandise, and at four o'clock, everyone would likely head to the Grange Hall for the play. She and Elaine needed to arrive there by three to start helping the actors with their costumes.

She took a fresh container of cookies from beneath the counter as two couples came over.

"I was hoping you'd be here today," Maureen Oakley said. "I'll have sweet tea and one of those adorable cookies." She pointed out the lake monster cookies to her husband, Alan.

He laughed. "Give me one of those too, Jan. Oh, and we've got to have some of those." He pointed to the dalmatian cookies. Alan was the proud owner of two dogs, a spotted Brittany spaniel named Dot and a German shorthaired pointer named Dash.

"Can we get a dozen of those to take home?" Maureen asked. "Our grandchildren are staying over. They'll love them."

"Sure." Jan gave them each a cookie with a napkin and opened a cardboard takeout box for the extras. "Tea for you, Alan?"

"Sure thing."

She was getting beverages for the second couple when Jack Weston stopped by Tara's booth. Jan smiled as she worked. Those two would make a match of it, she was sure.

When her customers had moved on, Jack called, "Hey, Jan! How are you doing?"

"Good, Jack. Want a Chick cookie? I made twelve dozen, and I only have about a dozen left."

"Wow." He sauntered over and smiled at the array of monster-shaped cookies. "I'll bet those are the hot seller of the day."

"They went pretty fast. What'll you drink with it? Iced tea? Lemonade?"

"I'll take some lemonade."

"Jack!"

Jack turned, and Jan looked up to see who was shouting his name.

Zale Atherton, Macy's daughter-in-law, ran toward them and skidded to a stop in front of Jack, gasping for breath.

"Shane just called me. He went home early to get a boat ready for a family in one of our cottages, but the family came back after fifteen minutes on the water. They said they saw the lake monster between our place and the outlet to the bog."

"Really?" Jack set his cookie on the counter. "Can I take a rain check on that, Jan?"

"I'll save it for you," Jan said. "Go."

Jack and Zale ran for their cars.

Elaine was back a moment later with a large bag of ice in her picnic cooler. "I just saw Jack tear out of the parking lot," she said as she lifted the cooler out of her trunk. "What's going on?"

"A family at Green Glade saw the monster," Jan said. "Jack's going over there."

Elaine's eyes widened.

"Why don't you go?" Jan suggested. "I'm dying to know if they find anything."

"Oh, but—"

"Mom and I can handle the two booths, and Paula's coming back," Tara said. "You go, Elaine."

"Are you sure?"

"Yes," Jan and Tara said together.

Elaine patted the cooler. "The ice is in here." She hurried back to her car.

ELAINE DROVE AS quickly as safety allowed out to Main Street. A few cars were leaving the school yard, but more were heading in. As she passed the tearoom, she noted that there weren't many cars out front. She'd expected that, with everyone over at the muster. Rose and Archie would be having an easy day.

She drove to the cottage road and saw a cloud of dust hovering over the powdery surface of the dirt lane that led into Green Glade. She couldn't be far behind Jack and Zale.

Sure enough, when she reached the group of cottages, Zale was pulling up in front of the office. Jack's pickup truck had rolled on down toward the dock. Elaine followed him. There would be enough room down there, where they loaded and unloaded boats, for her to park out of Jack's way.

Shane was just nosing a small motorboat in toward the dock with his cell phone to his ear. Jack met him at the end of the dock. Elaine scrambled out of her car and hurried down the length of the wooden wharf to join them.

"Did you find anything?" she called, puffing a little, as Jack climbed into Shane's boat.

"Come on!" Jack held out a hand to her, and Elaine jumped down into the boat, glad she'd worn her tennis shoes. Jack steadied her, and she sat down on one of the thwarts. As Shane gunned the motor, Jack leaned close and yelled, "Shane saw something. He was going after it when I called him. He thought it might be better to come back and get me. You stay low when we get near the bog, okay?" He handed Elaine a flotation cushion and clambered to the bow.

Shane guided the boat toward the bog with the throttle wide open. When they got close, he slowed down and eased into the channel that meandered through the bog. On either side, tall reeds rose, and stumpy pines grew up from clumps of grass. Wild rice bent its seed heads over the water, and Elaine spotted a couple of bluebird houses people had mounted out there for the songbirds.

Jack held up a hand, and Shane set the motor to idle. Jack pointed to his right.

"Easy now."

Shane kept the boat moving very slowly. They came to a place where hummocks of vegetation nearly clogged the channel, and to the side, jammed in between the cattails, was a raft about eight feet long, made of pine logs. On top of it sat a rather bedraggled lump of green canvas, wire, and wood.

Jack turned and grinned at them. "What about that, eh, Shane?"

"Looks like we found the monster's lair," Shane said.

Elaine squinted her eyes nearly shut and stared at the pile of floating junk. If she used her imagination, she could see how it might have once looked a bit like a floating—or swimming— reptile of sorts. Green. Bright green with smears of black and yellow. And bright-red eyes.

Jack looked at her. "Think that would scare a couple of seven-year-olds, Elaine?"

"Yes, I do. Especially if it reared up out of the water at them unexpectedly. But why is it all smashed now?"

"I think whoever put it here was finished with it and beat it down so it would be flatter and less visible."

"But where is he?" She swiveled to look at Shane. "Was it a he? Did you see someone put it in here?"

"I saw a small boat towing the thing," Shane said. "I called Zale and told her to get Jack. By the time I got my boat out to go after it, they were out of sight. I puttered down this way, watching the shore. I suspected they might be headed for the bog. But before I reached the outlet, Jack called and said he was on his way, so I went back to the dock to pick him up. I'd just got there when you came."

Jack nodded. "They towed it in here. And I think you're right, Shane. That was going to be the monster's last swim. But they were in a hurry. They must have known someone had seen them."

"Was it one person or more?" Elaine asked.

"I only saw one for sure," Shane said, "but there could have been a second person in the boat, obscured by that thing. I was too far away, and I didn't have binoculars."

"Well, why did they ruin it?" Elaine asked. "Even if somebody caught them, why smash it up? They could have used it for fun or for advertising."

"I don't know," Jack said. "We may never know. But I want to get it out of here if I can and take it to my garage and see what I can learn about it. Maybe something will give me a hint as to who built it."

"Okay," Shane said. "If you can get it out of there, I'll tow it back for you."

Elaine looked around. "Where's the nearest place the person towing it could dock? He got to shore without you seeing him."

"*Hmm.*" Jack pointed farther into the bog. "There's a spot where the bog edges the pine woods. You could put a small boat in there."

Half an hour later, they motored slowly toward the dock at Green Glade, pulling what was left of the monster. They were only a quarter mile out when Shane pointed across the lake toward the town boat landing.

"Something's going on over there."

Jack trained his binoculars on the area, frowning. After a minute, he lowered them and shrugged. "There's a lot of people, but I can't really tell what's going on."

When Shane moored the boat at Green Glade Cottages, Jack helped Elaine climb onto the dock.

Zale came running down from the office.

"You guys! You'll never guess what happened." She stopped short on the dock and stared past their boat at the bedraggled creature on the raft. "Wow! You found it!"

"Yeah," Shane said. "Not too impressive, is it?"

"So, what were you going to tell us?" Elaine asked.

"Oh. The firefighters."

"What about them?" Jack asked.

"Well, when word got around that people had seen the monster and you went after it, Jack, everyone rushed over to the town boat landing to see if they could see anything. And while they were out there, somebody stole all the fire department's ticket money from the muster."

"What?" Elaine looked at her watch. The muster would only just have finished.

Zale shrugged. "Tag had all the ticket money and the barbecue proceeds in a metal box."

"Surely he didn't leave it sitting there with no one watching it," Jack said.

"No, he gave it to Rachel to put in the safe at the fire station. But she said while she was opening the safe, someone shoved her and grabbed the box and ran out. She didn't see who it was—just somebody wearing turnout gear. She saw him run out the door, but when she got up and limped over there, he was gone."

"You think a fireman stole the money?" Shane asked, frowning.

"I don't know. Someone in a firefighter's coat, for sure. Dan Benson's over there talking to Rachel and Tag."

Shane shook his head. "Have you been here the whole time?"

"Yeah. I wanted to know what you found out. I almost took another boat and followed you, but I decided I'd better wait here, in case you called needing something."

"So how do you know about the ticket money?" Jack asked.

Elaine wanted to know that too, but the answer should have been obvious.

"Your mother called," Zale said, looking at Shane. "She was at the school grounds when it happened."

Elaine met Jack's gaze, and she could almost read his mind. Trust Macy to get the news out. She meant well, but she was probably the one who announced the monster sighting and sent the crowd to the boat landing too.

But why would she say the monster was near the boat landing? It wasn't—it was farther down the lake and on the other side, near the bog. Elaine turned and looked out over the calm water.

Something didn't add up.

CHAPTER TWENTY-ONE

Jan held an ice pack to Rachel Leon's head while Alicia Brooks got out the fire station's first aid kit. Trooper Dan Benson stood by patiently, and Tag King and Caden Gower stood watch at the door of the station, so nobody else except firefighters could come in.

"Thanks, Jan," Rachel said.

"Hurts pretty bad, huh?" Jan asked sympathetically.

"It sure does."

Alicia moved in with the first aid kit, and Jan stood back. She was privileged to be among the first on the scene because Dan and his wife, Charlotte, had been talking to her and Tara at their booths when Dan received Rachel's urgent call. She'd thrown caution aside and left Tara alone to tend both the jewelry and refreshment booths and hitched a ride with the fire chief.

A few more firemen arrived, and Tag assigned them to keep watch with Caden. He came over to join Jan, gazing anxiously at Rachel.

When Alicia had dabbed a small amount of blood from Rachel's head and applied a bandage, Dan cleared his throat.

"You should probably go to the clinic, Rachel. Do you want me to drive you?"

Rachel laughed. "I've got EMTs all around me. Thanks, but I think I'm okay."

"You might have a concussion," Alicia said.

Tag nodded. "You ought to see Dr. McInnis, just to be sure. They might want an X-ray."

"Is this my cue for a head X-ray joke?" Rachel asked with a wry smile.

A phone rang, and Tag strode to the desk and answered it. "Lancaster Fire Department." After a pause, he said, "What's wrong?" He listened for a moment. "We'll be right there."

He hung up and made another call. "Des, take the ambulance to the boat landing. Swing by here if there's nobody else over at the school grounds to go with you. Drowning scare. They pulled the kid out, but he may need treatment."

He hung up and faced them. "I guess you heard. The ambulance was still at the school. Des said Russell Edmonds was right next to him when I called, and they'll take the ambulance over."

"Everything all right at the boat landing?" Dan asked.

"Near drowning. A boy fell off the dock in all the excitement over possibly seeing the monster. I was told the sheriff's department has some men over there for crowd control."

"Okay." Dan turned to Rachel as the ambulance passed the station, siren screaming. "Let me ask you a few questions. That will get me started, and then you probably should do like the chief says and get over to the clinic."

Tag patted Rachel's shoulder. "We'll take you in style when the ambulance gets back."

"No way," Rachel said. "But if you insist, I'll let Alicia drive me."

Tag nodded. "I do insist—however you want to get there."

"I know you told me on the phone what happened, but I'd like you to go over it again," Dan said, looking down at his pocket notebook. "See if you remember any details you might have left out before. Anything."

"Well, Tag gave me the cash box at the end of the muster."

"Where was it during the events?" Dan asked.

"They had it at the gate, where they collected the ticket money."

"At the little booth on the driveway, where everyone drives in?"

Rachel nodded. "I think Mark Payson was in charge of it. They kept it for us all day. And Caden's wife, Tanna, collected money at the barbecue. When they were done serving, she gave that to Tag too."

Dan wrote in his notebook. "So, the cash box contained the gate receipts and the barbecue sales? How much?"

Rachel looked to Tag.

"It was over three thousand altogether."

Dan grimaced "I'm sorry. That's a big loss."

"Yeah, we had plans for it." Tag sighed.

"Let's not give up on the prospect of getting it back," Alicia said.

"Right. You carried the cash box over here," Dan said, looking at Rachel, and she nodded. "Was there anyone in the station when you got here?"

"No. It was locked up. All the calls would go through the regional com center. If there was an emergency, they would have paged Tag, the EMTs, and the crew leaders."

"We're a volunteer department," Tag reminded him. "We don't have the budget to keep someone here 24/7. Des Murphy lives the closest, and he's usually the first to open up when we get a call."

Dan made notes. "Who has keys?"

"Me, Des, and the town manager," Tag said. "I loaned mine to Rachel today."

Dan wrote it down. "So, Rachel, tell me what happened when you got here."

"I unlocked the small door and went in through the lounge and in here to the office. I set the cash box on top of the safe and started to open it."

"That's a pretty small safe," Dan noted, eyeing the box. They were available in any big box store or home improvement center.

"We don't ever keep much money here," Tag said. "Petty cash, and when the EMTs get paid, I put their checks in there until they pick them up. Everyone else serves on a volunteer basis. The safe is just…well, it's not really going to stop someone who's serious about theft. They could pick up the whole thing and leave with it. But it gives us the illusion of security."

Dan nodded, writing. Jan thought about the YouTube video she'd watched once while digging into another case. It had showed how easy it was to open a small home safe like that, but she didn't say anything.

"In this case," Rachel said, "they didn't even have to touch the safe. They just shoved me down and grabbed the cashbox."

"Did he hit you on the head?" Tag asked.

She made a face. "No, I hit it on the corner of the desk when I fell."

"How did they get in here?" Dan asked.

Rachel looked at him blankly. "I don't know. I suppose they followed me in."

"You didn't lock the door behind you?"

She scowled. "No. I should have. Hindsight is twenty-twenty, you know? I thought I'd just be a second, and it wouldn't matter."

"Are you sure he wasn't in here when you came in?" Tag asked.

"I suppose he could have been. But I did hear a noise behind me, and he couldn't have come in from the truck bays or upstairs. There was only the lounge and the door back behind me."

Jan glanced at the window in the door leading out to the truck bays. All of the fire equipment was over at the school today, so the garage part of the fire station was empty. They had wanted to make a good showing for the muster and let the residents see what fire equipment they had. Kids were allowed to climb on the ladder truck all day, under supervision.

"Okay," Dan said to Rachel. "You heard a noise. The door? Footsteps?"

"It was more like movement—clothes swishing or—I don't know. Just a quiet movement, and suddenly I realized I wasn't alone. But before I could turn around, someone slammed into me, and I fell."

"Did you black out?" Dan asked.

"Not completely. I guess you could say I was stunned." Rachel gave a nervous little laugh and put a hand up to the bandage Alicia had put on her head. "I saw stars too. That's not just a saying—it's true. I went down, but I turned and tried to see what hit me. The outside door in the lounge was closing. All I saw of the person was a turnout coat and feet."

"Was he wearing a hat?" Dan asked.

Rachel squinted, trying to remember. "I don't know."

"What about his feet? You saw them. Was he wearing boots?"

She frowned. "No. He had on running shoes. I'm not even sure it was a man. Could have been a woman, but I did see the Nikes."

"Okay." Dan closed his notebook. "You'd better get over to the clinic and get checked out."

Tag stepped forward. "I called Matt McInnis. He'll meet you and Alicia over there. He and Andrea are standing by to examine the boy who fell in the water too. Do you want me to come, Rachel?"

"No, you'd better get over to the school grounds. And—" She broke off and looked at Jan. "How long until the play? I have to do the makeup!"

Jan checked her phone. "We have a little over an hour. Just go and see Dr. McInnis. If you're late, Elaine and I will handle things until you get there."

"But your cookie booth—"

"My kids are here, and they'll help pack up the booth. Don't worry. I'm heading right over there now."

Jan tried to sound calm, but she was a little nervous herself. She and Elaine should be at the theater soon. The makeup wasn't complicated for this production, but they would need some time, especially if Rachel was delayed at the clinic. She hurried out to her car. When she reached the driveway to the school, she felt she was swimming against the tide. Dozens of cars were leaving the grounds.

After a short wait, she was able to get in and drive slowly to the line of sales booths. The vendors were packing up their merchandise. She found Brian and Van taking down the tearoom booth, while Nathan, Paula, and Avery helped Tara with hers. Amy sat on a camp stool nearby, and Kelly kept the twins occupied, kicking a soccer ball around on the grass nearby.

"Oh good, you're here," Brian said as she approached. "We packed up all the food and put it in Van's trunk. They said to break down the booth, and fire department volunteers will pick it up and take it to storage."

"Great," Jan said. "Thank you, guys."

"So, what's going on?" Van asked.

"And where's Elaine?" Nathan added, and the others came to stand beside him and listen.

"I was over at the fire station," Jan said. "Rachel Leon was injured, and someone stole the cashbox with the money from the tickets and the barbecue from her."

"Oh no," Amy said. "The firefighters worked so hard!"

"Are the police on it yet?" Van asked.

"Yes. Trooper Benson was there."

"Elaine went to Green Glade," Tara said. "We heard some-one had spotted the monster again, and she followed Jack. Then the word got out, and half the people who were here trooped over to the lake to find out if they could see anything. I don't know where Elaine is now. I expected her to come back before this."

"Green Glade?" Brian's eyebrows shot up. "We heard it was near the boat landing. That's not near the Athertons' cottages."

"Yeah," Paula said. "We almost went over there, but every-one was dashing for the parking lot, like a stampede. We decided to stay out of it."

"Maybe I should drive over to Macy's and see if Elaine's there," Nathan said.

"Hi!" They all turned to see that Elaine had driven up close to the booths and was getting out of her car.

"There you are," Jan said, a little relieved to see her in one piece.

Nathan strode over to join her. "Are you all right?"

"I'm fine," Elaine said. "Is Rachel okay? And did they get the money back?"

"She's at the clinic, but I think she'll be all right," Jan said. "And no, they didn't get the money back yet. We need to go home and unload everything and get over to the Grange Hall. If Rachel is late, we'll have to cover her makeup duties too."

"I could help you with that," Tara said.

"And we can go unload at the house," Brian added.

"I can go with them," Nathan said.

Jan looked around at her children and grandchildren. "You know what? I'm going to let you do that."

"That would help a lot," Elaine agreed. "Thanks. If anyone's hungry, get yourselves a snack."

"Oh please," Amy said. "I think we all stuffed ourselves on chicken and cookies and cotton candy and ice cream. I may never eat again."

"Tara, why don't you come with us?" Jan asked.

"Okay, Mom."

"Hey, did you see the monster?" Avery asked.

Kelly and the boys had come over to listen, and the twins' eyes grew round.

"Yeah, did you see it?" Max asked.

Elaine smiled. "As a matter of fact, I did. And you know what?"

"What?" Riley asked, his face full of wonder that threatened to become panic.

"It was a fake," Elaine said, smiling. "Someone built a green thing like a dinosaur or an alligator on a raft. It was hard to tell what it looked like exactly, because they'd smashed it. It was all broken. We think they did that before they shoved it into the reeds in the bog to make it harder to spot. But Jack found it."

"We heard it was at the town boat launch," Amy said.

"Nope. It was down in the bog, stuck into the reeds like someone was trying to hide it."

"Why would they do that?" Jan asked.

"Well, my theory—if anyone wants to hear it . . ." Elaine looked around at them.

They all cried, "Yeah!" and "We do!"

She smiled. "My theory is that whoever built the monster was finished with it. As soon as the crowd started dashing over to the boat landing, they got it out of sight. Maybe even before that—as soon as the guests from Green Glade got a look at it. All they needed was for word to get out that the monster was seen on the lake today."

"Why?" Avery asked, frowning.

"I think it was a diversion," Elaine said.

Nathan nodded. "Of course. It made the firefighters gather up their money and send it over to the fire station."

Elaine nodded. "The bank isn't open today."

Jan said, "Tag and the others were going to help with crowd control at the landing. He told Rachel to put the money in the little safe at the station. As soon as he heard what happened to Rachel, he and a few of the others went back over there."

They all looked at each other, puzzling over it.

"I don't understand why somebody said the monster was seen at the boat landing, when it wasn't near there," Jan said. "Why not tell people it was near the bog?"

"That's how rumors go," Paula said.

Van frowned. "Maybe they wanted a place big enough for a lot of people to gather."

"Then why not show the monster near the landing?" Jan asked.

"*Hmm.*" Brian looked at his mother. "Maybe because there's no place for the person putting it out there to hide by the landing, like there is at the bog."

"And by 'that person,' do you mean the thief?" Elaine asked.

Tara met Elaine's gaze. "The thief did all that so he could steal the money?"

"I don't know," Elaine admitted.

Jan didn't know either. Something was fishy, that was for sure.

ELAINE AND JAN gathered the things they would need and entrusted the money they'd earned at their booth to Brian. While Jan's children and grandchildren headed for the house with Nathan, the two of them and Tara drove the short distance to the Old Grange Hall Theater.

"You know, something's not right with that story about the monster being at the boat landing," Jan said as they walked toward the old white two-story building.

Elaine nodded. "I have my doubts if the thief would have time to tow the monster into the bog and make it back to the fire station in time to attack Rachel and steal the cashbox."

"Exactly."

"Well, Dan and Jack are working on it." Elaine smiled at her cousin. "The show must go on."

"Yes, but let's think about it while we get everyone's costumes ready and lay out the props," Jan said.

Diane was backstage when they arrived at the theater.

"Thank heavens you're here! I heard what happened to Rachel. We might not have our makeup artist."

"My daughter Tara offered to help," Jan said. "She's pretty good."

Tara stepped forward with a smile. "Just tell me what to do, Diane. I'm happy to help."

"Would you?" Diane's face was drawn tight. "I hope Rachel makes it in time, but I'm so nervous, I need the extra insurance. Thanks."

"Sure," Tara said.

"Her makeup area's over there." Diane pointed, and Tara headed for the station equipped with mirrors and bright lights.

The actors began drifting in. Elaine put an arm around Diane and gave her a squeeze. "It's going to be fine, Diane. Everyone will love your script, especially since we know now what the monster really was."

"We do?" Diane's forehead wrinkled. "What was it?"

"A fake, floating monster. Jack Weston found it this afternoon, while all the excitement was going on at the boat landing and the fire station."

"You'll have to tell me all about it later," Diane said. "Right now, I need to make sure all the actors have arrived." She stepped into the wings and looked toward the front door, where Jo Murphy and her sons were entering. "Oh good, the twins are here."

Elaine chuckled. "So we know where our version of the monster is. That's a help." She called to Nick and Chris, "Come on backstage, boys. Jan and I made a few adjustments to the costume after last night's rehearsal. I want to make sure it's right now."

Half an hour later, the curtain went up.

CHAPTER TWENTY-TWO

At dinner, everyone was still laughing and exclaiming over the production.

"Imagine a friendly lake monster with an agent," Tara said. "I thought Diane was very creative."

"Yes, and Chick could go on to become a movie star. I thought it was a great ending." Paula smiled and passed a basket of breadsticks to Bob.

"Did I tell you I went over to the boat landing this afternoon?" Bob asked Jan.

"I don't think you did. How did you know? I didn't think you were at the school grounds when the stampede started."

"*Stampede* is a good word for it," he said. "Bree Dickerson called me and said she'd heard a rumor that the monster was seen near the launch area, and hundreds of people from the school grounds went charging over there. She thought I'd want to know, because of my interest and the article in the *Courier*."

"What did you find out?" Nathan asked.

"Absolutely nothing. There was nothing there to see, except the EMTs putting a kid into the ambulance and a whole lot of disappointed people." Bob shook his head.

"I'm sorry the boy got hurt," Elaine said.

"They say he'll be all right," Jan assured her.

"Well, there were so many people over there trying to get a look that it's a wonder the dock didn't collapse," Bob said.

"What happened to the boy?" Kelly asked.

"He got knocked off the edge, and I guess he couldn't swim," Bob replied. "Somebody had pulled him out by the time I got there. I don't think he's hurt—just scared." He stabbed at a meatball with his fork. "And that film guy, Garrett, was there, sticking his camera in everyone's face and asking them what they had expected to see, and what they thought the monster looked like, and if they thought it was real."

"That strikes me as odd," Jan said.

Riley tugged on Jan's sleeve. "Grandma, can we go look for our turtles?"

"Ask your dad," Jan said. "Maybe he'll go down to the shore with you for a few minutes after supper."

Later, when the family had cleared out and Bob and Nathan had left with promises to see them at church in the morning, Elaine and Jan finished the kitchen cleanup. There wasn't much to do—Paula, Avery, Tara, and Amy had done most of it before they drove away.

Elaine hung up her apron and looked over at Jan.

"What are you thinking?" Jan asked.

"I've been thinking over the list of volunteer firefighters. I don't see how any of those taking part in the last event of the muster could have been out on the lake showing off their quasi monster."

"You're right," Jan said. "They'd have to be in two places at the same time."

"I'm not so sure about the theft," Elaine said.

"Me either. It looks to me like the person towing the monster around was not the person who stole the money. But the firemen's muster was over when the money was stolen. Anyone could have taken it while everyone else was out monster hunting."

Elaine sat down on a stool at the work island. "And why start a rumor that there's a monster near the boat landing when it was on the other side of the lake? No one could see it from the boat landing."

"Maybe they didn't want anyone to see them towing it around. It would be too obviously a fake, and everyone would know who was doing it."

Elaine shook her head. "But someone had to see it. You can't just go on rumors without someone actually seeing it at some point."

"And they did." Jan sat down at the kitchen table. "That family from the cottages started out in their boat, and they saw it."

"Yes." Elaine stared at her cousin. "I think whoever built the monster wanted someone to see it and spread the story, but not find the fake monster."

"Agreed," Jan said. "And it couldn't be a firefighter."

"Well, not if they were involved in the last few events at the muster, or even the barbecue."

Jan nodded. "It would take them a while to get to the bog—or wherever they were hiding the monster—and tow it down the lake until they saw someone in a boat."

"Right," Elaine said. "The thief, however, only needed a few minutes to get over to the fire station once the boat landing rumor was started."

Jan nodded. "So, maybe the person who built and brought out the fake Chick monster is not the same person who started the boat launch rumor."

"That makes sense to me," Elaine said. "The thief probably didn't even know that Jack had been called out to go look for the monster. He was concentrating on getting that money."

"I think the thief started the rumor about the boat landing," Jan said. "It would get people away from the school grounds and the fire station."

"Not everyone went over there," Elaine noted. "We know the thief didn't."

"Right. But the thief couldn't know what Tag would do with the cashbox once people started mobbing the exit."

"Unless it was Tag."

Jan's eyebrows shot up. "Tag wouldn't attack Rachel."

"I don't think so either."

"Besides, Tag was busy. He sent several firefighters to help with traffic control. And he went to the firehouse immediately when he heard Rachel was hurt."

"*Hmm.*" Elaine scowled as she thought about it. "The thief must have followed Rachel."

Jan nodded. "Or at any rate, he or she followed the money, looking for the best chance to take it."

"But Rachel saw a firefighter going out the door after she was hit."

Jan sat up straighter. "Correction: she saw someone wearing a turnout coat and sneakers. All of the firefighters taking part in the last muster event wore boots."

"Okay." Elaine thought about it some more. "The thief isn't necessarily a firefighter, then. It could be anyone who grabbed a turnout coat as a disguise."

"And there was lots of gear piled up on or near the fire trucks," Jan said. "Not just the Lancaster trucks, but all four towns. Face it, anyone could have grabbed a coat and slipped over to the station."

They sat there for a minute, not speaking while they turned the situation over in their minds. Finally Jan stirred.

"Do you think the monster was hidden in the bog all the time? Say, since the twins saw it?"

Elaine raised her chin. "No, now that you mention it. Jack searched the bog pretty thoroughly last week. He'd have found it easily if it was parked where we found it today."

"So where was it hiding in between appearances?"

"I'm guessing in a barn or a shed," Elaine said.

"And somewhere not far from the bog outlet," Jan added.

Elaine percolated that thought for about twenty seconds. "Caden Gower said we could look around his place. It's between the bog outlet and the boys' camp beach."

Jam stood. "Come on. There's still an hour or so of daylight."

ELAINE STUDIED THE rocks on the small beach at the Gowers' cabin carefully, but she didn't find anything that made her suspicious. She turned toward the cottage and mounted the steps on the slope.

"What are you doing up there?" she called to Jan.

Her cousin looked down at her from the cottage's porch that overlooked the dock and the calm water.

"Thinking. If I were going to build a make-believe monster, I wouldn't do it on the beach. Someone might see me."

"Okay, then, where would you build it?"

Jan frowned. "Like you said—in a barn or a garage or something."

"There's a shed behind the cottage," Elaine said. She had seen it when they arrived. The driveway to the cottage came in at the back of the structure, away from the water.

The sun was setting behind them as they walked around the building and approached the clapboard shed.

"It's got a padlock on the door," Jan said wearily.

"Well, of course," Elaine said. "They probably keep their canoes and firewood and—and—I don't know, maybe their Jet Ski in there, for all we know."

Jan walked around the side. "Hey, there's a window." She leaned toward the glass and shielded her eyes with her hand, blocking the colorful reflection of the sunset. "I think there's a boat in there."

Elaine joined her and leaned against the window, both hands curled beside her eyes.

"I see it. I wonder if it's the one I saw the day the boys got scared."

"*Hmm.* I think a boat this small would have had to tow the monster on the raft that you and Jack and Shane found," Jan said. "But the boat you saw rowing away from the boys probably had the monster inside it."

"True. Maybe it was a smaller version of the monster, or maybe they thought of the raft later, as an easier way to transport it." Elaine turned away from the window, her shoulders slumping. "Or maybe that boat I saw had nothing to do with it."

Jan walked slowly from the shed along the tree line. "We've got to be missing something."

Elaine sighed. "It will get dark soon. We might as well go home." She raised her head and looked toward the car. When they reached it, she took a last look around. "The other cottages aren't close."

"True," Jan said. "But still, I think someone would have heard pounding or seen something if that thing was built here."

"Maybe no one was staying in the next cottage. The Gowers don't stay in theirs all the time." She turned and looked at the woods on the other side of the driveway. "Hey, look. Is that a house over there?"

Jan came to her side of the car and squinted into the dusk. "It's some kind of building. Have you got a flashlight?"

"Yeah, hold on." Elaine opened her car door and took her flashlight from the glove compartment.

Jan had walked up the driveway to the dirt road. "Come up here. There's a path."

Elaine strode to her side.

"See?" Jan said. "It's almost a road through the grass and bushes, and someone's driven here recently."

They followed the track toward the structure. As they approached, Elaine realized it was a large building.

"Is it a barn?" Jan asked. "I didn't know anyone had a barn out here."

"Maybe it's where they store their boats and things," Elaine said.

They circled the building and came to a large double wooden door on the other side. As with the Gowers' shed, it was padlocked.

"Well, so much for this little jaunt," Elaine said. She played the flashlight's beam over the front of the building. "Do you think this is the Gowers' property?"

"I don't know," Jan said.

"Maybe we can look at the property maps in the town office Monday and find out who owns it."

"Hey, Elaine, bring your light."

Elaine hurried to join her. Jan was examining an area beneath a large pine tree. She pointed down at the orange pine needle carpet on the ground. Wheel ruts disturbed the surface, exposing dark earth beneath the needles, and several patches of color gave the pine needles new hues. Elaine trained the beam on them.

"Bright-green splotches, and one bright yellow." She snapped a few pictures with her phone, but the light wasn't good. She probably wouldn't be able to see a thing in them.

"Paint," Jan said. "It looks like someone brought something out here to spray-paint it."

Elaine studied the spattered paint's pattern on the ground. "Something pretty big." After a moment's thought, she said, "Do you think Caden was lying last night?"

"But he took part in all the muster events today."

"Are you sure?" Elaine asked.

"We can ask Tag for the roster for each event, to make certain." Jan started walking back toward the car, and Elaine kept pace with her.

Elaine blew out a slow breath. "If Caden did take part in those events, he couldn't have gotten the monster out of hiding today. But that doesn't rule him out for the thief. And what about Tanna? I know she helped with the barbecue."

"I saw her at the school after you left," Jan said. "She was there when Tag handed off the cashbox to Rachel."

"So..." They reached the car, and Elaine gazed down past the Gowers' cottage, over the lake to where the last golden rays of sunlight topped the trees on the other side. A loon gave its eerie cry, and she spotted the mother near the Gowers' float, with a chick swimming just behind her. "So, Tanna's also a possibility for the theft, but not the monster sighting."

"Could be a team effort," Jan said.

"We should tell Jack about this," Elaine said. "He could compare the paint on the ground with what's on the remains of the monster."

"Yes." Jan opened her car door. "But I also want to have a look at those rosters."

TAG BRUSHED BACK his light-brown hair. "I just don't believe it. Caden wouldn't steal the money. We've all worked hard, and he was helping us, every step of the way."

"We just want to see your lists of who took part in each event of the muster," Elaine said. "We're not accusing anyone, and seeing the lists might help us."

"How?" Tag asked. They were sitting in his living room, and he had offered them coffee, but Jan and Elaine had turned him down.

"First of all," Jan said, "we don't think that the person who towed the fake monster down the lake this afternoon is the same person who stole the money. That should be a relief to you."

Tag nodded slowly. "So, you think the paint indicates Caden has something to do with the monster sightings, but not the robbery."

"That's right," Elaine said. "The paint was on the ground near his family's cottage. We worked out the timing, and who-ever was towing that monster away after the people from Green Glade Cottages saw it could not have gotten to the fire station in time to steal the money."

"Okay." Tag's scowl didn't leave his rugged face. "I still don't like it."

"Neither do we," Elaine assured him. "But we've got to fol-low the evidence. It's the only way we'll get to the bottom of it."

Tag looked at Elaine and then at Jan. "Hold on."

He left the room and came back with a folder. He opened it and took out several sheets of paper. "Russell Edmonds kept track of who was in each event." He riffled through the rosters and paused. "Yeah, thought so. Caden was in both the last two events."

"There you go," Jan said. "There's no way he was down the lake getting that monster out."

"But you found paint that matches it on the ground near his cottage."

"That's right," Elaine said. "We called Jack Weston after we saw it, because he took the raft with the fake Chick to his place. When I called him, he said he would go take a look at the paint on the ground tomorrow."

"But building a fake monster's not a crime." Tag's blue eyes were troubled.

"No, it's not," Jan said. "We didn't call the police. If Jack thinks they're needed, he'll make that call."

"Okay." Tag looked at his watch. "It's not too late. I guess we can go and talk to Caden."

Elaine drove, and she and Jan followed Tag from his house to Caden's. Tanna opened the door.

"Hey, Tag." She looked puzzled when she saw Elaine and Jan. "What's up?"

"Can we talk to Caden?" Tag asked.

"Sure. He's upstairs with his brother. Jason suddenly decided to leave tonight, and Caden's trying to talk him out of it while he packs. I'll go get him."

Elaine looked at Jan. She saw a flicker in Jan's eyes that told her they had the same thought. Tanna ushered them into the living room and left them there.

"Tag," Elaine said quietly, "I don't suppose you know if Jason was at the school grounds during those final events?"

He eyed her thoughtfully. "No, I don't. He helped us set up this morning, but I didn't keep track of him. He couldn't compete, because he's not a member of our fire crew."

Tanna and Caden came into the room. Caden eyed the three of them.

"What's going on, Tag?"

"Well, we have some more information about that fake monster."

"Okay."

"Could we sit down?" Elaine asked.

"Sure." Caden and Tanna sat down on the couch, and the others took chairs, facing them over the coffee table.

Tag glanced at Elaine and said, "We wondered if you had a hand in building a pretend Chick monster, Caden. It's no big deal if you did. I mean, there's nothing wrong with having a little fun, but—"

Caden held up a hand and looked directly at Elaine. "I told you before, I had nothing to do with that. I did hear that somebody saw it again today, but trust me, I wasn't behind that."

"We know you weren't," Elaine said. "However, you told Jan and me we could look around near your cottage. We did that, and we found some paint on the ground outside one of the buildings that looks like a pretty good match to what was used on the fake monster. See, Jack Weston found the floating monster hidden in the bog today. I saw it."

Caden stared at her for a long moment. "For real? I heard tons of people went over to the boat launch but they were all disappointed, because nobody saw a thing."

"That's because they were in the wrong place at the wrong time," Jan said. "The monster was seen on the other side of the lake and farther down, toward the bog outlet, by some guests from Green Glade Cottages. Shane Atherton got a glimpse of it too. Then Jack and Shane and Elaine went down there and found it."

Elaine nodded. "But for some reason, somebody started a rumor at the school grounds that it was seen over near the boat landing. Dozens—maybe a couple of hundred—people dashed to the town dock to try to see it, when it was nowhere near there."

"Why would they do that?" Tanna's voice was quiet, barely a squeak.

"We don't know," Jan said. "We're pretty sure that whoever made the floating monster did not steal the fire department's money. But we're starting to think one of you two might know something about the floating monster."

"Not me," Caden said.

"Me either." Tanna looked frightened. "I took every cent of the barbecue money and gave it to you, Tag."

"This had nothing to do with the stolen money," Elaine said. "We're just talking about the make-believe monster."

"We didn't build it," Caden said.

"What about your brother?" Elaine asked.

CHAPTER TWENTY-THREE

C aden held her gaze for a long moment. "I…suppose Jason could have had something to do with it. You said you saw paint at our cottage?"

"It was on the ground outside that barn across the dirt road from your place," Elaine said. "We weren't sure if that was even your property."

"Oh, a red barn with a rolling double door?"

"Yes. You can see it through the trees from your driveway."

"That's not our barn," Caden said. "That's the Taylors' place. It butts up to the camp road there, but to get to their house, you go in off the West Cottage Road."

"Okay," Elaine said slowly. "Sounds like we were off base and off your land on that one. I'm sorry."

Tag said, "Wouldn't it be a riot if Sadie built that monster?"

Elaine froze for a moment as Tag's words triggered a new thought. "Not Sadie. But maybe we *should* go see them tonight. After the wedding tomorrow afternoon, her cousin Garrett and his friend will probably leave."

"Garrett?" Jan cocked her head to one side.

"Yes, Garrett, the obnoxious filmmaker."

"I thought he was pretty charming, actually," Tanna said.

"Yes, but he's always filming people whether they want him to or not." Jan looked at Elaine. "Are you thinking what I'm thinking?"

"He and his friend Adrian could easily have used Sadie's dad's old barn for a workshop," Elaine said.

"Yes, and it's so handy to the lake." Jan nodded. "It certainly bears investigation."

"But that doesn't help with the stolen money," Tag said glumly. "I'd really like to know who did that. Rachel could have been seriously hurt, and we'll have to start all over raising money for the repairs. We might as well say goodbye to the thermal imaging camera."

Jan cleared her throat. "I have an idea about that."

"You do?" Tag asked, a spark of hope lighting his eyes.

At that moment, Jason entered the room. He glanced at Elaine and Jan and nodded, then said, "Hi, Tag."

"Hey, Jason." Tag stood. "I hear you're heading out tonight."

"Yeah, I need to get home. I have to work Monday. This has been a nice little vacation, but it's time to move on."

"Where's home?" Elaine asked.

"Concord, Mass."

"Why don't you stay over and leave after breakfast?" Tanna coaxed. "You won't get home until midnight if you go now."

"I'll be all right," Jason insisted. "I'm always up that late. And the traffic's a lot lighter in the evening."

"So, are you all packed?" Caden asked.

"I think so. I've just got to get my swimsuit off the line out back."

"Oh, I threw it in the dryer with a few towels," Tanna said, standing. "I'll get it for you." She and Jason left the room, walking toward the kitchen.

Elaine shifted in her chair and looked toward her cousin. "Shall we give Sadie a call, or wait until after the wedding?"

Jan was staring after Tanna and Jason with a faraway look in her eyes.

Tag stood. "Right. I'm calling it a night."

"Wait." Jan swiveled her head to gaze at Tag. "Help me out here. How did Rachel describe the person who pushed her down and stole the cashbox?"

Tag shrugged. "Not much of a description. You were there. Turnout coat and running shoes."

"Nikes," Jan whispered. "She said Nikes." She looked at Caden and caught his gaze.

Caden stood slowly. "You think..."

Elaine looked at both of them. "I hadn't heard that detail. Your brother's wearing Nikes, Caden. And he's about to leave the state."

"No, he couldn't—" Caden's chin dropped.

"Couldn't he?" Tag stepped closer to Caden and said quietly, "Jan's right. Rachel did specify Nikes. And there were a lot of turnout coats lying around at the end of the muster. When I got back to the school after Alicia took Rachel to the clinic, Russell couldn't find his. Finally someone spotted it on the back of the tanker."

"I don't remember that," Caden said.

"You went over to the boat landing, remember? After Dan Benson was done at the station I sent you over to make sure everything was all right there."

Caden looked up at him. "Where was Jason?"

"I don't know," Tag said. "I didn't see him after the last events. People started mobbing toward the boat launch, and I was going to head over there, but then Dan called me and said to get over to the station. I don't think I saw your brother after that."

Caden sank back onto the sofa. "When Tanna and I came home from the play, he was here. That's when he told us he was going to leave tonight. I talked him into dinner with us first, but afterward he insisted he needed to go."

Tanna's voice came from the kitchen. "You sure that's everything?"

"Pretty sure," Jason said as they entered the room. He had a couple of items of clothing in his hands. "Guess I'm about ready, bro."

Caden stood. "Give me your keys. I'll go open the trunk for your bags."

Jason took his key ring out of his pocket and tossed it to Caden. "Be right out. Nice seeing you folks." He nodded in Jan and Elaine's general direction and went down the hallway toward the bedrooms.

Caden stepped across the room and handed Tag the key ring. "Go outside and call Dan Benson. I—I can't do it, but I think we need to."

"What's going on?" Tanna asked, wide-eyed.

Tag pocketed the keys. "Elaine, why don't you and Jan step outside and make that call? I'll stay a few minutes and try to help Caden keep Jason here without getting upset."

"Right," Elaine said. "Tanna, sorry to run out so abruptly. Caden can explain." She hurried to the door, and Jan followed her out.

Elaine and Jan got into their car, and Elaine placed the call. Dan answered right away.

"Dan, we may have found a clue to the theft of the fire department's money," Elaine said. She explained that Tag had gone with them to the Gowers' home. "Caden's brother is preparing to leave suddenly, and Jan noticed that he wore Nike running shoes. She and Tag both say that's important."

"Yes," Dan said. "I remember Rachel saying the thief wore that brand. I'll be right over."

"Please hurry," Elaine said.

"Now what?" Jan asked when Elaine had closed the conversation.

"Wait and pray, I guess."

Within five minutes, they could hear Jason yelling from within the house. Soon afterward, he came charging out the front door with a duffel bag in one hand and a backpack in the other. He did a double take at their car, scowled, and headed for the black pickup parked in front of Elaine's car.

"Uh-oh. We're blocking him," Jan said.

"Well, I'm not moving," Elaine declared.

"What if he rams the car?"

Elaine folded her arms and set her jaw. "You can get out of the way if you want, but I am not budging."

Jason tossed his bags behind the seat of the truck and bent low beside the open driver's door.

"What's he doing?" Jan asked.

"Probably looking for a spare key."

"Oh right. He's probably got a magnetic holder under the—" She broke off as Jason rose with something small in his hand. A moment later he got into the cab and started the engine.

Caden, Tag, and Tanna had come out onto the porch and stood watching. When the truck started, Caden strode to the passenger side and yanked the door open.

"Jason, come on. I'm not accusing you."

"Yes, you are. Now shut the door."

"You can't leave until Elaine does!" Caden yelled over the sound of the revving motor.

"Watch me!" Jason put the truck in gear and eased forward. He cut the steering sharply and was just able to squeeze off the driveway onto the grass beside the garage.

Elaine watched in disbelief as he drove a complete circle around Caden's house and came back onto the driveway facing out, behind her car and Tag's truck. But before he could drive out onto the road, another vehicle pulled up lengthwise, across the end of the driveway. Jason hit the brake just in time to avoid colliding with State Trooper Dan Benson's SUV.

CHAPTER TWENTY-FOUR

At the wedding reception Sunday afternoon, Sadie's mother stopped by the table where Jan and Elaine sat with Bob and Nathan and Mark and Bristol Payson.

"Thanks so much, all of you, for coming," Sharon Taylor said.

"Wouldn't have missed it, Sharon," Elaine assured her. "The wedding was lovely."

"Thank you."

"The refreshments turned out well too," Jan said.

Sharon rested a hand over her heart. "For a little while I was afraid it would be a disaster. But it all came out well, didn't it?"

"It sure did," Jan said.

"Well, thanks for jumping in to help. It's not a catered dinner, but people seem to be enjoying it."

"It's wonderful," Bristol said, "and you have plenty of food and a big variety of dishes."

Sharon smiled and focused on Bob. "So, Bob, did you get any answers about that lake monster business?"

"Funny," Jan said, "we found some paint on the ground outside your family's old barn."

"You wouldn't know anything about that fake monster that Jack Weston found stashed in the bog yesterday, would you, Sharon?" Bob asked.

She laughed. "Not I, but you might want to have a word with my nephew and his friend."

Jan looked across the room, where Garrett Wolfe was holding a microphone in front of the bridal couple and Adrian Holt was filming the impromptu interview.

"Are you saying that Garrett was behind all the commotion about Chick?" Jan asked.

"I don't know about *all* of it," Sharon said. "People just seemed to take hold of the idea and run with it, didn't they?"

"They sure did," Jan said.

"I don't understand why he would do that," Elaine asked. "Why build the thing and take it around the lake so people could catch glimpses now and then, and why give pictures to Lydia for the newspaper?"

"You'll have to ask Garrett," Sharon replied. "He loves making films, and he's passionate about the small-town dynamic in Lancaster. Oh, make sure you try the seafood salad. Priscilla Gates made it, and it's divine." She smiled and moved toward the head table.

"All right, it's time to get to the bottom of this," Bob said. "Excuse me for a moment." He got up and walked over to Garrett. A few minutes later, they both came back to the table, without Adrian and the video camera, for which Jan was grateful.

"All right, Mr. Wolfe," Nathan said. "You've had Jan and Elaine in a frenzy for two weeks. Time to 'fess up."

Garrett laughed. "To what? I heard the thief was arrested last night."

"He was," Elaine said. "The brother of one of our firefighters confessed to stealing the fire department's money. The firefighters got back every penny. But he had nothing to do with the lake monster, other than starting a rumor that it was at the boat landing. He did that to distract everyone— especially the firefighters and police, so he could get away with taking the money."

Garrett nodded. "That's about what I figured. Everyone was over there looking for a monster that wasn't there, and the firemen were busy with crowd control and the ambulance, besides cleaning up after the muster. But what does that have to do with me?"

"We know you built the monster on the raft," Jan said. "We found paint on the ground near Mr. Taylor's barn, which you used for your workshop. And the boys just down the lake at the summer camp found a piece of your painted canvas."

"Not to mention the scare you gave Jan's little grandsons last week," Elaine said.

He chuckled. "Okay, you got me. That was a trial run. Just about the first thing I heard when I got to town was how one of the selectmen saw something in the lake."

"You were at the tearoom the day Clifton reported his sighting," Elaine said slowly.

"Yep. And then some other guy saw it again."

"Chad Prentice," Jan said.

"Yeah, but the game warden told me he thought that sighting was bogus. He said it was late in the day and the light was poor, and, well, he implied that the fisherman wasn't quite sober, if you get my drift."

"Did those sightings inspire you to build a monster people really could see?" Nathan asked.

"Sort of. I thought it would be interesting to see how people reacted. My first version was a flop, though. I couldn't see how to show it without giving away my involvement."

"You rigged it up with a rope over a tree branch near our beach," Elaine said.

Garett gave her a sheepish smile. "Guilty. But that was after the underwater version."

"What?" Jan's brow furrowed. "You made one that went underwater?"

"I tried. I thought I could get a fisherman or two to buy into it. But it was too complicated to work it without being seen."

"But one guy did say he saw something under the water," Elaine recalled.

"Yes. That was Adrian. Not many people here would recognize him, so I had him put on a fake mustache and go into the diner and say he'd seen something."

"Oh man." Nathan laughed. "You went to a lot of trouble."

"That's nothing compared to the one Elaine is talking about—the one the little boys saw," Garrett told him. "Cute kids, by the way."

"How did you do it?" Jan demanded.

"It was an above-the-surface version, but it was awkward. I waited in the bushes half an hour for those kids to come out without a grownup, and then I yanked it up from behind the point. My monster scared the kids, but it was too small, and I could see that getting it in and out of the boat was too cumbersome. That version would never have fooled an adult."

"I didn't actually see it," Elaine admitted, scrolling on her phone, "but is this you?" She showed him the picture of the boat. "I took that just a few minutes after the boys saw the monster."

"Guilty. I got out of there fast. Thought I'd row out a bit and start the motor, but I couldn't get it going. I had to row all the way down to the bog. But anyway, I knew I needed a bigger Chick, and a better way to get around with the critter."

"So you made the raft," Elaine said.

He nodded. "It was all in good fun. I'm sorry if I scared the kids. I just wanted to see how people reacted."

"What do you mean?" Nathan asked.

Garrett smiled. "You'll see when I'm done editing the tape. We got some fantastic interviews of people who claim they saw the monster or were hoping to see the monster. Typical small-town attitudes. I love it."

"So you're putting together a film that makes fun of us all?" Bristol asked archly.

His eyes widened. "No, not at all. Actually, I'm celebrating the small town." Garrett laughed. "I was pretty disappointed that hardly anyone came out to see my monster yesterday, but then Aiden told me he got plenty of footage anyway, because so many people rushed over to the landing on the other side of the lake."

"So your whole film is about this fake monster and how people react to it?" Mark asked.

"No, the monster's not all of it, by a long shot. I've got the preparations for a country wedding, and the kids having fun at VBS, and folks cheering on their teams at the firemen's muster. Lancaster's a wonderful town, and I want to show it to the world." Garrett looked around at all of them. "I hope you folks aren't too put out with me. I had a blast, and it's going to be a good film. Might even win some awards." He grinned and walked back toward the head table.

"Well," Jan said.

Bob nodded. "I think I believe him, as crazy as it seems."

"Me too," Nathan said. "He's an artist, or at least he thinks he is."

"I'll reserve judgment on that until I see the film," Bristol declared.

Bob reached for his coffee cup. "When his film is released, if it's as good as he thinks it is, it might send a swarm of tourists to Lancaster, in which case we'd probably ought to write him a thank-you note."

Nathan laughed. "Well, in the meantime, Elaine and Jan have cleared up another mystery."

"What's that?" Bristol asked.

"The old chandelier in their house," Nathan replied.

"I finally got hold of Dennis Clarkson, who owns the old Dubois house," Elaine said. "He's agreed to let us have the matching chandelier." She left out the rest of the story about Anthony Nichols, his wife, and the flying sparks.

"I hope he finds a buyer for that old mansion who doesn't believe in ghosts," Bristol said.

Nathan laughed. "Not any more than they believe in lake monsters?"

Bristol chuckled. "Something like that."

"Where are you going to put the chandelier?" Bob asked Elaine.

"We thought in the east parlor. It's such a large room, I think the crystal and gilt will show off best in there."

"Sounds good," Bob said.

Jan looked across the room toward the windows. "Oh look!"

Nathan and Bob snapped startled gazes in the direction she had turned.

"Sadie and Jeff are going to cut the cake," Jan said.

Nathan sagged a little, then burst out laughing. "For just a moment there, I thought you'd sighted a lake monster!"

ABOUT THE AUTHOR

Susan Page Davis is the author of more than seventy novels and novellas in the historical romance, mystery, and suspense genres. Her newest mystery titles include *Beneath the Surface, Steeped in Secrets, Captive Brides,* and *The Labor Day Challenge*. She is the mother of six and grandmother of ten. A Maine native, she now lives in western Kentucky with her husband, Jim. Visit her website at www.susanpagedavis.com.

From the Tea for Two Kitchen
"CHICK OF CHICKADEE LAKE" SUGAR COOKIES

MIX THOROUGHLY:
¾ cup shortening
1 cup sugar
2 eggs
1 teaspoon vanilla

BLEND IN:
2½ cups flour
1 teaspoon baking powder
1 teaspoon salt

Cover and chill at least 1 hour. Heat oven to 400 degrees. Roll dough ⅛-inch thick on a lightly floured surface. Cut into desired shapes. Place on ungreased baking sheet. Bake 6 to 8 minutes, or until very light brown. Frost or decorate as desired. Makes about 4 dozen.

READ ON FOR AN EXCITING SNEAK PEEK
INTO THE NEXT VOLUME OF TEAROOM MYSTERIES!

Apart at the Seams
BY AMY WOODS

"This display could rival a Smithsonian exhibit!" Elaine Cook exclaimed to her cousin, Jan Blake, as they toured slowly around the local art gallery in the small town of Lancaster, Maine. The Lancaster Veterans of Foreign Wars chapter had teamed up with sisters Rachel and Elsa Leon, who owned and managed Whisper Art Gallery, to put on a weeklong event showcasing Heroes of Foreign Wars, and if the rest of the week continued as that Saturday morning, the exhibit promised to be a roaring success.

"It's wonderful to see these lives remembered," Jan said to her cousin. "The families kept so many mementoes of their loved ones who went off to serve overseas."

Elaine looked at her cousin, whose short hair featured only a hint of gray, like her own. Jan's blue eyes surveyed the large, open room in reverence. What Jan had observed was true. As they made their way around the gallery, Elaine saw photographs from Vietnam all the way through Iraq, articles of clothing worn by soldiers, newspaper clippings dating back to the 1940s, and tiny keepsake items such as jewelry, pins, and buttons. There was even a small shabby teddy bear, she noticed, perched atop a tattered green uniform jacket on one of the tables. Her heart melted at the images the bear brought to mind—had a child sent the stuffed animal with her father as a token when he went off to war? Or had a battle-weary papa brought it home with him to a wife or a waiting little one? Each proudly displayed piece held a heart's worth of memories, including Ben's camera, which Elaine had thought to add to a small display of his belongings.

Her late husband, who had been a lieutenant colonel in the US Army, had served all over the world, and photography had been a hobby of his. The camera, she'd noticed that morning, still held a full roll of film—the little ticker showed zero photos had been taken, and she smiled sadly to think of Ben loading the roll hopefully. It had been a while since his passing, and she'd even been blessed to fall in love a second time, but she knew now that she would continue to miss him every day.

The townspeople had been invited to contribute any relics related to overseas wars in which American soldiers had served, and boy, had they come through in abundance. Besides the displays, the Leon sisters had hung black-and-white photographs along the walls where they usually displayed the work of local artists, and American flags in various sizes adorned the rafters.

"Well," Jan said, taking one last look around before glancing at her wristwatch, "I think our short break is up. We'd better get back to our table."

Elaine nodded and she and Jan made their way to the table they'd set up near the front by the gallery doorway. As co-owners of Tea for Two, a tearoom they'd opened together a few years back in the large lakeside Victorian they also shared as a home, the cousins had volunteered to cater this exhibit free of charge. As their business had become more and more popular and seen growing success, Jan and Elaine did what they could to give back to their small, close-knit community.

As they drew near the table, Elaine admired the blue-and-white tablecloth Jan had chosen, and the red tea service she herself had picked out. Spread across the patterned fabric were miniature cupcakes with white frosting and tiny red and blue sugar sprinkles, alongside Jan's locally famous mini maple croissants and a tiered stand holding expertly sliced fruit.

A steady stream of visitors passed their table, and Elaine and Jan served tea and made sure there were plenty of treats available, restocking from the supply they'd brought anytime things got a little low.

Elaine was glad to see many of their friends from Lancaster stop by, like Shane and Azalea Atherton, a young couple who worked helping Shane's mother, Macy, run Green Glade Cottages. They paused briefly at the tea table to say hello. With the line for the refreshments moving along at a brisk pace, all Elaine had time for was a quick greeting, after which she noticed Zale had on a beautiful, delicate gold bracelet when the young woman reached for a cupcake. Elaine complimented the pretty piece of jewelry and Zale, blushing a bit, said thank you before the couple moved forward to allow fellow locals Ryan and Felicia Standish to grab some goodies. The day and the small talk flew by, and before she knew it the crowd thinned. Glancing at her watch, Elaine noticed it was almost time for the exhibit to shut down.

As the last few visitors trailed out, Elaine and Jan said goodbye to Cora Packard, a navy veteran and the VFW's chapter representative, as well as to the other chapter members that had come to help sign in visitors and answer questions that day.

"We couldn't be happier with how well opening day turned out," Cora said as she lingered at their table. Tall and trim in her uniform, with intelligent gray eyes and a presence that was kind but commanding, the fifty-something veteran made it easy to guess she held her own in a predominantly male profession. "I think this event will go a long way toward sponsoring the handicapped-accessible van we're hoping to purchase."

"We're so glad to help out," Jan said, shaking Cora's outstretched hand. "It's the least we can do to thank you for your service."

With the gallery nearly empty, they packed up Elaine's car with their supplies and the remaining food before heading over to touch base with Rachel and Elsa, who were busy tidying up.

Rachel smiled as Jan and Elaine approached, the corners of her eyes crinkling softly behind the lenses of her glasses. Her shoulder-length hair was pulled back into a ponytail, and she wore a white button-down top, a purple denim skirt, and brown leather sandals. Rachel's skin was tanned and her limbs toned from her work as a volunteer firefighter. Elaine guessed she was around forty or so, and she was a pleasant person to be around. She shared the loft apartment above the gallery with her sister, Elsa, whose paintings the gallery most prominently featured.

"What can we do to help?" Jan asked, rubbing her hands together. Elaine could see that both sisters were tired from running around all day, making sure that everyone's questions were answered and that things ran smoothly. The gallery did well on a regular basis, but it wasn't often as crowded as it had been with the special exhibit going on.

"I think that's it for today," Rachel said, holding out her palms.

"We're all pretty beat," Elsa added. She was the more confident of the two sisters, though both were smart, pretty, and kind, and they seemed happy with the lives they'd built and with each other's company. That day, Elsa had traded the flowy bohemian-style clothing she usually preferred for an outfit similar to Rachel's—a top and cardigan over a modest skirt. Elaine grinned to herself though, seeing that Elsa had still added a flower to the loose bun at the nape of her neck.

"Agreed," Rachel said. "I couldn't be more pleased at how the day turned out, and I think the VFW will be overjoyed at the generous donations we'll be able to pass on to them at the end of the week," she added, pointing to a jar sitting atop a nearby table. "But I think I could use a break."

"We'll all be glad for a day off tomorrow," Jan said. "But why don't Elaine and I come by tomorrow after church to debrief you on today, and help you set up for Monday?"

Elaine nodded. "That'll give us a chance to review and be ready for next week. I know it probably won't be as busy during the week as on a Saturday, but both the *Penzance Courier* and the *Weekly Wave* ran advertisements about it, and Cora said the VFW office phone rang off its hook last week with interested folks wanting to come by and see the displays."

"I have no doubt we'll get that handicapped-accessible van," Jan noted, sounding pleased.

Elsa and Rachel smiled at each other before Elsa said, "Sounds like a good plan. And I have no doubt the visitors' generosity has much to do with the deliciousness of Jan's pastries."

Elaine turned to see her cousin's expression brighten as Jan thanked Elsa for the kind words. Elaine couldn't agree more. When they'd first opened the tearoom, Jan had been a bit shy and reserved, but now she beamed when someone complimented her baking, and she deserved every word of it.

"Save a seat for us at church if you would, and afterward you can come by to talk about how today went and if we need to change or add anything for next week," Rachel said.

"Sure will," Elaine responded. She and Jan waved to the Leons and walked out to her car. Even after owning it for a few years, Elaine still liked the bright-red Chevy Malibu. The color was so cheery it always made her smile.

Elaine let the late-day sun bathe her face as they walked into the parking lot. The weather was another reason to smile. Late August in Maine was one of her favorite times of the year. Often the weather began to cool by then, with highs in the upper sixties to low seventies and lows near the fifties. It was comfortably warm during the day and the night air cooled things off so it rarely got too hot.

When they had climbed inside the car and buckled up, Jan said, "That was wonderful, wasn't it? Looking around at all those photographs...I don't often think much about all the sacrifice our soldiers make with the hope that those of us back home can live normal lives. I'm sure you do, though, because of Ben."

Elaine turned the ignition, enjoying the warmth of the car seats after they'd sat in the sun all day. Her late husband had traveled so much for the army that their family had never really put down roots. All the same, she had felt privileged to see such a great deal of the world. "I did, a lot, when we were in active service. Now, I think more about how nice it is to stay in one place for a while, and how blessed and comfortable our lives are."

"I had no idea we had so many veterans in Lancaster," Jan said. "When Cora called and we agreed to provide refreshments, I was a little worried we'd made too much, but I counted only three cookies left over! We'll have to make more for next week. With Labor Day coming in a couple of weeks, there might be lots of family members visiting for the rest of the summer who'd want to stop by the gallery."

Elaine glanced over at her cousin as the short drive ended and she pulled into the driveway at Tea for Two. Jan was positively glowing. "You're right. I hope you don't mind the extra busy-ness," Elaine said, feeling a little guilty as she was the one who'd said yes the instant she'd heard Cora's request, only running it by Jan afterward.

"Are you kidding?" Jan said, waving a hand to dismiss Elaine's concern. "I'm just glad to have new guinea pigs for my recipes. You keep me on my toes!"

Smiling, the cousins unloaded the trunk of the car and headed inside.

THE NEXT MORNING, Jan woke to strange silence. She usually woke with an alarm, and as she slowly opened her eyes, she realized it was far too bright in her room. She looked at her bedside clock and sat up with a start. She'd forgotten to set her alarm and slept late! After rushing through her shower, she dressed quickly in a cheery yellow button-down shirt and a soft gray cotton skirt, stuffing her feet into sandals. She grabbed her Bible, cell phone, and purse and hurried down to the first floor, taking the stairs two at a time.

"Elaine!" she called out. "I'm sorry, but I slept in. We've got to run if we want to get into church before the sermon starts."

She made her way to the kitchen, fully expecting her cousin to be there waiting for her, having already read the paper and eaten breakfast, but Elaine was nowhere to be seen. Jan was just about to go back up to knock on her cousin's door when she heard footsteps rushing down the stairs.

Elaine burst into kitchen. "Sorry I'm late," she said. "I slept in."

Jan couldn't help but laugh. "So did I! I thought I'd find you down here all ready to go, annoyed at having to wait for me," Jan said. "Need anything to munch on for the road?"

"Nah," Elaine answered, waving a hand as she opened the door. "I'll just eat when we get back."

Jan shrugged, deciding she wasn't too hungry herself. Her body hadn't quite figured out it was awake yet, so her stomach wasn't grumbling.

Once they'd gotten into Jan's old blue Camry, both women looked at each other and laughed again. "I can't believe we both goofed," Elaine said.

Jan shook her head and started the car before pulling out of the drive and onto Main Street. "I guess we were more tired than we thought. We were up extra early yesterday to start tea and pastries, and we didn't leave the gallery until after six, and the tearoom's been so busy lately with summer tourists that we haven't had a chance to really rest."

"Plus, we have the Labor Day clambake coming up in two weeks, and the planning has been busy."

Jan pulled off Pine Ridge Road into the Lancaster Community Church parking lot and found a spot. The cousins grabbed their purses and Bibles and went inside, quickly heading for a pew instead of stopping to chat as they normally would have.

"Remember, we've got to save seats for the Leons," Elaine reminded Jan.

"You don't think they're already here?" Jan whispered, trying not to draw too much attention as the notes of the first hymn began.

Elaine looked around at the mostly full pews. "I don't see them, do you?" she asked, biting her bottom lip.

They settled into a half-empty row and Jan glanced around as well. "No, I don't."

The cousins looked at each other. "Maybe the same thing happened to them—they worked even harder than we did, setting everything up yesterday. Do you think they could have slept in too?" Elaine asked.

"It's certainly possible," Jan answered. "Elsa had already hung most of the photos and paintings by the time we got to the gallery yesterday morning. I know she was so proud and honored when Cora asked them to host the event, but I think perhaps it was a little busier than she thought it would be. The gallery's successful, but from what the sisters say, it's mostly a slow and steady stream of tourists—rarely a huge crowd like yesterday."

"Hmm," Elaine murmured. "Well, I don't see anybody else who needs a seat, so I'll leave my purse here next to me in case they come in late."

Jan nodded, reaching into the wooden pocket of the pew in front of her to grab a hymnal, and Elaine did the same. After the congregation finished the first song, there were a few moments to greet neighbors. Jan said hello to Ned and Rue Maxwell, asking after their daughter, Melissa, a geologist. When Rue patted Jan's hand and turned to catch up with Alan and Maureen Oakley, Jan took a moment to look around again, hoping to spot Rachel and Elsa. Sure, it was possible that the younger women had just been too tired to come, but Jan had a strange feeling about it that just wouldn't let up.

"Have you seen the Leons yet?" she asked Elaine, who'd just finished speaking to Bristol and Mark Payson in the pew in front of theirs.

"No," Elaine answered, turning to check behind Jan. "I'm sure they just decided not to come today."

Jan frowned. "You could be right, but then why would they specifically ask us to save them a seat?"

Elaine's brows knit. "I'm not sure."

"I'm worried about them. It's not like Rachel or Elsa to back out of something, and they both have our numbers. I'm sure they would have texted if they weren't going to make it," Jan said, the butterflies in her stomach fluttering faster.

Elaine put a hand on Jan's forearm. "If you feel that strongly, let's go over and check on them."

Jan hesitated a moment, then nodded.

The cousins slipped out of their pew and made their way outside the church to the car. As Jan drove past the marina and into view of the art gallery, she gave a little gasp. Police cars with flashing lights dotted the parking lot.

FROM THE
GUIDEPOSTS ARCHIVE

This story, by Kathleen Dean of Fort Collins, Colorado, originally appeared in *Guideposts*.

Alan and I worked and prayed hard to be the best dad and mom we could be. But it had been a long, trying winter. Alan had a demanding job at a research lab, and we were both drained from taking care of three sick children, even more so from worrying about them. Five-year-old Max had to have his tonsils out, then both two-and-a-half-year-old Daniel and baby Andrea Rose developed serious ear infections. They had to have surgery. Finally things settled down.

One night after I gave the baby her feeding, I was getting some badly needed sleep myself.

"Monster! I saw a monster!" Daniel wailed. As he came scrambling into our bed I groaned and squinted at the clock. 2:00 A.M.

"There's no monster, Dan," my husband said sleepily. "Now go back to bed."

"Monster!" Daniel insisted.

Alan carried Daniel back to his bedroom. "See? No monster," I could hear him saying to our son. Not under the bed, not in the closet, not behind the chair. "Here's a hug. Now go back to sleep."

The next night the same thing happened. Daniel woke up and cried that he'd seen a monster. Again we assured him there was no such creature. We tucked him back into bed and he finally drifted off to sleep. But when it happened again the following night, I was beside myself. Alan and I limited the kids' television time and never allowed scary programs. We had tried to protect them. Still, our little boy's imagination was running wild.

What are we doing wrong? I wondered. Did Daniel have a serious emotional problem? Was it our fault? I combed our library for information about children's phobias and night terrors; I talked to friends and our pediatrician. Nothing they suggested seemed to help. Daniel kept seeing the monster, a swift phantom in the shadowy night.

I grew as anxious about bedtime as Daniel, except my monster was the fear that I wasn't a good mom. How else could I explain my son's terror and my inability to reassure him? Finally Alan suggested I take a break and visit my brother, who lived near a peaceful cove on Puget Sound. My mom came to stay with the children.

At my brother's, I walked on the beach, rocked on the porch and tried to put my anxiety about Daniel into perspective. "I'm at the end of my rope with Daniel," I told God. "Is it something I'm doing?" It was then I sensed an answer: *Just trust Me.* A week later, I came back relaxed, confidence in my mothering restored. During my absence Daniel had slept without incident. It's over, I thought.

But that night at 2:00 A.M. there was a familiar wail and a sturdy little figure in his red sleeper was back in our bedroom. "Mom! Dad! Monsters!"

I sat up wearily. *God, I'm trying my best to trust you but...*

Daniel was tugging at Alan's hand. "Come on, Dad," he said firmly. "Quick. There's a whole bunch of them!"

They hurried out of the room. Moments later I heard Alan gasp, then burst into laughter. "Kathleen, come here," he called.

Slipping on my robe, I hurried into Daniel's room. Alan pointed outside the window. "Look," he said. Clinging to the screen were three tiny creatures—baby raccoons. Close behind them on the porch roof lurked the night monster, complete with glowing eyes! For weeks the mother raccoon must have been padding back and forth across the roof carrying food to her babies. Now her babies had left the nest and joined her, peering into the window at Daniel's night light. "So that's what it was," I whispered to Alan.

We tucked Daniel in, and he agreed that his monster, and her little monsters, were not so scary after all—now that he knew what they were.

Isn't that true of most of our monsters? I thought, as I snuggled back into bed with Alan. Usually they disappear when we try our best and trust God to lead us when we are in the dark.

A NOTE FROM THE EDITORS

We hope you enjoyed Tearoom Mysteries, published by the Books and Inspirational Media Division of Guideposts, a nonprofit organization that touches millions of lives every day through products and services that inspire, encourage, help you grow in your faith, and celebrate God's love.

Thank you for making a difference with your purchase of this book, which helps fund our many outreach programs to military personnel, prisons, hospitals, nursing homes, and educational institutions.

We also create many useful and uplifting online resources. Visit Guideposts.org to read true stories of hope and inspiration, access OurPrayer network, sign up for free newsletters, download free e-books, join our Facebook community, and follow our stimulating blogs.

To learn about other Guideposts publications, including the best-selling devotional *Daily Guideposts*, go to Guideposts.org/Shop, call (800) 932-2145, or write to Guideposts, PO Box 5815, Harlan, Iowa 51593.

Sign up for the
Guideposts Fiction Newsletter
and stay up-to-date on
the books you love!

You'll get sneak peeks of new releases, recommendations from other Guideposts readers, and special offers just for you . . .
and it's FREE!

Just go to Guideposts.org/Newsletters
today to sign up.

Guideposts.   Visit Guideposts.org/Shop
or call (800) 932-2145

Find more inspiring fiction in these best-loved Guideposts series!

Mysteries of Martha's Vineyard

Come to the shores of this quaint and historic island and dig into a cozy mystery. When a recent widow inherits a lighthouse just off the coast of Massachusetts, she finds exciting adventures, new friends, and renewed hope.

Tearoom Mysteries

Mix one stately Victorian home, a charming lakeside town in Maine, and two adventurous cousins with a passion for tea and hospitality. Add a large scoop of intriguing mystery and sprinkle generously with faith, family, and friends, and you have the recipe for Tearoom Mysteries.

Sugarcreek Amish Mysteries

Be intrigued by the suspense and joyful "aha!" moments in these delightful stories. Each book in the series brings together two women of vastly different backgrounds and traditions, who realize there's much more to the "simple life" than meets the eye.

Mysteries of Silver Peak

Escape to the historic mining town of Silver Peak, Colorado, and discover how one woman's love of antiques helps her solve mysteries buried deep in the town's checkered past.

Patchwork Mysteries

Discover that life's little mysteries often have a common thread in a series where every novel contains an intriguing whodunit centered around a quilt located in a beautiful New England town.

To learn more about these books, visit Guideposts.org/Shop